TROUT

Trout

Colin Bacon

Elliott & Thompson
London

For Moth

With special thanks to Peter and Gordon.
(Not to be confused with the 1960s pop duo)

PART ONE

CHAPTER ONE

·

Striving to scoop up the endless dogends that clung to the raised paving slabs, Lurch steered himself up the Dale. But this was not the Dale that Lurch would have preferred. There was no babbling stream flowing between undulating hills. No people-carriers spewed out city folk wearing Berghaus fleeces and hiking boots, to paddle and play in the glistening pools. No cliffs of millstone grit churned up in some glacial age remained, just rows of back-to-back houses leading into industrial waste. A fly-over merged with the river basin where joggers jogged and bored adolescent boys fingered their girlfriends, as the river flowed murky on its way to the weir. Here, Lurch would stare at some sad victim of hopelessness as they floated by. Both sick with the past and searching for a cure.

Lurch shared a bathroom with a heroin addict. Their kitchen had been lost for years and the space left behind now resembled a motorcycle scrap yard. They never communicated, but preferred a stance of mutual suspicion as they passed on the stairs. Lurch was never that concerned about his environment. He never noticed the smell of drains or the roof that leaked through the wall at the back of his cupboard. He no longer cared much about anything, as he lay in bed waiting for the night to blot out his past, and listening to the Dale coming alive outside.

Once the Dale had been Lurch's whole life, but it always tried to drag him back into the mud from where it had begun. It had split his family apart, forcing them into high-rise flats and away from the substandard housing they had lived in for generations. Lurch despaired and had made it clear to everybody who would listen that at the first opportunity he would leave to find something better. His father had been a trolley bus driver and his mother worked in the town's cigarette factory. That was enough.

As Lurch headed up the street in a tattered shell suit clinging to his body for comfort, he felt in the midst of an invasion. He had woken late. Instead of trying to force the light back out between the curtains, he had opened his eyes and squinted through the window at the bus picking up passengers outside. Lines of grey faces stared blankly at the seats in front and he remembered the reasons for why he was filthy, cold and scraping the ice off a cracked window-pane. It was going to be a long battle, but one day he would resume his rightful place in a world that had, up until now, taken him apart brick-by-brick. Lurch had laid back in bed and issued a warning to the crack which stretched the length of his wall, as he covered his face with a grease stained pillow.

The Dale was overrun by immigrants and students. The smell of dope was in the air and brain cells littered the pavement. Shops selling exotic vegetables, and Halal butchers, spread its whole length. The corner mini-mart now stood where the hardware store had been and a mosque had taken over the Astoria cinema. Drunks swayed by bus stops abusing everybody and sirens filled the night air. Every type of human flotsam spilled out onto the Dale, blending with the coloured saris that massed at its edge. It was a place to meet and share experiences. The Holy Ganges, reincarnated in the East Midlands. They even brought their washing, but not to batter with a stone on the gravely bank. They had the convenience of Akmed's Washeteria and Mini-mart, situated in the centre. Owned by three Asian brothers, who judged their success by the numbers of girls willing to share the delights of their sleek, black Mercedes, the brothers had seen the advantages of employing Lurch the moment he had entered their premises, wandering down between the packed shelves straightening the washing powder boxes. He was obviously simple, the brothers guessed he would be cheap to run, and they had just let their previous employee go when her incontinence eventually overcame her stacking skills. So Lurch began a new career, working as an untouchable. He was never offered a wage, but instead took home as many out-of-date goods as he could carry. His sweet tooth ensured that the shop never ran short of Cherry Bakewell's.

The mini-mart opened early and closed when the streets were empty, which varied, depending on television schedules and what was worth going out to celebrate. Lurch's built-in telepathic system told him the punters needs before they knew themselves. He could have saved them time, taking the goods directly to them as they stood at the door but the brothers preferred to give the customers the chance to buy something else. Lurch crept around the shop replacing stock or unloading dodgy items from out of the back of a white van.

Sometimes the brothers' ageing parents were left in charge. They would stand behind the counter understanding very little as Lurch rushed about replacing goods as fast as they could be sold. Friendly customers appreciating their language problems would help out by shouting very slowly at them. They could deal with simple requests, but when confronted by comments in the local dialect, would just nod nervously. Lurch understood and came to their help one night when a drunk, returning from a stag party, stumbled in looking to buy some cigarettes.

'Ayup me ducks! Aya goreny snaats?' the drunk shouted.

The elderly shopsitters grinned at each other, then stared at the floor.

'Geeyus sumothem.'

The drunk pointed towards the ceiling as Lurch emerged from his hiding place and handed the man a packet of Marlborough.

'Ta very much me ducks,' said the drunk, before falling into the stationary department, realising his mistake and launching himself out into the night. Lurch returned to his cupboard and left the couple to contemplate whether the locals, as well as themselves, had a problem coping with English as a second language.

Lurch had just left the shop. Hugging close to the stone-fronted houses, he steered himself around the dog turds and broken beer bottles. He crossed the road in front of the doctor's surgery and swerved into one of the alleys that divided the back yards. These streets that once had been a haven of pigeon fanciers, were now the haunt of dodgy dealers and glue sniffers. Lurch had stopped caring about the area's decline, blind to anything except his basic needs. He plotted a course through the criss-crossing alleyways. A mist hung over the river valley as he negotiated the smallholdings that stretched along the water's edge. Along the river bank lumps of Hawthorn hid a small area, which projected outwards into the river, where local girls could supplement their benefit cheques, after a few cans of Special Brew.

Lurch loved the river. It was a symbol of escape. He would prostrate himself watching the swirling eddies making their way downstream as his arms stretched down into the water, one pushing against the current and the other loosely bobbing with it. Going with the flow. He could feel the water's energy pulsing through his body, giving him strength. Lurch also went there to listen to the hum of the city and to light fires, just above the weir. He loved lighting fires. They helped him forget.

Lurch opened a bottle of cider and glanced across at the block of flats rising up above the trees. His parents were still there, retired and angry for wasting each other's lives. At first drinking had helped, but it soon fuelled Lurch's depression and left him anxious and addicted to Valium. He was on the downward spiral towards self-destruction, but at least he was talking now, even if it was only to himself.

⸺

If anyone had travelled any weekday, in the distant past, on the 8:05 bus from one of the more leafy suburbs in the city, they would have seen Lurch wearing a raincoat and clutching a leatherette briefcase. He would be waiting to board the bus to work and although it was not very far to walk, Lurch always preferred to stand and wait for the 8:05. It began the day properly. It also gave him the opportunity to glare at the person who was inevitably sitting in his seat. As the big white bunker appeared, he stepped down out onto the pavement and disappeared through the doors and into 'his job for life' – or so he thought.

Then, of course, he wasn't known as Lurch.

Lurch had been christened Arnold, after an uncle who gained some family respect in the war by goose-stepping around the house with a small moustache painted above his upper lip. Such unselfish action for the war effort had the affect on Arnold's father of insisting that his son be named after him. Arnold hated his name. William or Henry would have been much better. Those names would have suited his expected future role. But Arnold had yet to learn that our destiny is never certain, and our lives can change as rapidly as the fortunes of football managers.

Arnold welcomed school, but with his future life in the balance, he decided that he would take no chances. He would be average, keep a neat pencil case, and cheat whenever possible. He would also split on his friends. This certainly helped his teachers to nail the miscreants, but it did not gain him any respect and never endeared him to anyone. Arnold could be very irritating.

One day, during playtime, he appeared out of a mass of charging bodies to report on an over zealous Japanese camp commander who was committing war crimes against our gallant tommies.

'Sir! Sir!' Arnold screamed, as the gang of half-starved prisoners tried desperately to erect the next stage of the Trans-Burma railway, before being called into second sitting.

'Sir, Ronald Barrow says I can't be a soldier unless I do Hari Kari with my testicles and go to Rangoon to get the clap.'

He leapt in the air, zig-zagging to avoid the rapid fire of pursuing machine gun bullets.

'Shit!' the teacher uttered under his breath, 'Fuck off and stick a hand grenade up your arse.'

'But Sir! I was supposed to be the one that blows up the end of the bridge, before the train comes and then gets put in the oven.'

Arnold was hysterical. The teacher blew the whistle and began sending the children in to wash their hands. He could see the situation needed diffusing.

But Arnold had not finished. There were still scenes to be filmed and Oscars to be won.

'But Sir! I can't wash my hands. I've got bamboo needles stuck in my nails and we want to escape into the jungle. Norris's dad's waiting with a aircraft carrier to take us back to Blighty.'

This, to a man who had been through the war was the last straw. Hollywood and history made him see red at the best of times.

'Attention!' screamed the teacher, as one-hundred and fifty children stared in terror at the sergeant-major he had never been, before ushering them into order and marching them back into school.

Of all the pupils that passed through the school system, at best Arnold was average, but he never had any doubts regarding his capabilities. In his own way he was still going to set the world alight. It was at junior school where he first began to see girls differently. He became clumsy in their presence and they mostly decided to ignore him. Arnold preferred to bury himself in his mother's breasts at any opportunity, and plan his future with ample support. The girls treated him with scorn, taking him behind the bike sheds to show him his inadequacies and never their knickers, as they were supposed to. He knew flighty girls like these would never be for him. One day he would find a girl who appreciated his qualities.

Arnold's dream was to achieve a position of responsibility and respect in a field where he would not have to think very much. He loved mundane things. Tidying bookshelves or washing paintbrushes, he was happiest sharpening pencils. This procedure had on occasions given him an erection, though he had not realised why. All he knew was that it was pleasant, and the more he sharpened, the nicer it became. He started sneaking into the classroom at break times and deliberately snapping pencils, frantically working them into a fine point before the lunchtime supervisors ushered him back outside. The teacher became suspicious when the thrice-yearly pencil stocktake revealed the class had gotten through twice the usual amount. All became crystal clear when a pupil noticed Arnold's erection whilst he was sharpening the crayons, and informed the class. From then on pencils were out of bounds. Not that it mattered. He had his own set at home always finely tuned and ready to break. His Christmas list was already made out and an electric pencil sharpener was its top request.

Girls were still a mystery. His friends were taking notice,

but he was still far from being interested. To him an erogenous zone was anything that needed organising. He could not see any future involving even a basic interest in female anatomy. If it could not hold a set of encyclopaedias there was no point. So Arnold spent his pre-adolescent years completely lacking insight into his sexual future. It would be much later before he came to recognise a woman's full potential, and even then she would have to provide her own filing cabinet.

Arnold did enjoy some aspects of his life at junior school, though it was not compartmentalised or receptive enough for his emerging organisational skills. To a degree, he felt spoon-fed. He loved being a dinner monitor, fetching the classes in order of age and wiping the tables and chairs after they had finished. Some children helped at lunchtime in order to get fed extra helpings of congealed custard, but Arnold did it for the experience alone. The pleasure stacking the chairs was what he craved. It was a bonus if he was required to get on all fours and climb under the trestle table to scrape at the vegetables that had been deposited there.

By the time he was eleven he knew he was now ready for senior school. It wasn't because he would find the work more stimulating, but because he would have to be even more organised. Now he had a homework diary and was required to change classrooms after every lesson, returning to his locker at regular intervals to get the relevant books. Although admirable, this quality to turn up on time with the neatest satchel in the world was not considered an indication of ability. He tried his best and his teachers saw no point in pressurizing him. He was useful in other ways, so why worry about the fact that he wasn't very bright? There would always be openings for an Arnold. Local government or the civil service would cherish him. So Arnold continued on his unique path, always knowing that he would find his niche somewhere.

For Arnold, puberty appeared suddenly. He had returned from a strenuous day at school and wanted to relax in his bedroom. He loved his own space and this particular day he was overcome by how neat and tidy everything was. This stimulus of ultimate pleasure instantly fuelled an erection, and coupled with the sight of his pencil sharpener, produced an uncontrollable desire to climb into the wardrobe of crisply starched clothes and masturbate. And so his mother found him, as the wardrobe gently rocked round the room, and enquired whether he wanted a boiled egg or cheese on toast for tea. Arnold groaned something about looking for a clean shirt and his mother left the room making a mental note that Arnold was probably suffering from growing pains. Arnold's desire for orderliness did not diminish with the onset of puberty. He did begin to take notice of girls, but the powerful desires experienced by his peers still eluded him, a lack of interest reciprocated by all of the sexually active girls in his school.

However, one afternoon during a regular visit to the local library to study the intricacies of the Dewey Decimal system, Arnold saw a vision that sent his hormones racing. Standing behind the counter, stamping books with ultimate precision, was a girl. Peeping through the stacks, he could see that she was wearing the school uniform of the grammar school. She was immaculate with striped braiding around her cuffs and lapels, and a perfectly white, crisply ironed shirt.

Now he took notice. She was even wearing a tie, though not like the girls did in his school, tied loose and ugly around their necks. Her's was pristine, with a neat tight knot close under her chin, without even a hint of a dinner-time stain. Arnold, however, did not focus on her physical attributes. He was transfixed by the way she was searching for book tickets in the filing cabinet. She opened the draws with such precision and fingered the tickets so perfectly that he began to experience those growing pains once again. She was perfect, like those robots Dan Dare was always trying to prevent taking over the world, but one without its square edges. Arnold was contemplating for the first time his ultimate erotic fantasy. Racks of books in alphabetical order containing justified text and perfect spacing. No bondage dungeon or black leather for him. His brow filled with sweat and he fought for breath as he heard the climactic thud of a date stamp hitting the page

Arnold knew that he had to speak to her. He would not be

able to concentrate on anything until he had, but how could he gain her interest. In the next week, he read fifteen books. Every day after school he watched as she licked her fingers, selecting the cards to place back in the covers. The stamp sent vibrations via the floor and up his leg to where his testosterone was stored, but still he did not know what to say.

'You're obviously a keen reader.'

Arnold was transfixed at the broad smile revealing a perfect set of teeth.

'Yes. I like books.'

'I won't keep you a minute. Only the cards seem to be all jumbled up. These are all blank. They often are when I get them out of the draw. The authors are in the wrong place. It's the librarians' fault. They put them anywhere. It can be really difficult to locate the cards sometimes.'

Arnold's brain went into overdrive. She hypnotised him with her hands as she re-organised the cards, better even than Maverick could. Arnold struggled to find something to say and inspiration appeared from nowhere.

'I've got an electric pencil sharpener that takes six different diameters and automatically stops when the lead achieves a perfect point.'

She carried on stamping. He waited for a reaction.

'That must be nice for you. Don't you find that you get through a lot of pencils though?' Arnold recalled his pleasure earlier when he had almost wiped out his entire tin of Lakeland Deluxe.

'I do, but it's a small price to pay. There's nothing worse than an untidy box of crayons. You just have to be very selective. I always like to keep mine at the same length though. It facilitates easy access to the tin.'

Now he was really talking dirty.

'It's mounted on my bed head.'

'What is?'

'My sharpener.'

'Why?'

He was obviously going to fast.

'So it's there when I need it. Do you work here every day?'

'Yes, but I'm finishing tomorrow. I've just done two week's work experience.'

Arnold took a deep breath.

'I was thinking of going to the museum on Saturday. There's an exhibition of costumes, with a selection of clothes fasteners dating from Neolithic times, all catalogued in complete chronological order. Would you like to come with me?'

'If you're sure you wouldn't be rather sharpening your pencils, I'd love to.'

They went to the museum. The following day he took her rowing on the local lake. She was meticulous and beautiful and made perfect symmetrical patterns in the water with the oars.

Their relationship became a weekly timetable of identical events with an itinerary planned to the finest detail. It respected orderliness, and suited them perfectly. On Saturday they would meet in the afternoon, walk around the shops and as the big clock in the square struck four, catch the bus back to Arnold's house. Here they would eat egg, chips and plenty of bread and butter. Arnold's father insisted on it. He remembered food rationing after the war and being full was still something of a novelty for him. It had to be dutifully consumed for no other reason other than that it had been prepared.

'Eat the bread and butter up before you finish your chips. You can't waste good food. There are people starving.'

So they would gulp it down with plenty of sweet tea, secreting crusts in their pockets, before eating the cream cakes that came out of a cardboard box tied up with string.

Arnold had always hated where he lived, but now it did not seem that bad. The square block of flats with protruding balconies and windows were for the short term at least, acceptable. His regimented life had a focus and girls with their hidden secrets now became a new obsession. What exactly was under those skirts and blouses, held together with zips and buttons?

He had a rudimentary knowledge of womens' bodies and what they wore next to their skin, but the endless variety of female underwear confused him. He would stare from his window looking at it all hanging out on the washing lines, marvelling at the variations of colour and style. He could not even work out where it was worn, let alone how they got it on or off. Everything was elastic and reinforced gussets. He had access to the usual selection of *Health and Efficiency* magazines but these were completely devoid of pubic hair. There seemed no advice available on how to approach a roll-on in full passion. And why were they called a roll-on. Was it because you rolled on and then rolled off? Like a ferry, with access from both front and rear?

When the summer came they went to the boating lake, allowing nothing to upset their regimented rules of courtship. Arnold was always polite in her parents' company and they considered him a good-natured lad, but in the confines of their front room about as interesting as a life insurance salesman. But he was now going steady, and for him it was nearly as good as it could possibly get. All Arnold wanted to complete the equation and balance the books was sex. Apart from a kiss on the cheek when they parted, and holding hands occasionally, they had no physical contact. They had slipped into a process that could not incorporate anything more.

The opportunity did not present itself until three years into the relationship. O Levels loomed and this necessitated a break in routine. Both of them had set their sights on steady careers which suited their personalities. She wanted to work in a library and Arnold fancied the planning department at the local council offices. Revision meant they were able to spend time at home on their own. It seemed an opportunity to Arnold; to relieve exam tension by experimenting with bodily contact. He was terrified at first, but true to character began planning, using a scale drawing of her bedroom and a slide rule. He had been stockpiling condoms in the hold of a model of HMS Victorious for some months, stolen from the dressing-table draw next to his father's bed, in such quantities that Arnold's mother was suspected of infidelity.

His first attempts at tooling up were pathetic and almost resulted in him being hospitalised. Initially he was shocked when he ripped open the packet and saw how small a condom was. Then he felt pleased. His dad obviously was not that well-endowed for a trolley bus driver. Maybe it was his continual exposure to electricity. Arnold came to the conclusion that it all came down to technique. He attempted to force his flaccid penis into the open end of the condom, using a finger. This proved fruitless, so he resorted to a toothbrush handle for added torque. This ripped the sheath as well as his foreskin, which erupted into a black blood blister, rendering him out of action for days. It was only on closer examination of the instructions, that he realised he had been using a finger sheath.

'Cover wound in a light dressing and place over finger if coming into contact with water'. There was no hint that it should not be used as a method of birth control. Eventually, Arnold became proficient when he realised that his penis had to be hard, and soon he managed to get up to four on at once. This resulted in a lack of feeling, but at least he knew there would not be a chance of an unwanted pregnancy. He had now mastered the practical, but that was only forty per cent of the marks.

When should he actually put the condom on? Obviously not after. Should it be during sex, just before, or a week the previous Thursday? Should he do it in front of her or turn around to face the wall? The whole process of anticipation turned into a nightmare, but he knew there was no turning back.

He muddled his way through. The first possibility he considered was wearing it before he went round to her house. The problem was that when he went soft, it slipped off. He came up with the brainwave of sellotaping it to his pubic hair, which was excruciating. He abandoned the idea after a couple of attempts, because any secondary erection could not be relied on to behave itself, and missed the open sheath by miles. He also found it difficult to explain to his mother what a condom was doing on the end of his shoe, as he crossed his leg during breakfast. He could not put on a condom whilst in the same house, let alone the same room as her, as she would see. There was only one option left.

His new strategy involved rolling on the condom and immediately slipping a heavy-duty elastic band over the end of his penis and down the shaft. This prevented the blood from escaping and meant that he could keep his erection for longer, without any direct sexual stimulus. Allowing for a fifteen-minute bus ride and twelve minutes walking, plus brief glimpses of the underwear section in his mother's mail order catalogue en route, he was confident of sustaining an erection for the entire journey. The unknown factor, which he gave the least consideration to, was the amount of time required once inside her house. Foreplay was not a word he was familiar with and he thought it would probably take about as long as blowing up a bicycle tyre.

He visualised the scenario. On entering the room she would be immediately aware of a sexual chemistry that had lain dormant in both of them. She would lead him to her bed and he would stick it in before they both returned to the table to continue studying the causes of the Franco-Prussian war. Everything was clear. He was ready for love.

The next day, after eating a light breakfast consisting of a four-and-a-half minute boiled egg, Arnold returned to his bedroom and checked his equipment. All his clothes were ironed and his shoes spotless. He stood in front of the mirror, stroked himself in a clockwise motion and slipped on the cause for the biggest boom in razor blade sales in post-war Britain. Then he rolled home the elastic band. Making sure he had adequate spares, he saluted himself in the mirror and headed for the bus stop.

Twenty-two minutes later, he opened her back door and climbed up the stairs to her room.

It was no surprise that the sight of two naked bodies involved in mutual body exploration caused Arnold to drop his revision notes and stare in amazement, before falling back against the door in horror. A vision of Hereward the Wake's two-handed sword Brainbiter came into Arnold's mind as he stared at the monster she was manipulating with obvious dexterity. Her hand was attached to Dennis, the ape-like son of the man who owned the boating lake.

She jumped up, covering herself with a sheet, but not before Arnold noticed something that was equally troubling to him. Her breasts were different sizes. All this time he had been going out with a girl that was not perfect at all, but decidedly lobsided. He knew that his scrotum was not symmetrical, so what would the babies look like?

'Why are you here Arnold? I thought you had your Biology exam this morning?'

Arnold resisted the obvious reply.

'No. We were supposed to be going through European history actually.'

'Well, I didn't think you were coming until this afternoon.'

'Unlike you.' This time sarcasm did get the better of him.

'Have you met Dennis?'

Arnold stared at the mesomorph on her bed. He remembered that they had called him Bigfoot. He was so hairy he would not be out of place living amongst the giant redwoods of northern Canada.

'Yes, at the boating lake. When he swung down to the water's edge to drink.'

Arnold was pleased with that comment. Dennis unfortunately wasn't.

'Fuck-off cunting fucker, or I'll dent your cunting fucking head in!'

Arnold had always marvelled at how certain people could communicate perfectly well by just using a more basic form of language. He had reason to remember Dennis as an expert. The previous summer, some poor punter had got fouled in weeds and was late returning his canoe. Bigfoot did not even wait for him to get back to the boathouse.

'Come in number fucking-cunting six or I'll kick your fucking cunt right off!' he shouted, grabbing him by the hair to haul him from the boat. Though a good three-feet off shore, such were the length of his arms that Dennis still managed to throw the poor rower head first over the turnstile.

Although this was not acceptable behaviour, it did have its advantages for the manager of the municipal lake and putting green. People were so terrified at returning their boats late, that they would nervously check their watches before docking ten minutes early. This suited Dennis and his father because it allowed ten hours' revenue from an eight-hour day, a business plan in the years of Thatcherism that could have earned them an award. It was even rumoured that one customer was so scared of Dennis that he returned his boat half- an-hour before he took it out.

Dennis rose from the bed and took an aggressive stance about a semi-erection's length away from Arnold's nose.

'I told you to fuckingfuckoffyoufucker!'

'Please don't hit me, but I just want to know what's happening.'

Bigfoot uttered a short grunt to signal his superiority and retreated to the wardrobe mirror to engage in some grooming.

Arnold began to experience severe pains, followed by numb genitals, as he turned red and tried to rip his trousers off. Dennis thought that he had become the centre of Arnold's passion and grabbed the eiderdown, before hiding behind the cupboard. Arnold was at last able to pull his underpants down and wrestle with his anaesthetized penis. He tore off the condom, but the elastic band had started to wear a deep groove into his crural ligament. He was turning purple. Luckily it shot off, giving his testicles a parting jolt as the rubber band headed towards the window. Arnold fell to his knees clutching himself, then vomited on the carpet.

'How disgusting!' the girl fumed, although she still had not really understood the reason for Arnold's behaviour. Arnold had the distinct feeling that she was going off him.

'Fucking cunting amazing,' grunted Bigfoot, realising he had just witnessed the infamous elastic band routine.

'But we were going to get married and now I've caught you doing it with him. I bet he's never ever even read a timetable.'

'You haven't caught me Arnold. I can do what I want. We've only ever been friends, and anyway caught me doing what?'

'Sex,' choked Arnold, trying to hide his emotions.

Bigfoot interrupted.

'What do you mean fuckingcuntingsexcunt? She's got the fucking painters in.'

'What painters?' Arnold looked round for evidence. 'They had the house done last summer.'

'He means I'm menstruating Arnold.'

'Not today, we should have been revising that tomorrow, for the volume and capacity exam on Thursday.'

'Not mensurating, menstruating, having a period.'

The only periods Arnold was familiar with lasted either side of lunchtime.

Feeling stupid and hurt he had experienced his first lesson in love and betrayal. Like a clairvoyant, the girl had given him an insight into the future. It was not going to be the first time he would feel cold steel enter his heart.

CHAPTER TWO

·

Arnold superficially attempted to overcome his grief by listening continuously to Christine Perfect singing *I'd Rather Go Blind*; his self-pity was brought to an abrupt halt when his father hid the stylus, mumbling something about rather being bloody deaf than blind. Sympathy was wearing thin. Arnold tried to rekindle his interest in construction kits, but it all seemed childish and anyway, his father always interfered.

Arnold painted the pieces meticulously before assembling them, but his dad would try to glue them first. It always resulted in conflict. 'The bloody boat's grey and the plastic's grey, so what's the odds,' was his father's attitude. He did not appreciate contrast and tone like his son. Arnold could spend hours mixing such subtle shades, using only black and white, that when the battleship was finished nobody would even notice.

'I can't see where you've painted it. It's still grey. What's the point in wasting all that time?' moaned his dad.

'But I can,' replied Arnold.

His father did not understand the intricacies of naval procedures, especially where painting was concerned.

'My bloody trolley bus is green. Nobody spends hours mixing up every green under the sun before painting that. It would be stupid.'

'How do you know they don't?'

'Because I've watched them. They open the bloody tin and paint it on. It's not a bloody work of art. They haven't got Picarseole down the garage, poncing around in a beret every time they want a bus painted.'

Arnold could see there was no point in arguing, but he still would.

'Anyway, I haven't.'

'Haven't what?'

'Painted it.'

'I just came in and you were mixing enough greys to paint a friggin' frigate.'

'That's what I am doing.'

'What?'

'Painting a frigate.'

'I thought it was a bloody battleship.'

'No, a battleship's got more guns.'

'So you haven't painted it then?'

'No.'

Arnold's dad reached down and snatched up the plastic boat, getting covered in grey paint in the process.

'I thought you said you hadn't bloody painted it?'

'No, I said I hadn't painted it using all the greys. I decided to take your advice and just use one colour.'

Arnold returned to touching up his turrets.

There was always tension in the house now. Arnold lacked motivation. He would spend hours in his bedroom tidying his shelves and staring out of the window, which aggravated his father even more. He constantly told Arnold that he was lucky, not like when he was a boy, but Arnold would have preferred to be a boy in his father's day. He was not interested in bowling alleys and coffee bars. He wanted to be involved in something useful, and he would, as soon as he got his exam results.

His broken heart had meant that he had found it difficult to concentrate for his exams, but he was still confident he would get good grades. He had already gained a preliminary interview for the local council and hoped to start the following September.

At the beginning of August, a letter arrived. It was good news, and by the end of the week he had acquired a sports jacket, cavalry twill trousers and a pair of brown brogues. The raincoat came last, as this was the most expensive item. It had a secret pocket with a key ring attached to the inside, on a button. The briefcase and watch would have to wait until Christmas.

And so Arnold left his childhood behind on a rainy September morning. It was no gentle transition, but abrupt and welcome. Now everything would progress as planned and he could begin organising the county's planning applications, hopefully in triplicate.

He continued to live at home and this arrangement suited

his parents as well as himself, as the extra money would be useful. Flats were not cheap and he needed to save, to put money away for his plans for the future. These plans would include a semi-detached house, south of the river, where he could park his car in the drive and wash it on Sundays, before he mowed the lawn. He became optimistic again about finding a wife who would cook in the evenings and have coffee mornings. They would own a Goblin Teasmade and make love in the garden by a plastic waterfall. His previous relationship had never been serious, but a childish attempt at living a fairytale. Next time he would not be so stupid. He was in Planning now and planning makes perfect.

Arnold's initial task was to learn all the more complicated duties of a clerical officer, but as these were minimal he progressed on to Stage Two rapidly, mastering those by the morning tea break.

He had fifteen codes to learn. Each had nine digits and commenced with three noughts, which were used when the application was transferred from the initial request to the official form. The applications were stacked on the left of his desk and when he had given them the correct coding, he had to place them in another tray on his right. As Arnold was left-handed, it seemed obvious to him to reverse the process. Six pairs of eyes stared down at his desk and then at each other. Arnold had got his answer.

'I'll just try and do it the other way round then,' he said.

The eyes rolled in unison and nothing more was said. He quickly learnt that this was how Planning Officers communicated. Sometimes it was preceded by a cough, the volume varying, depending on the request. Winter-time was always confusing. Staff did not know whether they were being given instructions, or a dose of the flu. It was a bad time to put in for a house extension as office juniors rushed around in confusion.

Arnold loved all the figures neatly displayed in identical columns. He did not need the pencil sharpener anymore, to bring his primal urges to the surface. Writing the numbers down was enough.

Arnold had no problems slipping into a routine. As long as he never ran out of ink, he had complete job satisfaction.

He even appeared on a recruitment poster, which was displayed in Job Centres as encouragement to the unemployed. The unemployed were not that impressed and Arnold's image constantly had snot flicked at it, as the masses waited to sign on.

But Arnold's dedication did not go unnoticed. He was regarded as a rising star and his numbers began to develop a flourish. This new confidence helped in his relationship with the rest of the workforce, especially the more mature women who had a tendency to find Arnold's awkwardness sweet. They even considered him handsome, with steady and sensible qualities; a mixture that could almost be considered desirable. He was still critical of the more 'common' women in the office, these mainly being categorised by the lengths of their skirts. He felt uncomfortable with the male banter that followed them around the office, especially when they had to bend over to use the filing cabinet.

He now decided it was time to invest in his own transport. He had caught the bus long enough, and he needed to begin stamping his personality on the world. He deserved a reward. One Saturday, he put down his paper and went out and bought a scooter. It was not new, and the sides were covered in dents that represented bank holiday skirmishes on Skegness seafront, but it was freedom. Mods and Rockers had been and gone, so Arnold felt safe that he would not be pursued by hordes of leather-clad Hell's Angels. With transport he could hopefully tempt Maureen, the new filing clerk, into the country to visit some of the stately homes. The scooter was fitted with a rack that could hold Arnold's briefcase in the week, and a picnic hamper on Sundays.

Maureen said yes, and on the first warm weekend of the year, they set off for culture and custard creams. Old habits die hard and Arnold's mum had packed the picnic basket, cramming it with bread and butter, which they managed to eject somewhere around Matlock Bath.

This brief relationship did not blossom, but it gave Arnold the opportunity to touch his first breast. That summer Arnold's score rose in leaps and bounds. By August, it stood at five breasts and a clitoris. The odd breast belonged to the girl in Highways, who took exception to his expectations and blocked him before he could complete the set. The clitoris was a major find, but it made him feel uncomfortable as he did not know what to do with it.

Life took a further upward turn when it was decided that his dedication should not go unrecognised. He was awarded the PUS in the local council's New Years Honour's list and officially Promoted-Up-Stairs. Arnold now found himself on the cutting edge of planning procedures, and directly answerable to the Fireman.

Called the Fireman not because he put out fires, but allegorically speaking because he started them, his official title was Enforcement Officer, and he had a position of great power. The Fireman could demolish practically anything he wanted. Anybody stupid enough to put up a porch or a garage without permission had to answer to him. Arnold's new responsibilities were to man the phone and take messages that were mostly reports on illegal structures put up by neighbours under cover of darkness. Arnold took his new duties seriously. His office was the size of a broom cupboard, but this added to the excitement. It was like being in a bunker and a member of a crack military force whose task was to direct the missiles. Even the phone had a different ring.

'Hello, Planning.'

'Is that Complaints?'

'No, this is…'

'I've gorra rat in mihouse meduck anit keeps coming outa 'ole in wall.'

'This is Planning,' Arnold said slowly.

'Aye, an it's a big bugger witha tail like an elephant's cock. I tried hittin' it witha spade burit shat on mi patio.'

'No, this is the Planning Department, I think you want Environmental Health.'

'Sorry mi duck, you'llav to speak up. I've got boils in mi ears ana think it might be because of the rat. The quack's gonna lance them tomorra. Can ya send somebody raand?'

'You've got the wrong department, you want Environmental Health.'

'Who are they then whcn they're at 'ome?'

'They're the department that deal with rodents.'

'I ain't got one o'them I've gorra rat.'

'Yes. They'll come round and deal with it.'

'Somebodies already bin raand. They killed bugger once, burrit come alive again.'

'Maybe it's bloody Jesus,' Arnold muttered under his breath. 'What do you mean it came alive again?'

'He come raand an' took it away. Then it come back.'

'Maybe it's another one.'

'It looks same.'

'But you don't want to speak to me, you want to speak to another department.'

'I am doing.'

'What?'

'Spekin to you, another department. He told me to spek to you.'

'What, Planning?'

'Yes, miduck.'

'Why?'

''Cause it's coming outa hole in next door's wall where he's gotis bantams.'

'What's a bantam?'

'Don't ya know whata bantam is, miduck?'

'Isn't it a motor bike?'

'No, that's a BSA Bantam, miduck. These are buggering chickens.'

Arnold had no idea why he was having this conversation, but he was a public servant and this was his job. For the good of the community, he took a deep breath.

'So what about the rat then?'

'The rat keeps coming outa hole in wall where chickens are, an' he shouldn't 'ave built it.'

Immediately alert, Arnold's missile finger began to twitch.

'Built what?'

'His chicken shed for bantams.'

'Did he not have permission then, to build the shed?'

'He tried to getit but they wouldn't givit im, so he built it anyway. I didn't care but that wa before mi boils, and now he won't takit daan.'

'Can you give me the address?'

'Aye, it's down Radford bottom, next ta allotments.'

Although it was not Arnold's responsibility to go into the field, he needed to experience what it felt like to personally confront the enemy, to see the white's of their eyes. Suddenly filling in the relevant form wasn't enough. He wanted to be away from the safety of the office and out there, facing bullets.

———

He pulled his scooter backwards onto its stand and banged on the door.

'Who is it?'

'Good afternoon, I'm from the Planning Department and I wonder if I could have a word?'

'Piss off!'

'Am I right in assuming that you applied to the County Council to build a shed at the back of your house?'

'What if I did?'

'According to our records your application was rejected.'

'Why?'

'Because it was considered out of keeping with the neighbourhood.'

'Why?'

'Would you mind opening the door please? You were given the statuary length of time to appeal against the decision.'

'What's the point in that? You still wouldn't have let me build it.'

'May I see it?'

'What?'

'The shed.'

'I didn't build it.'

'We have had information to the contrary. In fact, we believe that you now have a problem with rats as well. We are in a position to obtain an enforcement order to inspect your property, if we believe you have an illegal erection.'

'I need planning permission for that now, do I?'

'What?'

'A fucking hard-on. Every time I want to roger the wife I'm expected to send in a bloody form?'

'There's no point in being rude.'

'What if I just want to play with myself? Is it the same form or a different one?'

'What do you mean?'

'What if I can't get an erection. Will I be eligible for a rebate?'

'What do you mean, a rebate?'

'If I can't get a stiffy. Can I set it off against tax?'

Arnold tried to get back to the point.

'Have you or have you not got a shed in your garden?'

'Do I have to apply for permission to ejaculate? What about the wife? She comes sometimes as well? Not very often though, mind you, I think she's frigid, or maybe I'm not rubbing hard enough.'

'Look, are you going to let me see it?'

The door opened and Arnold was presented with two choices. He was face to face with a fifteen-stone lunatic carrying an axe. The choices were to turn and run, or to turn and run even faster. Before Arnold could make up his mind the lunatic stepped out of the way to allow his wife free access with a bucket of chicken shit.

Arnold didn't get the smell of ammonia out of his clothes for weeks, and decided that he would stick to filling in forms and answering telephones.

He did this with enviable commitment, and was rewarded again for his ability to remain sedentary for long periods of time. He had worked under the Fireman for six years and on his first attempt was promoted to an administrative officer. Now on a much larger salary, Arnold began to think seriously about marriage. Then Dawn appeared.

Dawn had been well tutored by her mother and they were in firm agreement on many things, especially husbands. Finding one with money and prospects was the main consideration. Looks and personality came last. It had not taken her long to consider all the possibilities, and Arnold was top of the list.

Dawn and her mother had recently moved to the area from the other side of England. She had come well recommended and had found a job easily. The references had been provided by her previous boss – and former lover.

Encouraged by her mother, she had got herself pregnant and the plan was that her boss would leave his wife. They had omitted to tell him the plan however, and when she announced that she was pregnant, he dropped her. He had met Dawn's mother, which was more than enough of a reason to come clean to his wife.

Dawn had an abortion, and five hundred pounds, to start a new life as far away as possible. With a reputation, finding a husband would prove difficult, so she was now prepared for a clean start. She just had to find the fool. Secrets and lies came easy to her. Arnold did not stand a chance.

'Hello, I'm Dawn,' she said to him on her first day, and from that moment he was hooked. From then on she played him like a lovesick stickleback.

Dawn was everything he desired. She was attractive, and although friendly to men, never flirtatious. All her attention concentrated on Arnold. She chatted to him about her work teaching the Sunday school class that she missed terribly, and asked him whether she should take lessons in self-defence, slowly crossing and uncrossing her legs. He was over the moon when she suggested a picnic.

The scooter had long gone, scrapped for cash soon after he had passed his car test, but until now he had not seen any purpose in buying a car. Dawn changed all that, and before the month was out he was the owner of a second-hand MGB and she couldn't wait to tell her mother.

Dawn's mother was very pleased with her daughter's choice. Arnold obviously lacked experience and seemed gullible, a perfect combination for a son-in-law, as far as she was concerned.

He also had money which could be converted into a house and possessions. She tried not to get carried away. There was still a lot to sort out if her daughter was going to keep her in gin for the rest of her life. She took every opportunity to tell Arnold just what a lovely daughter she had, and how Dawn had turned down numerous young executives who wanted to marry her. She was waiting for the right man and if he was lucky, Arnold might be the one.

Arnold never took Dawn home to meet his parents. Arnold's dad would have seen through her before she had climbed out of the car, but as he had no influence on his son it would not have made any difference. Anyway, his dad was not interested. Arnold had become 'a right stuck-up twat'. Arnold's mum would have reached for the bread knife and started buttering away, causing Arnold even more embarrassment, so he thought it was best that his parents left him to get on with it.

Arnold did not tell Dawn what his father did for a living as he did not think she would be very impressed. Dawn, however, knew all about buses, especially the lack of luggage space, as she had spent many evenings after school under the stairs with the driver of the bus that took her home.

Once, when they were waiting at traffic lights, Arnold glanced up to see his father grinning at them from the cab of his trolley bus. He ignored him, but this only encouraged his father to wind the window down.

'Ayup, Arnold.'

His father never said 'ayup'. He was considered quite a well-spoken man.

Arnold turned away, but his father became more determined to get his attention.

'Ayup Son. What you bin up to?'

'Nothing really, we've just been for a drive in the country.'

There was no way that his father was going to behave himself. This was too good an opportunity to miss. His stuck-up son with a posh bird, and at his mercy.

'What you driving that fartbox for? Have you changed your job?'

'Who is that man, Arnold?' Dawn had stopped flicking her eyelashes at the workman, who had his hands in a metal box next to the traffic lights, and was now listening. Anyway, she had always found bus drivers interesting.

'What does he want? What's a fartbox? It sounds crude.'

Arnold wanted the lights to change so he could be off. He revved the engine hard in an attempt to drown out his Father's voice. But his father had been a lifelong football supporter and was having none of it.

''Ave you changed your job then son?'

Arnold accepted defeat and decided to come clean.

'It's my Father. He drives a bus, for the City Corporation.'

Arnold need not have worried about what she might think. She was not interested, as long as his father was not a beneficiary in Arnold's will. Dawn turned her attentions back to the workman, and Arnold faced his father.

'No. You know I haven't changed my job. Why?'

'Because that's what hairdressers drive. A fartbox, just like that. Can you give me a perm while we're waiting?'

Arnold prayed for the lights to change.

'Anyway Tarquin, do you do highlights? I bet you're handy with a hairnet.'

Arnold flicked the gear stick back into neutral. Everybody was getting impatient and the drivers began to sound their horns. The workman stopped altering the time sequence for the traffic lights he had been repairing. Dawn smiled and tossed her hair back as the lights finally changed. Arnold accelerated away, leaving his father hanging out of his cab flicking a V-sign.

Arnold and Dawn were now an item, and once again Arnold had a relationship that was evolving into a closely structured routine. He would pick her up on Saturday afternoons and they would go into town to shop, before returning to her house for tea. In the evening, they usually went to the cinema and held hands in the back row. Their fondling never progressed much further. Arnold had too much respect for her, and she was biding her time. She knew that once they had sex, he would be committed to immediate wedding bells. She was in no hurry, as she was seeing a carpet fitter three times a week, who was hung like a donkey. He had come round with an estimate and finished up laying more than the berber twist.

The nights he did not see Dawn, Arnold would plan the layout of their dream kitchen-diner, with sliding doors opening onto a patio. He would soon be moving upmarket, and could forget the pokey flat he had lived in all these years, in an area overrun by dropouts.

On Sunday lunchtimes, the two lovebirds drove out into the country to visit a pub. As he was driving, Arnold only ever had a half, but Dawn would manage five or six large vodkas before the bell was rung at half-past-two. They then returned for Sunday dinner, prepared by Dawn's mother.

The quality of the meal varied, depending on how long she had spent down the Legion. In the afternoon, they snuggled up on the settee to watch a film, whilst Mother snored on the easy chair. Sometimes they kissed during the adverts.

After tea, Arnold returned home for an early night, leaving Dawn to wash her hair, while waiting for Donkey-man to come round.

She realised that their courtship needed to progress, when Arnold returned unexpectedly one Sunday evening. He had got very excited about an advert in the local paper for some new Wimpy houses which were being built, and maybe this was the time to seriously think about their wedding.

He drove round and parked his car. Opening the back gate, he was startled to see Dawn with her head forced up against the kitchen window and her hair covering her eyes. Her face was blotchy and she was sweating heavily. He could not see clearly into the kitchen because of the steam, but her eyes were closed tightly and she was making a noise that sounded like a pig.

Luckily for Dawn the lights were turned off, or Arnold would have seen the donkey behind her as she was bent over the tumble dryer. The donkey spotted Arnold and collapsed to the floor, grabbing his trousers and crawling towards the front door. It took Dawn a moment to realise that she was alone, as she was still in a high state of arousal, but when she opened her eyes she focused on the face of her future husband.

'Hello Arnold.' She was still gasping for air.

'Are you alright Dawn? You don't look well.'

'I'm fine. Yes I was just… er… looking for… erm… drying my hair, with the tumble dryer. Yes, my… um… hairdryer's broken.'

She felt for the control and turned it on, the blast of hot air reminding her that she was not wearing anything below the waist.

'I'll come to the door, hang on.'

Dawn could only find her knickers in the dark. She put them on back to front and unlocked the door.

Arnold could not wait to show her the advert. He noticed she was wearing her undergarments in an unusual way, but as he was about to ask her to marry him, it did not seem to matter.

He got down on one knee.

'Dawn, will you make me the happiest man in the world and marry me?'

'Yes, of course I will Arnold.'

As she spoke she felt something warm and wet run down the inside of her thigh.

They waited for Dawn's mother to return from the pub before celebrating with a bottle of Leibfraumilch. Arnold drove home in a dream, and Dawn could not believe her luck.

Arnold now had the wedding to organise. The following morning he went to the stockroom and commandeered a brand new set of felt-tip pens and a large piece of acetate sheet. He carefully cut the sheet into identical sizes and divided each one into time scales. He had different colours for every conceivable action and event associated with a wedding. Red for the cars, blue for the service, yellow for the reception and orange for the honeymoon. He drew graphs and flow charts representing everything from the picking up of his wedding suit to the precise location of the buttonholes. When these were placed on top of each other the whole day became instantly clear. Nothing was left to chance, and everything was coupled together with its own individual six-figure code.

But not everything went quite so smoothly.

The wedding was due to be held the following May, but Arnold was having mixed feelings about whether they should get married in a church or a registry office. A church wedding would mean inviting his entire family. This was certainly not a good idea, but a registry 'do' did not seem grand enough. Eventually, the decision was taken out of his hands by his future wife and mother-in-Law. They did not want him frittering away more money than was absolutely necessary, so he was persuaded to decide on the registry office. But he did insist on formal dress.

Arnold did not have a stag night. Nobody expected him to. The thought of going out with his work colleagues terrified him, and he was probably very wise. He would have been a perfect victim to fill up with beer and be left, tied naked to a lamp-post. He spent the evening before the wedding walking up and down the landing in his morning suit, perfecting his speech and deciding which side to dress. His father attempted a man-to-man talk after a couple of stiff whiskies, but decided it was best to let sleeping dogs lie.

Dawn went out with three of her girlfriends. They went for a Chinese meal and started off drinking barley wine, before progressing to snakebites. She did not need to have her drinks spiked with anything, and at closing time suggested the nearest nightclub. They danced and screamed the rest of the night away, and Dawn had a snog with a welder. She resisted the temptation to go home with him, but at the end of the evening, Dawn and her friends took turns with two squaddies behind the Palaise de Dance, before throwing up in the back alley, amongst the dustbins.

Arnold still managed to spend some money on his wedding day. Dawn had a pink Rolls Royce to bring her from home, and to take them to the reception held at the Masonic Lodge. He felt very honoured to have this venue for the celebrations, and gratefully accepted it as a favour from his old boss, the Fireman. They only had a finger buffet, and the crabsticks were a trifle flabby, but the couple were toasted in champagne and had provided a litre of Hirondelle for every four guests.

There was no official best man and, as Dawn's father was not there, no speeches. This was perfect for Arnold. He only wanted there to be one speech, and that was going to be his, and he had been planning it for years.

He tapped on a bottle with a spoon and slowly the room fell silent.

'Ladies and gentlemen…'

He was interrupted by Dawn's mother who shouted, 'Speech', at the top of her voice, before toppling off her chair.

Arnold ignored the disruption.

'Ladies and gentlemen. Thank you all for being here today and sharing with me the most wonderful day of my life. When Dawn consented to be my wife, I was the happiest man in the world. All my life I have waited for this moment and now all my wishes have been granted.

'My work has always been very important to me and I hope I have always done a good job…'

Arnold paused here, waiting for the obligatory cheer, but none was forthcoming, so he continued.

'My work has been my life and I'd always hoped that one day, I would find someone to share it with. So when Dawn appeared I couldn't believe my good fortune. We fell in love, and today our lives are linked in a spiritual bond of harmony, only found in fairytales and legends.

'When Orpheus fell in love with Eurydice, he captured her with his lyre, but she was stung by a viper and died. But Orpheus could charm rivers with his lyre, and Hades gave in.'

Arnold's Father who was also a little worse for wear, shouted, 'Who the bloody hell was Orpheus? Does he work for the Planning Department?'

Arnold's mother dug him in the ribs.

'No, shut up. He was a God, Father.'

'What, like Marlon Brando? He put a horse's head in a bloke's bed, for sleeping with his fishes.'

Arnold was not going to be put off.

'Like Eurydice, Dawn captured my heart and my lyre captured hers, but unlike Orpheus, I am not going to turn round before I bring her home. She will not vanish, but we will live in harmony forever, and my head will not be cut off by the women from Lesbos.'

By now he was exhausted and sat down with a sigh.

'So there,' were his final words on the matter, and everybody clapped, relieved that Arnold had stopped.

It was only fitting that Orpheus should take his Eurydice to the Greek Islands for their honeymoon, but the gesture was wasted on Dawn, who was more interested in the waiters. They did however have a wonderful week, and Arnold was at last able to consummate his love.

Dawn did not really notice. On the first night, she got stuck into the Domestica and when they went to bed, she could hardly stand. Arnold put this down to nerves, as he fumbled with her clothing. She did not forget the lines she had been rehearsing the entire plane flight, and managed to remain word perfect.

'Be gentle with me Arnold, it's my first time,' she groaned as she turned out the light, just managing to remove her hot pants, and throwing them into his lap before passing into a semi-coma. She still managed to brace herself as he moaned into her ear,

'Don't worry darling, I'll be very gentle.'

Dawn, being no stranger to having a man on top of her, went onto automatic pilot and slid herself down the bed to meet him. Arnold realised that he was close and pushed harder as instinct took over, and he began to thrash about like a snake in full battle with a mongoose. It was a short conflict. He thrust downwards, Dawn thrust upwards and it was all over. He lowered himself gently onto her body and kissed her ear. Dawn farted, and as her head rolled to one side, began to snore.

Arnold knew that wedding nights could be difficult. It could not be easy for a woman to submit herself completely to a man. Arnold was determined to be a loving and under-standing husband. Dawn would need time to adjust to his new dominant role.

They spent the week visiting archaeological sites in the morning and beaches in the afternoon. Dawn was not very impressed with the state of the buildings that Arnold kept dragging her to see. The Greeks could not have been very good builders, as the supposedly impressive examples were all falling down. The local Taverna owner looked after his property though. She did not need a structural survey to determine that, and he was only too happy to give her a guided tour, when Arnold went to look for souvenirs.

Returning home, they moved straight into their new house. Everything was as Arnold wanted it to be.

Dawn had been so considerate about letting him decide on the colours and style for the main rooms, but because he did not want her to feel left out, he had suggested she should take charge of the bedroom. She had chosen white veneered chipboard in a Regency style, with matching fitted wardrobes. Apparently, Dawn had found a carpet fitter who was prepared to do a cheaper job, if he could work in the evenings. So Arnold had agreed to her choosing the floor coverings, and she had even been prepared to supervise the work personally.

That first evening, Arnold gave her a Goblin Teasmade.

After a few days at home helping to get the house straight, Arnold went back to work. Dawn did not even return to clear her desk, and she kept the car. Arnold thought he would prefer a wife at home, to keep the house tidy and to kiss him goodbye in the mornings. Maybe she could start going to church again, and take an interest in the local community. Anyway, she needed time to adjust to married life before they started a family.

MARRIAGE TO DAWN – ARNOLD STYLE – DAY 1.

7:30 Alarm. They wake up to a cup of Earl Grey. Dawn goes down stairs to prepare Arnold's breakfast and to make his packed lunch. Arnold enters the kitchen at 8 o'clock and after a full English breakfast, leaves for work. Dawn sets about tidying the house and thinking about dinner.
5:30 Arnold returns home to find Dawn in the kitchen ready to serve dinner. They have a small sherry together and Arnold tells her all about the day he has had. After dinner, Arnold helps her dry the pots and they go into the lounge to watch TV. Arnold reads the paper.
10:00 Arnold makes a pot of tea and they retire to bed to make love, before falling asleep in each other's arms.

MARRIAGE TO ARNOLD – DAWN STYLE – DAY 1.

7:30 Alarm goes off. Arnold wakes up to a cup of Earl Grey (if Arnold's bought any), and depending on whether he has set the Teasmade the previous night. Dawn tells him to get his own breakfast; she's not moving for anybody. Arnold enters the kitchen at 8 o'clock, grabs a bit of toast, makes his own packed lunch and leaves for work.
5:30 Arnold returns home to find his wife and mother-in-law drinking their second bottle of wine. There is no dinner and certainly no conversation. They go into the lounge, leaving Arnold to make himself some beans on toast and to read the paper.
10:00 Arnold retires to bed.

His preconceptions about married life were not destroyed immediately. At first, Dawn seemed satisfied in her new role of wife and housekeeper, and Arnold was justifiably proud of her. She kept the house tidy, and to show his appreciation Arnold bought her flowers every Friday.

If Dawn wanted to go out for a drink or to the cinema, Arnold was only too pleased to take her. She had her own chequebook with no limitations on spending, and he loved going out with her on Saturdays, into town to buy clothes. But what Arnold wanted now above anything else, was a child.

Dawn knew that she would never love Arnold. Like her mother, she had been used by men all her life and coupled with her inherent bitterness, could never feel deeply for anybody. But she was still going to get what she considered rightfully hers, and she did not care how she did it. This was going to be all about having fun and being in control, and she could only despise the person who was too stupid to see it.

It was going to be enjoyable work. She was not prepared to simply put Arnold out of his misery. He was going to suffer slowly, whether he deserved it or not. But first she needed to test the water.

Arnold hardly drank alcohol, and at first it did not matter to him that Dawn occasionally had too much. Nobody was perfect and life was for enjoying, but now, when she drank she became short-tempered. This would make Arnold more miserable, which irritated her even more.

One evening he came home and she was in the kitchen, preparing dinner. The sherry bottle was open and as he bent over and kissed her, she turned away.

'Fucking dinner's ruined.'

He had never heard her swear, and it took him by surprise. He did not care there was no dinner.

'Why? What's happened? Are you feeling alright?'

'I'm alright, it's the dinner that isn't.'

'Well, never mind. We can have a Chinese.'

Arnold began to get excited at the prospect, and she sensed it.

'But I've spent all afternoon getting it ready and it was going to be really special'

'Well, that's great. I'm sure it'll be delicious.'

'It's burnt and I so wanted it to be nice.'

She began to cry. Arnold had never seen her like this and he put his arms around her.

'Don't worry. I know it'll be fine. Let's eat, I'm starving.'

She seemed comforted by his concern and opened the oven to get out the cottage pie she had made. It was his favourite meal and she knew that he would not let her down. She had spent hours slowly letting it burn, to get it exactly right. It had been taken out of the oven several times during the afternoon, in case it was spoilt too soon. Too much and it would have been inedible. Dawn was not one of the three bears and Arnold certainly wasn't Goldilocks.

'I don't really feel hungry now Arnold, but you eat it if you're sure it's not that bad.'

She poured herself another glass of sherry and sat facing him at the table, testing him.

'I'm sorry it's a little bit burnt, but I'm sure you'll still enjoy it.'

Arnold had no choice. She must be upset otherwise she wouldn't have opened the sherry. It tasted awful, but he did not want to upset her again, so he ate what he could and put down his knife and fork.

'What was it like? Terrible, I suppose.'

'No. It wasn't that bad, not bad at all.'

She took another gulp of sherry, letting it linger in her mouth.

'You only ate it because you thought you had to, didn't you? You didn't enjoy it.'

Arnold was out of his depth and he did not know what to say. He just wanted it to stop.

Dawn was testing the water again.

'I didn't have to eat it. I wanted to, honestly. Let's just forget about it. Let's leave the washing up. I'll do it later.'

Dawn had no problem forgetting about it. It was Arnold that could not sleep for worrying. It was not going to be the first time he went to bed, next to her, listening to her breathe, as he lay there unable to sleep.

Insidiously at first, his aspirations were eroded away. Everything could be fine, and then for no apparent reason everything became tense and confusing. He was aware of the atmosphere as soon as he opened the door, and the fluttering in his stomach would increase. He felt like she had cast some spell on the house that was making him permanently anxious.

She knew as soon as he appeared at the door whether the spell was working. His degree of agitation determined her next move. It could be carefully orchestrated into a scenario that would leave him utterly bewildered by bedtime.

If he looked worried, she turned on the charm and stroked his hair. Feel his apprehension melt away. But Arnold was no psychologist. Unused to examining extreme emotions, he was unable to tell how his mind was deliberately and cold bloodedly being twisted into knots.

She would bring up the subject of children. Arnold desperately wanted them, and it suited Dawn to let him think that she felt the same. Arnold had equally shared her apprehensions about the pill. He was happy to carry on using condoms. Then, as soon as she felt ready, it should be relatively easy for her to conceive.

One evening, she took him deeper than ever before, and he stammered for the first time. She announced she wanted to get pregnant as soon as possible, and Arnold instantly felt relief and joy. This was what had been wrong. Deep down she had wanted a baby. It was her hormones acting out of control, which had been making her act irrationally, but now she understood the cause and was allowing her maternal instincts to surface.

Dawn saw it differently. She just felt the time had come to experiment further. It would make a great book, though taking notes would interfere with her enjoyment. For Dawn had been on the pill most of her adult life, though she had never told Arnold; she didn't want him to get the wrong idea about her.

She allowed two weeks before she told Arnold the good news.

'Arnold. I think I'm pregnant.'

'Why do you think that?'

'Because I'm two days late and I'm always on time normally.'

'That's wonderful.'

Girl's names flowed through his mind.

'It's too early to tell for definite, but I'm sure I am.'

Three days later she broke him the bad news.

'Arnold. I'm sorry. It was a false alarm.'

'Well, never mind. There'll be plenty more opportunities.'

He was very disappointed, but at last they had a common aim. Dawn allowed him three more brief insights into fatherhood over the coming months. The second time, she was pregnant for six weeks before 'loosing it'. They didn't make love often, but one night she wanted him so badly they had passionate sex. The next night, he returned home carrying roses and she told him she had violent stomach cramps and had started to bleed heavily. She had lost the baby and blamed it on the sex the night before. He was devastated. If he had been more considerate, it would never have happened.

She began excluding him more and more from her life, but he was so besotted he preferred to believe everything was normal. Arnold would often return home to find Dawn and her mother together drinking. They would disappear into the living room and leave him sitting at the kitchen table. Other nights, Dawn would not be there at all. These were the worst, as he wondered where she was.

The fluttering in his stomach became an ache, and he had his first anxiety attack.

Arnold decided to go to his doctor. He knew he must not bother Dawn. She had enough problems, but he did tell her that he had been prescribed Valium. It would only be for a short time until things improved. Dawn thought it was a good idea, as she now needed to rise to an even bigger challenge if she was going to counteract the effects of prescribed drugs.

On Friday nights the local pub held weekly discos, and Dawn liked to go. Arnold did not mind. It was what she wanted. He would stand at the bar with his beer as she disappeared with friends for a dance. He did begin to notice that she was spending more time hanging around the DJ, and it made him feel uneasy.

But one night near the end, he glanced over to the booth where the DJ stood. He was not there and neither was Dawn. The ache from his stomach spread into his chest as he scanned the dance floor. She wasn't there. The pub was like a labyrinth, and all the rooms disappeared into darkness. His head started to pound in time with the music and as Marvin sang, 'How sweet it is', the bass hit him like a train, and he pushed his way back to the bar.

Symptoms that affect the mind and body when they suspect betrayal, attack instantly. There is no comparable disease, and no cure. Jealousy and fear infect the mind. The body shakes with emotion and panic spreads as the virus takes hold. An holistic nightmare, but with no waking up in a warm bed.

Arnold's mind fought for an explanation. She would return in a minute and everything would be fine. It was some time before Dawn appeared from around the end of the bar, with the DJ. His hair was black and wiry and he smelt of sweat.

'Hi Arnold! This is Darren, he's the DJ and he thinks I ought to be a professional dancer.'

'Hello,' Arnold said, holding out his hand.

'Oh yeah, right, OK.' Darren made a vague attempt at a handshake.

'Better go anyway. I've got to finish my set. See you.'

He walked back to his booth and Arnold fetched the coats.

His mind was racing and his stomach ached as they walked home. She suggested chips. He said no as he led her by the arm and through the Precinct. She felt his fear, and smiled as they walked in silence.

He slammed the door shut and could not wait any longer.

'I tried to find you. Where were you?'

She was not in the mood to make excuses.

'I was sitting down having a drink with Darren and his friends.'

'But I looked all over the place and you weren't there.'

'Where do you think I was then, outside with him?'

Arnold had not even thought about this possibility. The panic rose again.

'I don't know what you're worrying about. We spent most of the time talking about you. Don't worry, I told him we had a really good sex life.'

'But why did you talk to him about that?'

'We just did. We talked about a lot of things. He's really interesting.'

'But I'm jealous. I can't help it. I'm really jealous.'

'What do you mean? You've got no right to be jealous. How dare you!'

Arnold began to cry.

'I can't help it. I love you and I'm jealous.'

'Well, you shouldn't be. Anyway, he does a disco out of town on Saturdays and he wants me to go.'

'What? When? Am I invited?'

'No. You wouldn't be interested and there'd only be room for me.'

Arnold felt an electric shock shoot through his neck and into his head.

'But you're not going to go are you? You can't, you're married. I won't allow you.'

But Arnold knew that he had lost. There was no way that he was ever going to stop her doing exactly what she wanted.

As his fears continued about his marriage, more pressure was applied on him at work. He had always loved his job and despite his personal life was able to maintain standards. But now his leadership was being tested.

Once every ten years, a major event in the calendar of public services took place. It was called the Land Use Survey. County records were brought up to date and everybody had to be on their toes. This was achieved by hours of fieldwork. It required an enormous input of manpower and could not be covered by the permanent staff, so temporary help was drafted in. These would-be surveyors had to be fit and intelligent, but the main requisite was that they were conscientious. Arnold was given the job of recruiting them.

It filled Arnold with dread. He had worked for years with little change, and he did not consider himself a manager. The job centre bombarded him with recruits about whom he had no clue. They all had long hair, stacked heeled boots and wore shaggy coats that smelt of goat.

But he built his team. They were allocated the old pavilion on the edge of the playing field, adjacent to the main building. The field had been compulsorily purchased, destined for a car park, but its small colonial-styled changing hut still had a part to play in the county's development strategy.

Arnold was allowed to take his desk with him. He placed it in the room as far back from the window as he could. There was a kettle and a lavatory, and one room still contained a bath, but the balcony was the bonus. It faced the river and was an ideal spot to roll up five Skinners, when one needed to take a well-earned rest from map duty. A combination of youth and intelligence equals drug abuse. Most of the newly appointed team smoked large quantities of Lebonese Gold, and the habit was not going to be affected by the constraints of work. As the weather got warmer, somebody had the idea of bringing a cricket bat. Runs and dope were scored together, in the afternoon sunshine.

Other things though, did not run so smoothly. Everybody wanted to survey the areas nearest to their homes. This meant they could stay in bed longer. The team soon realised they would be long gone before any of their gathered information was made public, so they opted for a surveying from bed approach. Why get up to tramp around in the rain when it could be done under the duvet?

Arnold was in no state to realise what was going on. Trying to deal with his personal life, his team saw him as a soft touch. They never meant to upset him, but he represented all the things they were rebelling against. The idea of a Straight being in charge was never cool, and they were not going to be part of The System at any cost.

Dawn continued to tear him apart. She would now sometimes stay out all night.

'I'm going out tonight with some of the girls and I'll stay at Mums', and she would be gone, leaving Arnold drained and afraid.

Once, he tried phoning her. All he wanted was to hear her voice.

'Hello. Is Dawn there? It's Arnold.'

'No. She's not here. Why should she be?'

'I thought she was staying with you tonight?'

'No. She's gone to her friend's house.'

'Have you got the number? I need to speak to her.'

'I have, but I've lost my address book.'

'What's her surname?'

'I don't know.'

Arnold knew she was lying.

He grabbed his car keys. He knew where most of her friends lived. He thought he might see her walking, laughing with them. He also might see her arm-in-arm with some stranger, leading her away. He felt sick and turned the car around.

'Hello. Has she got back yet?'

'She's not here and she's not going to be. I've told you, she's staying with a friend.'

'Well, if she does come back, can you tell her to phone me?'

'She won't, and anyway you don't bloody own her. She's got a life apart from you.'

Arnold did something he had never done before. He reached for the gin bottle and got drunk. As he sat there, he looked around at their belongings. He could remember where everything had come from and what it had cost, piecing together their whole relationship through occasional tables and the three-piece suite. He picked up the teddy bear he had given her on their first Christmas together. He had sent away for it after seeing an advert in a magazine. It doubled as a pyjama case and she was always cuddling it. He put the bear up to his face, smelling the fur. The zip was open and as he pushed his hand inside, he felt a plastic packet. He pulled it out and placed it on the table.

It was a packet of pills with the days of the month printed on its side.

———

Dawn poured herself another drink as she lay on her mother's settee, watching television. Why should he know where she was? It was far more enjoyable that he did not. He wasn't going to treat her like the other bastards did.

Arnold went to bed and slept like a condemned man awaiting his early morning call.

———

Arnold's office was in the hands of anarchists. Progress was slow and lunch breaks long. Somebody had discovered the rough land surrounding the field was a perfect habitat for cultivating magic mushrooms.

He still spent time over in his old department, but Arnold was feeling more and more uncomfortable. His colleagues would make sarcastic comments about the commune, and life with the hippies.

He now started experiencing panic attacks, and severe mood swings at work. Sometimes he could not care about anything, and he would become paranoid and angry with everybody, calling them useless. What did they think they were playing at, wasting public money and treating him like a fool? When he got really angry they would tell him to chill out, which annoyed him even more.

What Arnold could not see was that these changes of mood usually followed tea breaks. This was because the workforce were adding something more than sugar to his coffee in an attempt to sweeten him up.

He now ate lunch in the canteen, but the staff continued to make jokes at his expense.

'I suppose you'll be wanting something vegetarian now Arnold. I hear you're starting to grow rice out the front of the pavilion, either that or pot.'

He grew tired of the jokes and resorted to taking very short lunch-breaks. He did not like leaving the pavilion unguarded at lunchtimes, after he had returned once to find Maria naked in the bath with a young man wearing a top hat, and nothing else.

'Hi Arnold. This is Roger. He's a guitarist.'

Arnold had worked this out for himself, as the young man was balancing a guitar on his knees and strumming the chords to *Brown Sugar*. Jane was holding what Arnold perceived as a reefer in one hand, whilst giving Roger hand relief with the other.

'Hey man. Why don't you join us?' said the Top Hat.

'I'm going outside and when I come back, I want you gone and Maria back at her desk.'

Arnold walked back to the main building and through the swing doors. He then turned and marched back to his desk. He had made his point and they would have to respect him for it. There was no way he was going to put up with that sort of behaviour whilst he was in charge.

He had never known the room so quiet. Every head was bent over, working furiously. He felt embarrassed at his outburst and pretended to look for something in his desk. Maria meanwhile started to achieve a particularly earth-shattering orgasm. It sounded like there were two whales in the next room, and then water began to wash under the door.

Somebody shouted 'There she blows!'

Arnold pretended not to hear, and searched through his desk again. The Top Hat appeared with Maria, and everyone cheered as they disappeared out the door. The strains of *Midnight Rambler* were heard fading into the distance.

At ten-thirty every day, Arnold made himself a cup of tea and sat with the rest of the team for the morning break, before going to the lavatory. This coincided with the Red Brigade going for a joint. What he never noticed this particular break-time was the dried-brown fibrous vegetable matter that had been slowly infusing in the kettle, most of the morning. It was not a strong dose, but anything would be strong for an Arnold. Especially an Arnold that was already half-way to being certified.

This day they did not leave, but hid outside, before creeping back and tying up the toilet door. Arnold was stuck. They considered it a practical joke, but to someone close to a breakdown it was another major factor in pushing him nearer the edge. When he could not open the door, Arnold suddenly became overwhelmed by the events of the previous months and broke down.

Nobody was there to witness it. Alone, locked in the lavatory and hysterical, he lay on the floor and sobbed. It seemed everything, even his chosen vocation was destroying him, and his entire life had been wasted. His emotions changed from fright to anger in a second. It was only a matter of time before he was found out and disgraced. The team he had chosen had undermined his authority and respect. The work was shoddy, incomplete and unacceptable. He battered down the door and stood there, staring as the mushrooms started to hit the spot. All his paranoia surfaced at that moment and he felt an overwhelming desire to run.

He headed out from the door and across the playing field, towards the river. Five stoned figures resembling meercats knelt up in the long grass, and watched him disappear into the distance.

If Arnold had been in a state to notice, and he had looked downstream, he would have seen the block of flats where he had spent most of his life. Here, the river ran fast and wide as it flowed under the bridge that carried traffic from the south into the city.

Arnold did not know where he was going. He just needed to run. If he ran far and fast he might be able to exorcise the demons that were inside his head. If he exhausted himself, he might feel calm.

So he ran until his energy deserted him, and he could not run anymore. But the switch had been pressed in his brain and it could never be turned off. Arnold would never be considered sane again.

He lay on the edge of the bank with his hands dangling in the water. The rush had gone, but his mind still jumbled together all the events of the previous months, and at that moment love and hate merged together.

All he wanted was to go home and be with the woman he loved. She would make it better; would tell him that she loved him and everything had been a mistake. She would never betray him.

His twisted thoughts carried him back to the nights he had spent crying, lying next to her in bed, feeling the creases of her nightdress.

She was a whore.

She had hair like gold and he had captured her back from Hades to be with him forever.

But where did she go at night, when she said she was with her mother.

Her mother, the bitch that stank of drink and fucked anybody.

Two bitches, both on heat and begging for it.

Taking the pill and on the game.

They were going to have a large family, at least three.

Arnold climbed over the fence that ran adjacent to the main road and started to run again.

He felt alienated from reality, as if he was floating in a bubble and looking down at himself from space. If he wanted to change his destiny now, he could not. His fate had been determined years ago, before cream cakes and bread and butter. The metamorphism had started, and Lurch was emerging, with vacant eyes and a shell-shocked soul.

It was not very far, and it was still early, so she would still be there. Maybe they might make love in the garden, like he had always wanted to.

He dragged his shoes along the ground as he ran. The tears were streaming down his face as he stared at the world through drug-dazed eyes.

Arnold knew when he saw the black car parked outside his house that it was time. He polished the car's front wing with his sleeve and looked up at the window.

The spare key was hidden in the garage, and he reached over the mower and lifted up the fuel can to retrieve it. It was full. On the wall, next to the dartboard, was his tool cupboard. He had found it in a second-hand shop. It was an old kitchen unit with sliding glass panels, and Arnold had meticulously painted the outline of all his tools on the back panel in orange paint. He was proud of it, and had recently added another shelf for all the screws that he had been collecting over the years.

He slowly considered the shapes, weighing them up in his mind, before reaching up and choosing a 16oz. professional claw-hammer with a black rubber grip handle, which he slid into his pocket.

Arnold opened the back door and looked around. There was a bottle of spirits with three glasses on the table, and his blue rinsed mother-in-law, semi-conscious on the settee. A cigarette had been left to burn on the edge of the table, and the rosewood veneer was charred. He walked over and dropped the cigarette in the ashtray, before placing the glasses in the sink.

For the first time in his life he believed he was seeing everything clearly. At that moment the only thing he had ever been sure about was that Sunday followed Saturday. His senses became acutely focused on what he was about to do.

He climbed the stairs withdrawing the hammer from his trouser pocket.

He did not hesitate at the top or have second thoughts. In front of him was the mirror and he saw their reflection, and heard her making sounds that she had never made with him. Arnold thought the mirror could do with a clean.

She was on top of him, facing the wall. Her eyes were closed and her head was bent back as she rocked gently from side to side.

Arnold could not see his face, but he could see he was wearing a gold signet ring, as Arnold raised the hammer above his head.

There was no doubt in his mind that at that moment he wanted to kill her, but he knew he could never bring the hammer crashing down onto her skull. He was a useless fool who was even incapable of feeling hatred. He was more concerned about the mess it would make, scraping her brains from the bedroom wall. He allowed the hammer to fall silently by his side, as he turned and walked back down the stairs.

Arnold wiped the table, and then went to the sink before washing the glasses thoroughly and returning them to the cupboard. But then again, Arnold was always meticulous. He could still hear sounds coming from upstairs and he felt sick, as he looked around the room at the pathetic possessions he had proudly gathered around him.

Dawn's mother's mouth was open and her stockings were gathered around her ankles. She was snoring. Now Arnold could feel hate. It welled up inside, and he wretched as he stared at the woman who had helped to tear him apart. Her rinsed hair glowed purple, as he brought the venom up into his throat and vomited onto the carpet. Again he felt calm and focused. He would have his revenge, and this time he would not back down. He went into the garage and picked up the can of fuel and carried it back into the kitchen. He trickled the petrol around the living room, making a perfect elliptical arc around the settee and finishing at the back door. Dawn screamed with ecstasy as Arnold lit the match.

He sat on the garden wall and began to count. The Fire Brigade arrived seven minutes and forty seconds later. Arnold had no intentions of going anywhere as he was having a well-deserved afternoon off. He reached into his pocket and began witling at a pencil with his penknife.

The police found Arnold with the can of petrol. He admitted to everything but kept muttering something about a Goblin Teasmade.

He got a suspended sentence and a psychiatric assessment. The court order prevented Arnold from coming within a mile of his home. He would have preferred prison but instead, he was sentenced to a life back in the tower block with his parents. Neither really understood the circumstances of his breakdown, but at least the return of their son gave them something to focus on. Arnold relied on Valium to help him deal with the trauma of deceit as he began to obliterate the past from his mind.

PART TWO

CHAPTER FOUR

·

Gordonski had been sitting in the snug of The Duke of York most of the afternoon. He was fond of The Duke of York, and had started going there as he began to surface from a deep depression. Then, he had been a pathetic shadow of a man, spineless and weak, but the desperate need to re-invent himself had honed his body as well as his mind, and he now resembled a redundant prize-fighter, punch drunk with past glories and alcohol abuse. The rumours about his identity had persisted for weeks. He was a drugs dealer, or even a drugs squad officer, depending on the moral stance of the observer. Either were fine for Gordonski. It enabled him to invent his past as required.

He had appeared one winter and immediately retired to a corner in the snug underneath the dartboard, where he sat staring into his pint. From that moment, whenever Gordonski was present in the bar, the dartboard was redundant. Then around Easter, he came into the pub and bought the regulars assembled around the fruit machine a drink. He was friendly, amusing and extremely courteous to the landlord's daughter, who was struggling to carry the crates around the back into the yard, and had just announced that she was ten-week's pregnant. He always came in alone and could stay for hours, but whenever he left it was always begrudgingly, to appease his better half. Nobody was sure whether she was a figment of his imagination, as her name changed as often as his moods. But if she did exist, she cer-tainly must be a saint to be prepared to put up with Gordonski.

Over the coming weeks, the customers began to learn about Gordonski's past and although the basic story never faltered, the finer details could be elaborated on, or some-times forgotten, depending on his mood, and Gordonski's mood changed with the seasons.

If he came into the bar and ordered a drink, the signs were good, but if he went and sat under the dartboard, they took him his pint and nothing was said. These were the days he would stare into his glass and endeavour to battle with the demons that were biting at his heels. These were the times he was best left alone.

A psychopath with a heart of gold. Aggression tempered with compassion. Courted for his wisdom and avoided for his temper, Gordonski definitely had a split personality, but it had not always been a medical condition, and he attracted troubled souls like a magnet. They would wander in off the street and he would draw them to him, as he leaned over the table offering them the benefit of his troubled soul.

Gordonski's greatest love, apart from telling stories, was starting fires. He rated this as one of the most exciting things in the world, but that was before he progressed onto making bombs. There was always an audience prepared to listen to his exploits, and whether the stories were truth or fiction was irrelevant. He found recalling his life cathartic, and he had long since convinced himself that it was the truth. His creativity in fabricating lies was astounding, and as he amused the customers standing around the bar, his fingers constantly itched for his lighter. Becoming a pyromaniac suited his revised personality, allowing him greater creativity to expand on his past. In reality it was fire that had helped to bring about his downfall, but that was one story he did not like to recall. Fire could be relied on to obliterate the truth, and the truth was something Gordonski did not want to remember.

The landlord once asked him when his love of fire had started. Gordonski accepted the offered pint, and rolled himself a cigarette.

'I was about five. My dad was asleep in front of the fire, so I set his slippers alight. They went up a fucking treat.'

The voices around the bar grew silent. The football scores could wait.

'So then I stayed just long enough for the flames to reach his turn-ups, and chucked a cup of cold tea over him. He thought he was fucking spontaneously combusting. It was brilliant. I was even given some money to buy sweets.'

'Didn't you think he'd catch you? He couldn't have been that stupid.'

'He didn't have a fucking clue. There was even a fireguard

in front of the grate. I mean, if I hadn't acted sensibly, the whole house might have gone up.'

'So that's how it began then, your love of fires?'

'Yeah. My estate backed onto some fields, and at the end of the summer we'd make dens out of the haystacks. I got this great idea to start torching them.'

The darts team were having a practice night but they had now abandoned their game, and were packed in next to the jukebox.

'I'd wait until dark. My mates would place bets on how long it took for the Fire Brigade to come, and I'd get half the pot. I even used to dance on the top with the flames leaping around me and flick V-signs at them, as they drove up. But they never caught me.'

'They must 'ave known who you were.'

'No. It was dark. They couldn't see.'

'You're a fucking crazy man, Gordonski.'

'God, it's the best buzz in the world. I went out the next day. Had a phoenix tattooed on my arm.'

These stories entertained the wheelers and dealers with whom Gordonski now socialised. They respected his solitude when the seat under the dartboard beckoned him, but bought him drinks when he entertained them. Few bothered whether the stories were true or not. They would always be willing to listen, especially after committing an arduous benefit cheque fraud, or at the end of a hard night's thieving. Fence a few microwaves and listen to some anecdotes. It was a very civilised lunchtime, and Gordonski's tales made a change from dead cats in Chinese restaurants.

'So what happened? Didn't you ever get caught?'

The landlord already knew this bit, so Gordonski allowed him to answer.

'No. He fucking didn't. He always got away with it. Tell him what you did then, Gordonski.'

Gordonski reached inside his pocket and pulled out a folded sheet of newspaper and placed it on the bar. It was ripped and faded and showed the burnt out remains of a church, with a fire engine parked in front of it. Above the photograph was a caption.

ARSON ATTACK ON LOCAL CHURCH

'Was that you? Did you set fire to it?'

'Well, I liked being a major celebrity, didn't I? I'd got a taste for it.'

'And tell him when you did it. I love this bit.'

'On fucking Armistice Day, just as they were sounding the *Last Post*. I lit a poppy and threw it into a pile of knitted squares which the church was going to send to some fucking earthquake victims in South America. It didn't take long for the fire to spread, but by then I'd slipped back home to make the old dears a cup of tea.'

'Well, they must have thought it might be you, if you came back just as the church was set on fire.'

'They'd no idea. They were having their Sunday morning shag. They only ever had it off on a Sunday, and it was always between half-past-ten and eleven. They weren't going to admit that to the police.'

'And did the police think it was you?'

'They called to ask me where I'd been, but the old dears wanted to keep their secret so I had a cast-iron alibi, but everybody knew it was me.'

'So are you still doing it then?'

'Can't help myself, but it's not like I'm a drug addict. For fuck's sake, you don't catch Aids from petrol cans.'

Gordonski placed a cigarette in his mouth and adjusted his lighter. The nine-inch flame kissed the tip with perfect precision.

'Lets face it, there's no equivalent of Methadone for me. I can't break the habit by reducing the size of the fire until I'm content with a fucking nightlight. I know I shouldn't light fires, but I can't stop.'

'Couldn't you have tried therapy or something?'

'Fuck that. I knew that wouldn't work. I tried self help.'

'What was that then?'

Gordonski reached for his pint and winked at the barman.

'I worked on a cure myself. It fucking nearly worked as well. I connected my bollocks to the mains and gave myself mild electric shocks whilst watching *Towering Inferno* but the wires shorted and I set fire to my bed-sit.'

'God, you must have been mental.'

'And I invented the concept of nicotine patches.'

The barman leaned closer. He had not heard this bit before.

'I stuck firelighters on my arms. It was an attempt to reduce the addiction slowly. The fucking smell was foul, and one night I left them on too long and set fire to myself. It was a battle of wills. The fix of the fire versus third-degree burns.'

'And who won?'

'The fucking burn's won. I had to go to casualty.'

'And what happened then?'

'I just pretended I was simple. The bloke behind the counter said, "Name?" And I said Gordonski Von Trapp, and he replied, "What, like *The Sound of Music*?" That's correct, Traat, I answered.'

Gordonski often called people 'Traat'. It was actually 'Trout' pronounced with an accent. Nobody really understood why he pronounced it 'Traat' or even why he should want to refer to anybody as a fish. If asked, he would say that a trout was worth more than two roach and a gudgeon and he got the idea from a Captain Beefheart record.

'So the nurse said, "It's a bit of an unusual name, Von Trapp."

"My grandfather wrote it."

"Wrote what?"

"*The Sound of Music,* Traat."

"Rodgers and Hammerstein wrote *The Sound of Music.*"

"That's right. He was my grandfather."

"Rodgers and Hammerstein were two people."

"That's correct, Traat. Rodgers was my grandfather and Hammerstein was his brother. Rodgers and Hammerstein Von Trapp."

"How are you injured?"

"I set fire to myself."

'I showed him my arms.'

"How did you do that?"

"I had a firelighter taped to my arm."

Gordonski picked up the pint. It had been placed on cue, in front of him by the landlord. He drank half of it before putting it back down onto the bar. He studied the assortment of scallies that were gathered around him.

'I tell you what. The nurse asked me to take a seat but I knew I wasn't going to have to wait long.'

The customers in The Duke of York also learnt from Gordonski that he had once been a street fighter, on the housing estate where he had lived as a child. Here, older men past their prime, lived their dreams through younger eyes, and Gordonski had been taught to fight for his patch.

His street-fighting days ended abruptly when he was smashed in the eye by a bricklayer, and the injury seriously affected his sight. Two specialists were unable to help, and he was told to accept that the damage was permanent.

'So what did you do?'

Gordonski then allowed his fans to have an insight into the sensitive side of his personality.

'Well, I'd spent enough time stripped to the waist and knocking the brains out of neighbours. I decided to consolidate my horticultural skills by growing orchids in the lean-to greenhouse, at the back of my parents' house. I took the time to contemplate my future.'

Gordonski's audience would not want a story to end, but he would make them wait for the next instalment. The next day, they would be sat round the bar, waiting for him to arrive.

'Come on, Gordonski. What happened next?'

'Well, when they told me that I couldn't bare knuckle fight any more, I decided to start wearing gloves. I got a job as a boxer in a fair ground. The punters were paid five pounds to go three rounds, and I got a percentage of the takings. I took the rest in cider.'

One of the customers considered himself a cartoonist, and had drawn a picture of Gordonski flexing his muscles in front of a circus tent.

Gordonski stood up and raised himself up to his full height.

'Imagine the scene. The Barker standing in front of the curtains, decorated like the American flag. He presses the klaxon for attention. "Now then gentlemen, who of you out there sees yourself as a fighting man?" I'd then appear as *The Great Gordonski,* from behind the curtain.'

Gordonski was so convincing, the barman actually remembered seeing him.

'I'd look like a fucking cross between Spiderman and Quentin Crisp, and amaze the crowd with a display of shadow boxing. The theme to *Grandstand* blasts out from a pair of speakers. I'd wink at the blokes and blow them kisses, and they'd shout, "Fuck off you bastard poof, where's your handbag?" I'd dance about a bit more, enticing them to knock me for six.'

'How many fights did you have? Did you ever get hurt?'

'No way. There'd always be some twat with an eye for stardom, but they were always given good advice.'

'What, kick you in the bollocks and run?'

'No. They were told to take a fall. They'd still get half the money.'

'How did that work then?'

'Simple, the first round was a draw, the second theirs on points, and in the third I'd tap them on the chin, and they'd hit the deck. They got to keep their heads and some of the money.'

'Didn't everyone know it was a fix?'

'No. It always worked. When the twat started to do well, the crowd got excited and put on more bets, especially when they thought he was winning.'

Gordonski added some visual drama and entertained the group around the jukebox, to a display of dazzling foot-work.

'Sometimes, unfortunately, the boy saw his supposed advantage as a weakness in my fitness regime. You could always spot the ones desperate for glory, but they were always given a second chance.'

'What? Told to go to the toilet and not come back?'

'No. They were told before the start of the third to come out, take it on the chin and hit the canvas.'

'I bet there were some who didn't.'

'Unfortunately for them, there were. They thought because of the last round, I'd had it.'

'Poor sod'

'Yeah. He'd rush out to claim his Lonsdale belt, and I'd knock him senseless.'

There was always a brief show of appreciation after Gordonski finished one of his stories, but then the cider was bought and the jukebox turned up, leaving Gordonski to plan another chapter in his muddled past.

Gordonski reached for his glass and attempted to juggle his thoughts into order. He was in one of his darker moods, as he sat in his chair in the snug, staring at the light that reflected off the dartboard and into his eyes. He glanced at a man with lank hair tied back in a ponytail, who had bought a drink, and settled down on the next table. He was obviously troubled. Gordonski felt he knew this, having developed what he believed was the ability of second sight, a gift he had inherited from a deeply traumatic experience. It became more acute, the more he drank.

Like the Duke of York, 'when he was up he was up, and when he was down, he was down'. The result of amphetamine abuse, which left him with chronic mood swings, Gordonski always knew when a low was coming. It would follow a period of normality, but this never lulled him into a false sense of security, because he knew what was around the corner. His depression could last for weeks. He would spend his time watching daytime TV, and listening to Leonard Cohen in an attempt to induce himself back to sanity.

Gordonski could see in the man's eyes that he had a troubled soul and a story to tell, and Gordonski loved stories. Despite the intensity of his own mood, he could never resist administering a helping hand to a disordered mind.

The troubled soul glanced across at Gordonski. He saw a man wearing a black leather trenchcoat that was so distressed it was inconsolable, with a belt that was missing its buckle. If anybody asked Gordonski the reason for the coat's dilapidated state, they were told it was because he had been dragged for a mile behind a motorbike, when the owner had caught him trying to steal petrol. He hadn't needed the petrol for his own vehicle because he couldn't drive. It was because Gordonski had just had an uncontrollable desire to start a fire.

'Have you ever listened to Debussy?'

Gordonski sat down opposite the man staring into his face.

'He's a fantastic composer. I listen to him all the time. We were born in the same town. His music's very peaceful.'

The man did not like attention. He rarely spoke and even the social workers preferred to leave him alone, but Gordonski was quite capable of learning everything he wanted to know. He had been there himself.

'My grandfather used to cut his grass.'

The man staring down at the tabletop, reluctantly allowed his eyes to focus away from the ashtray and onto Gordonski's missing buckle. He had wanted to be left alone, but he also felt the need to confess, to obliterate his nightmare. He needed a priest, and Gordonski was only too eager to administer the last rites.

The man raised his head and leaned back on his chair. He stared at the bullet head, that was shaved so close it revealed a scar stretching from his left eye to his chin, and an ear, which was missing its lobe. Gordonski was making a clicking sound, by poking his tongue inside a cavity caused by a broken tooth.

'Woman was it?'

The man quickly looked down at the table again.

'Yes, how did you know… have you had problems… with women?'

'Only once. How long had your's been up to no good?'

'How did you know she was?'

Gordonski knew, just like he knew when the bus was about to come around the corner. It was because he had the gift of knowing and a compassion for listening. Suddenly an image of a woman's face inserted itself into Gordonski's mind and he fumbled for his lighter. She was from a story he had read in a magazine, left in a dentist's waiting room. A story that he had spent years trying to forget, but would never quite go away.

'It happened to me. I nearly went to prison.'

'What happened?'

'I started a fire and tried to burn the bitch.'

'Who?'

Gordonski's mouth went dry. A twitch spread down his cheek and joined his mouth in an act of solidarity.

'Oh bollocks, nobody. I'm talking crap. It's in a story. She was in a story, just a story I read once.'

Gordonski's hand reached for his glass, and he started to shake.

'So, who was your girlfriend shagging?'

'My friend. I'd known him for years. I thought she loved me. We were going to get married.'

So Gordonski listened, as images of his own past flashed in front of his eyes, and he remembered a life he had read about in a book of fairy tales.

The man was fighting away tears.

Gordonski touched his hand. He knew the man had made up his mind, and there was nothing he could do.

He went to the bar.

'Pint of cider… Hang on a minute.'

Gordonski turned around to ask the man what he wanted to drink, but he had gone.

He was found three days later in a reed bed, at the foot of the weir.

—·—

Gordonski opened the door and stared at the mat. It had WELCOME written on it in four languages, and he knew one of them was English, and two others, French and German, but he was not sure of the last one. He thought that it was probably East European. He was living with his girlfriend called Amanda, and she was getting really annoyed with him. He steadied himself before entering the hallway.

Amanda had met Gordonski at a club, where he was working as a barman. She fell for him immediately. It was not difficult to understand. Although he no longer had the physique of a fighter, he was still handsome, with eyes that could stimulate as well as any vibrator. His forté was mixing cocktails, and he had a separate routine for each one, dancing around the optics and pouring the shots as he gyrated to the Happy Monday's.

The night Amanda saw him first, his hair was long and platted with beads and he was wearing a kilt, Doc Martens and a black T-shirt, with 'I'm A Fucking Maniac' printed on the front. He looked like a punk participant in the Braemar games, rather than a barman in a nightclub. But that was what the owner wanted. Something to keep the punters amused, as he snorted another line in the office.

Gordonski always kept the women customers happy. They talked to him about pre-menstrual tension and the problems of sanitary towels, especially if you wanted to wear a thong.

East End villains and South American dictators, although teddy bears in the bedroom, can still nail a friend to a coffee table. The women that fell for Gordonski were attracted by his gentleness, as well as his collection of baseball bats.

It was not that Gordonski had ever contemplated annexing Poland, but he had this presence that made men proceed with caution. Women could not see it, but they should have, for even Gordonski was not aware of what he was capable of doing.

He had a presence that women could not resist. They could be strong and in control, or hurt and vulnerable. Gordonski had the charm to win them all round. He was sensitive with an air of danger, but he would never let them down. They could lean on him in times of trouble, and he would protect them. The sex was fantastic. He was considerate and exciting, leading them through fantasies they had not even dreamt of. Rasputin Gordonski, in tartan.

Unfortunately for them, it never lasted.

Amanda stayed behind after the club closed, and everybody played musical joints. Rizla's were stuck together and passed along the bar as the music played, and when the tape was turned off, the person left with the uncompleted joint had to add something. Any combination of pharmaceuticals was acceptable, and it led to weird experiences that could never be repeated. Chemical Liquorice Allsorts. You got what you got, and you took your chances.

Amanda took her chance, and it included Gordonski. He was taken home for sex, and made to wear a construction worker's helmet that she had found on a building site.

Gordonski became very attached to it, and he bought an ex-army canvas bag from a surplus store to keep it in. He carried it everywhere and it became affectionately known as *The Shagging Bonnet*.

Amanda should have known better. She had a good job and was in a steady relationship, but she wanted excitement, and Gordonski seemed to fit the bill. He was certainly not a long-term proposition, but some months later, and minus the boyfriend, Amanda met Gordonski again and everything changed. She was out with her friends from work, and they all thought he was amusing, as well as attractive. She did not think that all her friends could be wrong, so she decided it was time to get the builders round again.

Amanda pushed her way into the cocktail area, where two girls in leather skirts and boob tubes were working their way through every conceivable mixture imaginable.

'Hi Gordonski.'

'Amanda hi. How are you? It's good to see you. I've really missed you.'

Amanda was in no doubt that he meant it, and since splitting up with the computer programmer, she had thought about him constantly.

'I'm fine. How are you?'

'Kool and the Gang thanks. I've been a bit down, but everything's great now.'

Gordonski was coming out of a deep depression, and going for counselling. He did not tell Amanda that, because he did not want her to worry. Anyway, he had been feeling much more positive recently.

'I'm on a night out with some of the girls from work, and we fancied a dance. I didn't think you still worked here.'

'Yeah, I'm still here. What are you doing afterwards? We can have a drink if you want.'

'Fine. I'll see you later.'

They saw a lot of each other later, and Gordonski moved in with Amanda. The canvas bag was hung on a hook under the stairs, and its contents were kept under the bed.

Gordonski liked living together, and he felt that Amanda could be the one. Living together reminded him of childhood and feeling safe. Initially the women loved it too, but then he would do something to make them re-evaluate the relationship, like urinating over them in the middle of the night, or getting them addicted to speed.

Three months later, Amanda lost her job and had a habit, which kept her up for days at a time. Gordonski never had to force his girlfriends. He was not some evil dealer that got them into drugs so that he could manipulate their lives, and take their money. They took the drugs because they wanted to. But then he would always try to take them that one step beyond.

One of Gordonski's many problems was that he suffered from terminal hedonism. His girlfriends' excesses gave him the will to take himself further down into the abyss, and he viewed their possible addiction as a mission of exploration. He should then, at least, have warned them of the dangers of going too far, but he never did. Eventually they saw the light themselves, and he was shown the door.

'Hi Amanda, I'm back. Hey, do you think that's Czechoslovakian written on the mat?'

Gordonski knew he was in deep trouble. He practised taking his coat off and hanging it up on the peg a couple of times, before entering the room. Amanda was sat facing the door and she was holding a glass of wine.

'Where the fuck have you been? You said you'd only be gone a few minutes. It's eight o'clock now.'

Gordonski sat down on the settee and placed a plastic bag on the table. It contained two large bottles of *White Lightning*.

'I'm sorry, but I had this really weird experience. I met this guy who'd been fucked off by his girlfriend, and I felt like I was reading him his last rites or something. He was really screwed up.'

'What, more than you? You went out at eleven o'clock to get a paper and a packet of fags, and it's eight o'clock now. I've been sat all day wondering whether you'd been run over by a bus. Instead, you've been abducted by aliens and had your brain removed.'

'No, no really. It's true. She'd been shagging his best friend for months. They were about to get married and he was really fucked-up. He'd just finished telling me about it, and then he just disappeared. It's like he chose me to be the keeper of his story, and I'm fucking going to remember it – to use for the good of others.'

'Well, get a pointed hat and a cloak, and get yourself a job on *Jackanory*.'

'Don't you understand what's happened? I'm part of a chain. Somebody's future could depend on me accurately passing the story on.'

'No chance! Chinese whispers have never been one of your better skills. Write it down. You'll have forgotten it by the morning. So that's where you've been all afternoon then, in the pub listening to some piss head.'

'I've told you he had a story to tell, and I was there. He trusted me and one day I'll pass it on to somebody else.'

'Alright, bloody tell me the fucking story? Tell me then.'

'I'm not telling you.'

'Why not?'

'Because you're not the right person.'

'What person?'

'The person who'll benefit from it. I'll only repeat the story to someone it might help.'

'It might help me.'

She knew it wouldn't.

Amanda was becoming accustomed to the lapses of sanity which followed his drinking sessions, but they no longer amused her. He would disappear for hours and come back drunk and talk in riddles. They never did anything together, and sex was not worth the effort.

At first he had been caring, with a sense of humour that made her laugh out loud, but now she could not find him amusing at all. He lost his temper and was irritating. He would recall a story he had heard, or tell her something he had done, but it never made sense. It was like listening to a stand-up comic, but never understanding the punch line. His stories needed subtitles.

Amanda thought back to when they first met. She was happy enough in her relationship, and she enjoyed her job.

It had simply been a case of lust, which had developed into something more. In the beginning of the relationship, he had been considerate and loving. Quite quickly, everything had changed, and Gordonski had become obsessive and abusive towards her.

'You just don't fucking understand. What's for tea?'

'Arse'oles.'

'Don't be so fucking stupid. What is there to eat?'

'Arse'oles'

'What? Fried arse'oles, grilled arse'oles or arse'oles with sautéed fucking potatoes, or maybe just fucking uncooked arse'oles?'

Amanda walked into the kitchen.

'None of your *Nouveau Cuisine* then? Not arse'oles lightly caramelised, and served on a bed of Thai rice with stir-fried arse'oles and rocket. To be followed by a summer pudding containing fifteen different varieties of arse'oles in season and raspberry coulée. All washed down with a bottle of 1956 Chateau Neuf De Ringpiece.'

She poured herself another glass of wine and wondered why she was having a relationship with a man who seemed determined to push her to her limits. She only used to drink at weekends. Now, she needed two bottles a night.

This was Gordonski's real party-trick. His ultimate challenge. To take a non-drinking virgin who had never had a cigarette, and turn her into a chain-smoking nymphomaniac with an alcohol problem. Women did not deserve his respect. He would show them the way forward and at first they appreciated him, but it would not be long before they were whinging and finding fault. It was bound to happen, and they soon found it difficult dealing with his excesses. This was when he realised the relationship was doomed, and as far as he was concerned it could not end fast enough. There would always be another lost soul around the corner, needing to be saved. So his habits would become more extreme and his methods more manic, until the women saw the light and he had to begin the process all over again.

Gordonski knew exactly why he did it. Women always hurt him. So they deserved some of their own medicine. His relationships always followed a pattern. When one ended, he immediately looked for somebody else to help him recover. His grief never lasted. Gordonski was incapable of reason. He had tried that a long time ago, and it had nearly destroyed him.

Amanda smashed her glass onto the table.

'There was nothing wrong with me when I met you. I just fancied you. You were really nice. Why have you turned into such a shit?'

Gordonski shook his bottle of cider and opened the cap. Three litres of chemical fizz erupted out of the top.

'If you're not happy, fuck off!'

'I can't live with you anymore, Gordonski. You're doing me in. You'll have to go and find somewhere else to live.'

Gordonski laughed. He had experienced this moment many times before and it always made him smile.

'O.K. Kool and the Gang.'

That night, Gordonski went out and set fire to Amanda's shed.

———

It was not detox that Gordonski was seeking to achieve as he set fire to Amanda's shed, but it was the closest he would get. He had never managed to stop starting fires, though he had scaled down. He was now only setting fire to what belonged to his ex-girlfriends.

Apart from the shed, his score included a cuddly toy, two laundry baskets and a caravan. The caravan belonged to a policewoman, where they had spent weekends together. He was especially proud of the job he had carried out on her. She was addicted to speed within a month, and was a long time recovering.

Gordonski varied what he burnt on the amount his girlfriends had suffered. He did not go easier on the ones he hurt the most. Temporary addiction to amphetamines equalled a caravan, alcohol dependence a garden shed. The more work he put in, the bigger the fire.

———

The next day Gordonski returned to his own flat. He paid the rent because he knew he would always return, and there was nothing about this current relationship that had given him reason to contemplate giving the landlord notice.

He knew he was about to enter a period of deep depression and had to prepare himself, if he was going to get through the next few days.

'Ten large bottles of strong cider and two hundred cigarettes please, Traat.'

This usually was enough to see him through the worst.

'I hope you've warned the neighbours.'

The owner of the off-licence was packing the bottles into a cardboard box. The fact that he did not get a reply should have been enough to make him realise. Gordonski was not in the mood for conversation.

'I usually find that it saves a lot of hassle if you warn them first.'

Gordonski finished putting the cigarettes away in his pockets and raised his head.

'What are you on about, Traat?'

'I just said about warning the neighbours.'

'Are you being deliberately fucking evasive, or are you going to tell me exactly what you're talking about. Warn the neighbours about what? That I'm a fucking psychopath, and I'm going to hack them all to death with a samurai sword, or tell them that there's a meteor storm about to land on their fucking heads, and they've only got four minutes to get their cars in the garage. Maybe I should warn them that road works are starting next Monday on the M5 at junction 28, and there'll be a contra flow system in operation for most of the week – or that the fucking price of stamps is going up again. Warn them about fucking what?'

Gordonski felt for his lighter and looked around for the best place to start a fire. The shopkeeper felt under the counter for the cricket bat he kept for emergencies.

'I'm sorry, mate. I was just trying to make conversation. I thought you were having a party, and that's why… er… you were buying all the booze.'

'What sort of insurance have you got on this place?'

Gordonski appeared calmer, and the shopkeeper relaxed.

'What sort of insurance? You mean like building and contents, and that sort of stuff. Well, I've got the normal sort of cover like theft and accidental damage. Why? Are you in insurance?'

He let go of the cricket bat and picked up a packet of Mintoes which he always kept by the till, and offered one. Gordonski refused the offer.

'What about fire insurance? Have you got plenty of that?'

'Yes. It's in with the buildings and contents insurance. Why? Can you offer me a better deal?'

'No, but I can offer you some advice.'

'What's that then?'

'Finish packing my stuff and give me my change, otherwise I'll come back later tonight and set fire to your fucking shop you bastard, but I'll make sure I'll warn the neighbours first, and then they can all come out and watch you burn.'

Gordonski headed for home. The shopkeeper locked up for the night and went to check the small print in his insurance policy.

PART THREE

•

'Come on. Spicy mushrooms or felafel?'

'I don't want spicy mushrooms or felafel. I want Cajun fries. No I don't. I want crêpes with banana and maple syrup.'

'Oh yeah. Crêpes or chocolate fudge cake, but before that I want chiapatta rolls with mozzarella and fresh basil.'

'Alright, but let's go to the cider tent first.'

'Good idea.'

Two middle-aged men were weaving their way through the maze of tents, avoiding the guide ropes as they made their way down the hill. The Vale of Avalon stretched out to the right, and Glastonbury Tor was visible on the horizon.

'Thank God! Only one more day of body abuse and then back to normality.'

They both carried wine boxes, one white and one red, and lit up a joint as they negotiated the dusty track towards Bartertown. They resembled Victorian explorers searching for the source of the Nile; one in a yellow kagoul, and the other in an ex-army poncho, bought especially for the expedition. They both experienced dread as they contemplated the day ahead, and had to sit down for a drink of wine.

Music pounded from every direction. Thousands of people wandered about looking for food. Lines of bedraggled men and women trudged back up the hill, like returning soldiers from a period of duty on some First World War battlefield; but their tired bodies were a result of all night raving, rather than the horrors of war. The Victoria Cross has never been awarded to a participant of Glastonbury, but perhaps it should be. Anybody who has survived three days at the Glastonbury Festival has easily done the equivalent of a major campaign, and ought to be treated with the deep respect, worthy of a Chelsea Pensioner.

The whole site was a mass of sludge. Everybody was wearing this season's new black, slimy-brown. Young conscripts who had arrived ill-equipped, in platform shoes and summer casuals, had merely changed one uniform for another.

It did not matter whether you were wearing *Paul Smith* or *Topshop,* you were still covered in shit, and missing your mum. Waterproofs were priceless, and the drug pushers who stood on the main thoroughfares shouting, 'Acid, Whiz, E's, Skunk,' were now being joined by the rubber dealers screaming, 'Wellingtons, Pacamacs.'

'What you got man?'

'Wellingtons.'

'How much?'

'Twenty-five pounds a pair.'

'Are they good?'

'Yeah.'

'Can I just have one for fifteen quid?'

'No you can't. Have you only got one fucking leg?'

'No, but I lost all my pills and I haven't got much money. I can only afford to buy one.'

'I'm not selling pills. I'm selling Wellingtons. Wellington boots, not bloody Ectasy. You know Wellingtons? That you put on your feet when it's raining. Fuck off!'

A police helicopter flew overhead, and a drunken biker exposed his backside as the dealers pulled their hoods tightly around their heads.

The two men were not covered in mud, and they had Wellingtons. They had been coming to Glastonbury for fifteen years, and had experienced every type of weather. They knew exactly what to bring. They had clothes for every climatic change, and even carried a compass in case their navigational skills were affected by mud blindness and they could not find their tent.

Nialls, the younger by ten months, had bought his *Helly Hanson* waterproofs two days before, from the same shop he purchased his *Royal Hunter* boots. His hair was long and thinning, and his short stubbly beard counter balanced his encroaching forehead. He was slim, good-looking and would have undoubtedly led the Charge of the Light Brigade if he had been alive, or so he thought. Malcolm was taller and heavier, with a round face and short cropped hair. Apart from the poncho, he was wearing a pair of navvy's boots with reinforced toes. He bought them at a farmers' shop, and had had them for years.

Nialls met Malcolm when they were thirteen and thirsty for life, at the school badminton club the day President Kennedy was shot.

Despite the fact they were at the same school, they had never spoken to each other, before that momentous day they crouched down facing each other in the gym. It was an inter-house tournament, and Nialls had been the choice to lead his team to victory. Malcolm had been chosen because his house tutor was a newly qualified teacher, and keen on encouraging self-esteem. It did not matter if it deprived his team of the trophy. So Malcolm, overweight and breathless, conceded defeat against the dashing Nialls, and they shook hands under the net. The rest of Malcolm's team groaned in unison, as the teacher experienced his first pangs of self-doubt.

Malcolm had joined the school two years before. Nialls, who had been there since leaving his infant's school, had already surrounded himself with a circle of friends. Their paths had crossed, but Malcolm had showed little interest in the sports star of the lower school. Nialls pretended not to care, but it secretly unnerved him that someone with a flagrant disregard for calorie intake, should not want to pay him the respect he deserved.

It was their mutual interest in the joy of shuttlecocks that eventually brought them together. Nialls was looking for something new to satisfy his over-active hormones, and despite his lack of athletic prowess, Malcolm was rumoured to have a girlfriend. Nialls was still flirting with boys and he knew that if he did not do something quickly, his masculinity might be put into serious doubt. So began a tenuous friendship that had lasted into middle age. They would lose touch for long periods, regrouping when their contrasting personalities needed to complement each other's individual quests.

Nialls' family were middle class and could trace their lineage back to slave traders. His father was a surgeon and his mother, a prominent exponent of women's rights. She lectured all over the world, and one of her novels had just been made into a film. Nialls' ancestors had once owned a fleet of ships and lived on an estate outside Bristol, but after the abolition of slavery, they moved into pottery manufacturing. It became a tradition that the eldest son should go into medicine.

Malcolm's family, as far as anybody knew, had worked on the land. His great-grandmother had been sent away to escape the advances of the local vet, who was known to have already fathered at least two illegitimate children. She was extremely beautiful, and obtained a position in a factory that made feather boas for the gentry. She soon caught the eye of the owner's son and they were married on New Year's Day. Later that year, the factory went bankrupt, a victim of changing fashion and foreign imports. Their daughter married an optician with a modest income, and the family inheritance eventually allowed Malcolm's father to open a chain of hardware shops. The venture thrived, and Malcolm was sent to private school.

It was a strange combination for a friendship. Nialls could never let his confidence falter, and he never sort sympathy, particularly from Malcolm. Malcolm, however, had required sympathy many times in his life. He particularly needed support now, but as usual, Nialls was demonstrating a lack of understanding, coupled with complete indifference. Despite this, they had continued to intertwine through each other's lives, forging a relationship that would outlast any marriage.

'Let's just have one glass of cider and then head back. I'm really fucked. I don't think I can take anymore.'

'Malcolm, you're such a lightweight. I thought you'd be up for a double drop tonight. Last evening, main stage. Where's your Glastonbury stoicism gone?'

Nialls knew that he would get his way. Malcolm was feeling vulnerable and needed a friend. He would not want to go back on his own to a deserted camp.

The cider tent was the first or last outpost, depending on the altered state of your brain, as you stumbled upon it. Conveniently sited at the entrance to the main stage, it granted you that final hit before you wandered into the largest mud bath ever seen. There was even a canoe, using the crowd for slalom practise, weaving in and out of the pylons, as the band played on, Straw had been scattered on the ground, and here, accountants and 'travellers' shared cigarette papers, but little else, and students in rugby shirts wearing silly hats ate baked potatoes at three pounds a time. The aroma of spiced cider and grass filled the air.

The cider tent was not strictly a tent, but a bus covered in brightly painted apples, advertising its contents. The destination board on the front read, NOWHERE, in gothic copperplate. It had been added by the owner's daughter, who was studying graphic design. Maybe it had once been a tent, but now it was definitely a bus, with a tent attached to it, and it was the Mecca of the New Age pilgrims searching for inner peace. Ignore the healing fields and the biodegradable toilets, this was where you came to be enlightened. Thousands massed in front of it, from early morning until late, when the flaps would come down like sleepy eyes winking with bloodshot intent, as the unwanted pints were abandoned on the ground.

Nialls loved coming to the cider tent because it buzzed with life. Traumas unfolded in front of his eyes, as friends became enemies or even lovers, as the alcohol fought for supremacy. Stories were written and plays performed, as the actors came and went. Life ebbed and flowed, in a sea of paper cups and plastic trays.

Nialls had another reason to keep coming back to the cider tent, and that was because he fancied the owner's daughter. She had smiled at him one night, and from that moment he was convinced she fancied him. She had actually been laughing at him tripping over one of the tent ropes, as he tried to negotiate the conclusion of a wonderful evening. But the drugs had kicked in, and he was convinced that her smile was a reflection of her passion, rather than pity, as his head appeared grinning inanely over the counter. The next day the seed had been sown and he would always be convinced that she gazed at him longingly, from behind the barrels of Special Vintage.

Nialls elbowed his way to the front of the queue and bought two pints of medium cider. He glanced into the murky background of the tent and thought he saw a figure quickly slip behind one of the barrels.

Malcolm had managed to find a seat. There was a row of

railway sleepers mounted on concrete blocks around the edge of the field. One had just been vacated by a figure in a sleeping bag, who had rolled off the edge and into the mud.

Malcolm took his opportunity and sat down. There was a fence around the edge behind the seats, and as Malcolm waited, he watched the figures in the next field sliding about, out of control. There was only one thing worse than battling through mud at Glastonbury; that was battling through mud to get to the toilets. A line of petrified faces stood balancing on milk crates, set at right angles to the rows of blue boxes, pulsing with methane. Deep furrows were worn into the ground, and each toilet had a personal flume leading directly to its door. This required anybody who was desperate enough, to launch themselves from the relative safety of numbers onto the downward slide to Shitsville. The stench became more overpowering the closer you got, but it did not prevent a skinhead in Union Jack underpants from enjoying a Donner Kebab, whilst waiting his turn.

Nialls returned with the drinks. He reached into his pocket and topped them up with some brandy he carried for emergencies.

'Fucking Hell! This gets worse every year. I'm not drinking cider anymore. I'm going to stick to beer.'

But he didn't, because standing in a beer tent was never half as much fun as being here, sitting around a field of mud watching the shell-shocked recruits enjoying a bit of leave.

'Come on Malcolm, let's go up to the sacred field. It's the Summer solstice so it's bound to be a bit of a laugh.'

The prospects of struggling through more mud to reach a man-made stone circle could only be considered after drinking copious amounts of cider. But at least they would be able to get some food on the way. They set off up the main avenue and through the market, past an inflated rhino, towards the healing fields. The rhino was floating above a stall supporting an environmental group, but it had a slow puncture and its majestic horn now hung flaccidly downwards. It resembled a prawn, rather than the noble beast of the African Savanna, and as the stall was not getting the attention it deserved, it had converted itself into a rave tent.

Nialls and Malcolm settled for garlic mushrooms. This was one of the few stalls that one could reach without waders. Fate had placed it on a few square metres of ground that had raised it fractionally higher than the surrounding stalls, and it was reaping the benefits. The stall's name had been changed to NOAH'S ARK, and had begun the weekend as a noodle bar. It had quickly sold out of those, and was now selling anything it could, by buying low from the less fortunate store holders in the vicinity.

The light was fading and the drumming was getting louder. A wicker man was blazing at the entrance to the sacred space, as Malcolm and Nialls approached the hill. Groups of musicians sat hunched over drums, all banging out individual interpretations of *Stairway to Heaven*. The Chief Druid was trying to keep them in time with a metal gong. He was raised up on a platform above the largest stone, and he was chanting. A group of young women wearing wings, were offering Tequilla out of water pistols, at one pound a shot. They kept fluttering back to Fairyland to get refills from a man in a buckskin jacket, who was sitting on top of another stone. He was grasping a bottle, and desperately trying to prevent his hair from igniting, as the sparks were whipped up by the wind.

'Come on, Nialls. Let's go back to the cider tent.'

'No way. We'll only get stuck talking to some twats inevitably called Andy or Steve, who are from Bristol and have run out of dope. We'll just head back.'

The music was still pulsing around the hill in waves as they made their way back up to the camp. The ground that had begun soggy and wet on the Friday, was now thick and heavy. It stuck to their shoes, pulling them back as they peered through the flares and smoke, looking for their field. A Crusty, with a dog on a rope and carrying a rainstick, tried to sell them some hash cakes. Market forces had forced him to reduce his prices and the Crusty was now working to a very tight budget. His professional cliental were now beginning to leave, and were more concerned about the lack of power in their phones, than buying from a dodgy dope dealer. It was Sunday night, and they could not be late for the office the next day. Nialls, in an attempt to avoid him, had tripped over the man's rainstick, and now slid into a couple eating a Pot Noodle over a primus stove.

As they entered the gate into their field, they could see someone standing amongst the dying embers of their fire. His face was smeared with charcoal and he was waving a burning cross. Nialls and Malcolm approached with caution. The rest of their friends were lying around the fire in various states of stupor, and one of them managed a cursory greeting as they stepped into the circle.

'Hi guys! This is Gordonski.'

Nialls gave the man the once-over. Gordonski was wearing a battered leather coat, and there was a bottle of cider sticking out of its pocket. Gordonski threw the cross down into the fire, reached into his pocket and brought out a can of lighter fuel.

Nialls sat down on a log and warmed his hands.

'So Gordonski. What the fuck do you do?'

'I start fires.'

'Are you particular, or do you just start them anywhere?'

'Anywhere that's Kool and the Gang, Traat. Fancy a drink?'

Nialls had an aptitude for picking up eccentrics. He was the Mr Toad of human resources. He loved anybody that could guarantee him pleasure, and as long as they provided it, he was their friend. Gordonski looked like he was going to fit in admirably. He was certainly entertaining, and definitely had the gift of storytelling. He kept them mesmerised for hours.

Gordonski recalled many stories that night. He told them about a man he had met when he had been crossing the Andes on horseback. The man was living in a stone hut on the side of a mountain, and had wandered the world for years. He had lost his job and his life, a victim of a vicious woman and her calculating mother, driven to the brink of suicide.

Malcolm had an enduring quality that often touched on gullibility, and he was moved by what he heard.

'Bloody hippies. If they hadn't got him stoned and locked him in the toilet, he'd never have gone home and found her.'

'Malcolm, you're such a twat. She wouldn't have stopped. He was bound to catch her eventually.'

Gordonski took out the can of lighter fuel and poured some onto the dying embers. He flicked his tongue through a gap in his teeth.

'Anyway, Traat, tomorrow I go in search of revenge, and if you'd like to join me you'd be more than welcome.'

'Revenge for what?'

'Revenge for the poor bastard who wasted years of his life sitting in some fucking shed in the middle of nowhere. Somebody has to pay.'

'So where are you going?'

'Tomorrow, Traat, I am travelling to Devon where I hope to obtain a position in a spiritual retreat for women in crisis, or so it says on the advert. I gather they're planning an eclipse festival and are in need of a general handyman, something that I am well qualified for. I hope to be successful in my interview, otherwise I might have to burn the place down. Anyway, I've already spoken to them on the phone and they seem quite impressed with my previous experience.'

Nialls decided that he liked Gordonski. He had definitely detected a hint of mysogynism, and that would do for a start. He always felt flat after Glastonbury. Gordonski might be able to offer him something to look forward to.

———

Nialls was fingering his split ends, whilst observing his sore throat in the mirror, when his mobile rang. He had just opened his bank statement and was feeling depressed.

'Hi, Traat! It's Gordonski. Do you want to hear some good news?'

'Anything that makes me forget the amount of money I'm paying out to past wives.'

'How do you fancy a day or two in the country? You can exercise a bit of revenge.'

'Always ready for that. What you got in mind?'

'This place is unbelievable. It's run by three women who don't know whether to save a whale or adopt an Albanian orphan. They're so trying to be Right On in everything, they don't do anything properly. The only thing they agree on is they don't like men, but I've caught them looking at me once or twice, and they're not short of an erect nipple or two.'

'So have you worn the shagging bonnet yet?'

'Not yet, but it won't be long. One's called Lynette and weighs about seventy stone.'

'What's she like then?'

'Can't say that I really want to find out.'

'So what are we going to do?'

'They're running a course in two weeks based around the solar eclipse. It's three days of workshops culminating in a big eclipse event. There's going to be camping and some fucking drumming group is going to be here as well. Why don't you both come? They haven't filled all the places yet, and we could have a really good crack.'

'Yeah! Good one. Give me the details. I wanted to see the eclipse anyway. You're in exactly the right place.'

'There's one slight problem.'

'What's that?'

'Only single women or couples can apply. No single men allowed, except me of course.'

'Well, that's fucked that then.'

'No. I've thought of that. It says couples, so you two can be a couple.'

'How do you work that one out, then?'

'Just fill out the form pretending that one of you is a woman. There are plenty of names that can be either male or female, and then when you get here they're not going to turn you away. They need the money. You can always be gay. They won't see a couple of fags as a threat, and by the time they do, it'll be too late.'

'So what's going on?'

'I don't know. It could be anything. I'm just the gardener. Tolerated because I'm sensitive, and was abused by my father.'

'You never said.'

'Listen, the only abusing that went on in my house consisted of my right hand, and an etching by some restoration artist depicting the Great Fire of London. They only gave me the job because they allowed themselves to be sympathetic to a victim of a cruel father. I apparently managed to escape his disgusting advances by locking myself in the greenhouse.'

'So what are you saying?'

'It allowed me to develop my horticultural skills. Also I've told them my name's Thrower.'

'Why's that an advantage?'

'Percy Thrower was the first superstar gardener. He had groupies and everything, and he happened to be my uncle.'

'God, you're a fucking chameleon, Gordonski. What did they say to that?'

'I told them he was into organic gardening, but only his close family knew about it. They were well impressed. I think I might blow them up.

'What?'

'Nothing, just a thought. I can see them now.'

'Who?'

'The three witches.'

'Why, where are you?'

'In the shed in the garden.'

'What are they doing?'

'Well, at the moment they appear to be dancing around a bush.'

'What?'

'They think it's got healing properties.'

'Why?'

'Because I told them that Percy was a white witch, and used to conjure up the healing properties of the mystical Rowan tree.

'What's a Rowan tree look like?'

'I don't fucking know, Traat! It just looks like a bush to me but they haven't any idea, so they can believe what they want. It's keeping them happy. I'm going to plant something else in its place tonight. That should really do their heads in. Can you bring some Potassium Pomangernate down when you come, and some weed-killer?'

'I suppose they don't allow chemicals?'

'I suppose they don't, but so what?'

'The weed killer… for the garden?'

'Not the garden. That's to make a bomb. I've been in touch with Belfast Rob.'

'Who the fuck's Belfast Rob?'

'Belfast Rob is who you see when you want to make a bomb.'

'You're joking?'

'Of course I am, Traat. But bring it anyway. It's really good for erigaceous shrubs, especially Azaleas. Give me a ring when you've got the forms. See you.'

Gordonski put his mobile down, and began to study the wiring diagram he had been sent that morning from Belfast Rob. It all seemed very complicated, but if a bloody bog trotter could blow up half of Ireland, he should have no trouble constructing a device that might make the earth move at an appropriate moment. He might even use the shagging bonnet. He could pack it with Semtex, so that it exploded on orgasm. It could be a post-coital, sperm reactive system and he might be able to sell it to any number of terrorist organisations.

Gordonski drew on a joint and concentrated on what was going on outside as his nose started to itch. One of his more amusing qualities was his laugh. It began, sounding like he was suffering a severe head cold, before allowing a succession of exhaling sniffs to quickly accelerate into a high-pitched screech.

Lynette's dress resembled a copy of one of the more ample designs of marquee, and she was clutching a bunch of twigs. The three women were chanting a tune they had learnt from a tape of Native American songs, obtained by mail order.

'Contact the dead with this easy-to-listen compilation of Red Indian funeral chants. Bring the death of Chief Sitting Bull to life and into your living room. From the same record label that brought you Fosters and Allen'.

Lynette's partner, Simon, was sitting crossed-legged, hitting a gong. He was completely out of time, as the women simulated the action of buffalo majestically roaming the plains.

Gordonski had resisted the temptation of impersonating Buffalo Bill, instigating an early seasonal cull with his spade.

He was loosing it, fast, and he stuffed his fist into his mouth to stifle any sound.

It began to rain. Three golfing umbrellas appeared, but there was not enough room for Simon, and he was now running towards the potting shed.

'Fucking Kool and the fucking Gang.'

Gordonski tied a sack around his waist before opening the door. He had to look the part.

'Hello, Gordonski. I was wondering if I might have a talk about the plans for the garden. Incidentally, why do they call you Gordonski? Is it your real name?'

'Actually Simon, it's my adopted name. Everyone knows me as Gordonski since it was changed by the Dali Llama, after his last reincarnation.'

'You've met the Dali Llama?'

'Yes. When I was over in Tibet, doing his garden.'

'You used to do the Dali Llama's garden?'

'For a long time. It's because he used to know my great-grandfather, and knew I liked to specialise in water features.'

'But the Dali Llama must have been born years after your great-grandfather died.'

'He was. Well, the one now was, but one of the others was around. You know how it is. He just keeps being re-born. When you think he's gone, he comes back. I'm not sure whether it was the last one or the one before that, but he went to the same school as my great-grandfather. They played with each other for a time, before the monks came to take him back to Tibet.'

'That's amazing.'

'Yes. Apparently he was a very happy boy. His name was Ronald, and his father worked for the Co-op until the monks told him his son was the reincarnated spiritual leader of the Buddhist faith. They all had to move.'

'That's fantastic. Does Lynette know? You must have an input at our next awareness session.'

'I'd rather you didn't say anything to anybody just yet. I have to feel grounded, get my energies working for the good of the community.'

'Can you do that, Gordonski? We had a healing session today. To ask the Land spirits to help us prepare the ground for planting. That's what I wanted to discuss with you. Do you think we could grow rice here?'

'Simon, you could grow anything here if you follow the correct path. When I left the Dali Llama's garden, he had the best selection of Brassicas in the entire Himalayan range. That and Cannabis Sativa.'

'What, dope?'

'Of course. It's part of the staple diet of the monks. They mixed it with the fermented juice of a species of crab apple, indigenous to the mountain region.'

'What, a type of cider?'

'Exactly. I think we should seriously think about getting a stock in.'

'I don't think that would go down very well. Tara doesn't really agree with alcohol any more, or smoking. She used to have a serious problem.'

Gordonski instantly warmed to Tara. He'd have her back in rehab before the month was out, with a bit of luck.

'Anyway Simon, we can always discuss it later, but the first job is to get the ground ready to plant the vegetables and herbs. Fancy a joint?'

'I'd love one, but Lynette would kill me.'

Gordonski thought she probably did that regularly, but he was never in a hurry to persuade anybody to do anything against their will. In his experience, they would always return when their need was great, and Simon was going to be no exception.

'Well, if you ever do, you know where to come. It can't be easy living with three women all the time, despite your spiritual bond. You're always welcome in the potting shed.'

———

Nialls returned to looking at himself in the mirror. He was vain, and liked to check that everything was where it should be. His hair certainly was not. It was almost non-existent, and he had spent the previous fifteen years slowly watching it fall out. He had not been granted the privilege of rapid hair-loss, where there can be acceptance of reality as hair disappears, almost overnight. His head had shown no compassion. He was first aware of its intentions when he was approaching thirty, about to be divorced for the second time. Actually, the process had begun after the breakdown of his first marriage, but he had been drunk for so long that he had never noticed.

Nialls had been in love three times, four, if you include with himself. His first wife took his children and money, the second just the money and the third anything else that was left. The whole experience had shaped him into the man he was today, and he was not going to appear on *Tricia* advocating the sanctity of marriage.

As his bitterness grew, his charm had increased and it was now honed to a fine point. Stable relationships were out of the question. He preferred to behave like a pinball, ricocheting about the local bars, hunting for prey. Once he had chosen a victim, he could spend weeks planning his future moves with careful precision. Flowers and champagne were given at every opportunity, as he attempted to wear the victim down, bit by bit, until they were ready to be flown to Rio de Janeiro, with a suitcase full of baby oil. Nialls was an expert and his prey never stood a chance.

He always picked the same type of women, certainly not stupid, just gullible enough to fall for his well-practised approach. His initial behaviour would allow them a tantalising insight into their future. They were usually recovering from a damaging experience with a solicitor called Rupert, and Nialls would help them to rebuild their self-esteem. He had a friend, an anaesthetist at a private hospital on the outskirts of the city, who was always coming into contact with women looking for a boost, after a bad experience. The first thing they did was to book themselves into the local clinic for cosmetic surgery. Nialls would then search them out, in one of the select bars they frequented.

He was an expert flirt and would prowl the tables armed with a bottle of *Becks* and a property magazine.

'Hello, aren't you a friend of Norman Thargs Wanker Twat-Abbott? We were at school together.'

'Sorry?'

'I'm a friend of Norman… Norman Abott. Weren't you at his party the other week? Do you mind if I join you? I'm called Nialls.'

'I don't know. I might have been. Is he in Advertising and lives in The Park?'

'Yeah, along with every other twat that shits money.'

'Sorry. It's difficult to hear through this noise.'

'Yes, he does. Aren't you called Celia?'

'No, Samantha.'

'Is that Welsh?'

'I don't know. The name was very trendy in the Sixties, apparently.'

'So what do you do, Samantha, for a living?'

'I work for my father.'

'And what does he do?'

'It always sounds so silly when I'm asked that. He's in ladies underwear.'

'Sorry. Why is that silly?'

'Well, I say he's in ladies underwear and people usually say something like, does it suit him?'

'Sorry?'

'They think I mean he wears ladies underwear.'

'Does he?'

'No'

'Oh I see. Ladies underwear. Oh, now I get it. I bet that causes some laughs.'

'It does actually.'

'Can I talk to you banally for the next half-an-hour, and take you home and finger you rigid?'

'I'm sorry this music is far too loud. What did you say?'

'Do you fancy a meal? Only I was going to go for something to eat. I've heard the Grill Room is really good.'

'So have I. It's supposed to be excellent.'

Nialls picked up his beer and spoke into the neck as he turned and looked around the bar.

'Yeah. It's only twenty-two pounds, fifty, for battered fucking cod and chips.'

'Pardon.'

'Apparently the fish is amazing. It's lightly marinated in

an egg and flour mixture, before being cooked in oil they import from Rotherame.'

'Rotherame?'

'Yes. In Tuscany.'

The scenario then followed a pattern. Nialls would secrete more oil than the fish had absorbed, and tell them about his latest development of environmentally-friendly loft apartments. He would casually mention his BMW, suggest lunch on Sunday, and possibly a day at the races the following week. His behaviour would be utterly honourable. There would be no suggestion of hand relief after the four-thirty at Doncaster, as he drove them both home with the hood down, avoiding the motorway. He would give her the compilation tape that he had personally recorded for her. He kept the master copy in his sideboard, along with the blank tapes.

This approach would continue for as long as it took Samantha to begin to question his sexuality. Women might have been badly treated in a previous relationship, but they had just spent three thousand pounds having their tits done, and they wanted to know whether he could tell. Nialls was a master at timing. He knew by the gentle urgency of a pelvic thrust as he kissed them goodbye, or the heaving breasts as he brushed an imaginary hair off their shoulder, that they were ripe.

He cancelled the next couple of dates, due to intolerable workload. It always had the desired affect. The next time he saw the girl, it would be the time for him to unleash his secret weapon.

Nialls found sex a let-down. He had found all his wives sexually dominating, as they had insisted on every aspect of lovemaking being done in a particular way. They needed to feel sexy, and there had to be the right amount of foreplay, usually after a candlelit meal, to get them in the mood. He always felt pressured. There was so much emphasis on what he should be doing to enhance their pleasure, he never felt they cared about his own desires. They basically made him feel inadequate. After three failed marriages, he had decided that enough was enough. Unfortunately, the re-occurring stress had led him into a downward spiral of alcohol and cocaine abuse, but he was still determined to get his revenge.

That was why he had spent hours perfecting his multi-faceted thumbing technique. Like Little Jack Horner, he knew when the plum was ready. Samantha would be as ripe as a turkey for Christmas.

Expecting the usual evening, she opened the door to see Nialls, without any bouquet. She only managed a cursory greeting before being picked up, carried into the living room and dropped on to the settee. What she experienced then was a session of alarming digital perfection. When is a thumb not a thumb? When it's on the end of Niall's hand.

He was a master puppeteer and he controlled the next twenty minutes, as she became Sooty to his Matthew Corbett. With a final flourish and a flick of the wrist, he was gone. Samantha had desperately wanted more, but it was too late. He had given her his entire Thumbs-Up repertoire and it was time to leave, as the final applause faded away in the distance. Like Zorro, he disappeared into the night.

Chapter Six

·

'For God's sake, answer your fucking phone! I know you're there. You're in serious danger of being a twat again. It won't get any better unless you listen to me, I'm an expert remember?'

'Fuck off.'

'About time. You never reply.'

'I've been busy.'

'Doing what? Talking to yourself, 'cause that's about all you can do now you're on your own. You haven't forgotten you're on your own now, by any chance, have you?'

'Bollocks.'

'No. No chance of that.'

'What do you want?'

'I had a call from Gordonski today.'

'What did that mad fucker want? Don't tell me he wanted to invade America.'

'He got the job in that alternative healing place. He thinks we should go down there for a few days for the Eclipse Festival.'

'Why would you want to do that? You think it's all a load of crap.'

'No. I've never said that. I'm always prepared to keep an open mind. It might be good for me to cleanse my body and mind. Anyway, remember the pact the three of us made at Glastonbury?'

'God, what fucking pact? We were all completely wasted. You make us sound like the Three Musketeers. Only in your case, it's not all for one and one for all, but just all for me and fuck anybody else.'

Malcolm was finding it difficult dealing with his life at the moment, and Nialls' comments were like a red rag to a bull. He blamed his present misfortune on his ex-wife's obsession with anything New Age, and the coven of women she had surrounded herself with, as she had taken him apart brick by brick. She had become obsessed with anything alternative, and he had been drawn into her world before she had left, leaving him to deal with the consequences.

Nialls hoped that with a little persuasion, Malcolm might sink to any number of untapped levels of depravity. He had worn his hair shirt for too long. His bitterness was on the cusp between despair and anger, and ripe enough to be now steered into an obsession. Nialls, of course, would be there to help.

Nialls had never been remotely interested in anything alternative, and had always found Malcolm's involvement with anything spiritual, irritating. Now, he could deal with the only two major faults with Malcolm's character. His complete misunderstanding of women, and what Nialls called his 'dowsing and tarot' mentality.

'Apparently, there's a ley line running right through the middle of the house, and the energy is really strong. It's just what you need to get rid of some of that latent aggression.'

'I don't give a shit about anything like that anymore.'

This is what Nialls wanted to hear. The weak link in the team was going to come up to scratch.

'But what about Yin and Yang and the Japanese garden in your back-yard?'

'I knocked it down, and built a huge fucking barbeque pit. It's big enough to roast a whole cow.'

Nialls remembered Malcolm's pathetic attempt to create a Japanese water feature, by knocking down the outside lavatory and connecting the water supply to a spouting dragon he had bought from Homebase. Because he wanted to be environmentally friendly and conserve water, he had kept the cistern, and it had to be continually flushed to get the desired effect. At least he had removed the toilet-roll holder.

'So. Are you up for it then? It's time for you to do something positive, rather than mope around like you have been doing for the last six months. You need to get out there and stand up for yourself.'

'What have we got to do?'

'Gordonski's sending us information. Sounds brilliant. I think we ought to go. It would give you the chance to see everything in a different light. Instead of being brainwashed, you can now tell them they're talking a load of shit. You need to exorcise your demons, and stop being a boring fart.'

'Alright. I'll come, but don't expect me to sit there and take it all. Especially if I have to listen to some spaced-out woman with an orange face, due to ingesting too much Beta Carotene, acting as a medium for some Egyptian Pharaoh. God, I've listened to so many Pharaohs endlessly spouting on about how we should look after the planet, and be compassionate to our fellow man. How compassionate were they being when they forced the entire Jewish race into slavery? About as compassionate as Hitler.'

Things were certainly beginning to look promising, and Nialls felt it was right to mention the little game they were going to have to play.

'So, you want to go then?'

'Yes. Definitely, can't wait, despite the fact that Gordonski is a complete mental case.'

'Right, we're on then. There's just one small problem we have to overcome.'

'What's that?'

'We've got to pretend to be gay.'

'What?'

'Apparently, the course is only for singles or couples, and if you don't want to wear a twin set, being gay is the only option.'

'Can you tell me how I pretend to be gay? You'd better not expect me to hold hands with you.'

'We just pretend to be deeply in love. You can do it.'

'And at the first opportunity, you'll start turning your charms onto some poor unsuspecting woman who's given up men. Then what will they think?'

'Well, that I've seen the light and my dabble into poofter-dom was just a misguided phase.'

'And what am I supposed to do when you turn your back on me, and start getting friendly with the woman who was married to an unfaithful sewing-machine rep?'

'I'll tell them you're a complete bastard who led me to believe that I could only find love in the arms of a man. That you cheated on me with a florist called Tony, and your first session of self-awareness made you see that you couldn't lie to me. I'll realise that I was never really gay at all. Meanwhile you can go and help Gordonski in the potting shed. You could always have therapy to help sort out your devious ways. Anyway, there's Simon.'

'Who's Simon?'

'He's the partner of one of the women who runs the place. I'm sure you could persuade him to fancy you, if you got too desperate from missing me.'

'I'm not listening. I don't know why I want anything to do with this. Just phone me when you know something.'

Malcolm put down the phone. He was hungry and fancied a fry up. For years, he had been a dedicated vegetarian, but now he had nothing in his house, unless it contained at least some percentage of animal. He had once marched for animal rights and was prepared to save the whale single-handed, but now he fancied a job on a whaling ship, and loved watching the video of *Moby Dick*. He had ripped up all his flowerbeds and was abusive to anybody from the National Trust, who tried to sell him a flag when he went shopping at Tesco's.

The house had once been full of pictures of Sai Baba, and posters of *Desiderata*. Now, in their place, were those diagrams which butchers have on the walls of their shops, showing the different cuts of meat. Malcolm had bought them from an auction, along with a butcher's block, and various implements used in an abattoir. He had arranged these in a display on the wall of his kitchen, next to the photographs showing intense battery-farming methods on a Norfolk chicken farm. The centrepiece of the entire display was a framed picture. It showed Malcolm holding a 'succulent drummer' in one hand and a chicken, injected with sixteen pints of silicone, in the other.

Slowly, over time, he had changed from being a caring conservationist, to a fanatical fighter against anything to do with saving the planet. He prowled the supermarket recycling centres at midnight, blocking the holes up with cement he kept in buckets in the boot of his car. His car had a large sign in the rear window. It said, FUCK ANYTHING WITH FLIPPERS.

This complete reversal in beliefs was apparently normal. His psychiatrist had encouraged him to follow his natural instincts. It was common to be suffering from an aggravated phobia against any number of things that could have contributed to a breakdown. As Malcolm's wife had been heavily into saving the planet, after she left him, he was left devoid of any of their previously shared beliefs.

At first he kept up the subscription to *Kindred Spirit* and spent hours reading about the crap in his food, but slowly, it dawned on him that carrying a copy of *E for Additives* around was ridiculous. But it was when he bought his first bottle of non-organic wine that the metamorphism really kicked in. He was watching a documentary about seal culling, and would normally have got angry, but after the second bottle of wine, his angst against the inhumanity of man began to dissipate. He bet the hunters didn't care about additives. It was additives he needed to help him see everything clearly, and from that moment, every time a seal appeared on the screen, he hurled his Fertility Stick at it.

His wife had sent away for the Fertility Stick when they were trying for a third child. She had read the advertisement in the personal column of a magazine, and it had offered the bonus of a packet of sand from Ayer's Rock. Apparently, the sand is known by the aborigines to enhance sexual performance and increase the chance of conception. The mailing address was somewhere near Walsall, but that did not offer a problem of authenticity for either of them. It was only whilst recently browsing through a copy of *Fetish Monthly* that Malcolm had seen the same address, advertising leather bondage equipment.

It was the night when the conjunction of the planets meant that she was probably at her most fertile in all of her five previous lives, that the Fertility Stick came out of the wardrobe, and the builder's sand, from some West Midland gravel pit, was sprinkled around the bed. Malcolm had wanted to watch *Match of the Day*, but that was definitely out of the question. He was summoned up to the bedroom, and handed the all-powerful Sperm Stick, as he preferred to call it, and a Sony Walkman, which she used for her guided imagery journeys.

'Put this on', she said. 'The music will help you to absorb the energy. It's traditional Aboriginal folk tunes.'

If this was an attempt to gain more Antipodeans'

ambiance, it certainly failed. She had made the mistake of buying a tape of Australian folk tunes, thinking they were Aboriginal in origin. Unfortunately, they consisted of a selection of Rolf Harris hits from the Sixties, and the thought of performing to *Two Little Boys*, with or without the Fertility Stick, destroyed the moment for Malcolm. He turned the volume down so that it was barely audible.

'Can't we just lie in bed together, and touch each other's genitals.'

'No. Sit down on the floor, and imagine you're on walkabout in the outback. The elder is telling the story of Dreamtime, and how the earth began.'

Malcolm closed his eyes, but all he could hear was Rolf singing about billy cans and billabongs.

'Now, tell me what you can see and feel.'

Malcolm closed his eyes and tried to concentrate, but he could not see anything vaguely reminiscent of the creation of the universe. It was not that he did not believe. He just found it harder to accept everything as easily as she did.

'I think I can see a dingo wandering across the desert.'

'That's fine. It will probably lead you on a journey. Don't be afraid to follow it.'

Malcolm tried to follow it. But suddenly he remembered the Dingo Baby case, where a baby had been snatched out of a tent in the middle of the night by a dingo. Not the sort of image ideally suited to aid an attempt at conception.

'I think if we have a girl, we should call it Matilda.'

'Is that what the dingo has told you?'

'Yes,' he lied, as the Rolf Harris track faded away.

'This is the time. We have to make love now. The dingo has led me to an oasis. It's a sign.'

Malcolm had been fiddling with himself behind the bottom of the bed. He had an erection that would not last and he wanted sex. He leapt up from the floor, dropped the Fertility Stick, hoping that his pre-coital ruse had been successful.

'Quick, you've got to put the stick on the pillow facing towards Ayer's Rock, for conception to take place. It says so in the instructions. It has to be facing that way.'

Malcolm had no idea of the right direction. If she did not

conceive tonight, it would be blamed on his lack of geographical knowledge, so he aimed it in the direction of the bedside table and hoped for the best.

She never did conceive, but instead began an affair with a white Rastafarian called Denzil, who worked as a plasterer, and ate frozen faggots. Denzil pretended he was a vegetarian. He only kept a cupboard full of pulses for show, so that she would notice them before he took her into his bedroom to show her his artex ceiling, whilst Malcolm was at work. Malcolm's wife knew that Denzil was lying, but he had a cause, and a firm commitment in recognising an oppressed minority, as well as an enormous nob.

Malcolm could never really understand the concept of a white Rastafarian. Accepting Haillie Sellasie as God is fine if you are black, and your culture stretches back for thousands of years, but being a second-generation plasterer, whose lineage evolved from a peat bog, did not seem to work. Even if you've got the hair cut. Anybody can wear the England kit; it doesn't mean that you are an international footballer. Punks with Mohicans never felt the urge to paddle up North American rivers to trade beaver furs. To them it was a straightforward fashion statement, but apparently not for Denzil, who in unadulterated admiration named his first child, Dopey, after Bob Marley's ganga habit.

Malcolm opened the fridge and got out the ingredients for his meal. Today he was going to have fried black pudding, with streaky bacon. He varied his breakfasts daily, steadily building up the fat content through the week, so that by Saturday he was prepared for his Cholesterol Dream. Today was a Wednesday, so it would only be moderately high in fat. He needed to feel gastronomically contented today, because he was about to be analysed by a yoghurt weaver in Polyvelt sandals.

Malcolm was becoming somewhat frustrated with his psychiatrist; he felt he was pouring his heart out to a man who was more fucked-up than he was. Today was his six-monthly assessment, and his recent pension application was going to be the main topic of conversation.

Malcolm had applied for early retirement from his teaching job, on the grounds of ill-health. He had never really enjoyed his work, and had only become a teacher because of the holidays which the profession offered. As the years progressed, he began to realise that he disliked all children, with the exception of his own, and when his marriage collapsed, he did not see the point of carrying on. So he decided to go crazy.

It did not prove difficult. His breakdown was completely involuntary, but he managed to return to work after two months, but by then, everything just seemed pointless. On his own, he needed to begin again, doing something new that did not include teaching the workings of an Egyptian irrigation system to eight-year-olds. They were still having problems with their own irrigation systems to be remotely interested in the complexities of the Shaduf. But first, he had to convince his bosses that he was unable to continue teaching. He had to sow the seeds of doubt. He hoped that he had been reasonably convincing during the final months, before eventually succumbing to madness, and frothing at the mouth during hymn practice.

Before eating his breakfast Malcolm changed into his I'm-so-off-my-head-I-don't-care-what-I-look-like-outfit. This consisted of a pair of old corduroy trousers and a worn cardigan. He had deliberately nurtured this dishevelled look, because he wanted to give the impression he no longer took any pride in his appearance. After finishing his meal, he dribbled some fat down a trouser leg and gave his shoes a scuffing against the wall. He finally practised his troubled twisted-soul face in the mirror, before roughing up his hair and heading off for his interview.

As he left his house, Malcolm began to twitch. The mental health unit was not far, and it required practise to bring the twitch to a peak at the right time. He otherwise might arrive looking like he was having a fit. All that was required was a facial tick, followed by a spasmodic shake of the head. He would vary the latter depending on the intensity of the question, and today he would find out whether his hours of rehearsing had paid off.

'Malcolm. You can go in now. Interview room three.'

Malcolm gave the fat on his trousers an extra smudge, and walked in to the room to face the Spanish Inquisition.

'What we're here for today, Malcolm, is to try and assess the state of your health, so that we can consider your application for early retirement. I know it's difficult, but try to relax. We're not trying to catch you out, but we have to go through certain procedures.'

Malcolm increased the twitch to four beats in a bar. All his interview techniques flashed through his mind. He remembered about eye contact, and how posture was of prime importance in assessing a person's confidence and suitability. He just had to do everything in reverse.

He slumped down in his chair, and tried to focus on everything in the room at once, jerking his head from side to side. He looked everywhere, except at the three people sat in front of him, who were now forced to contemplate the sanity of the third teacher that day.

'So how are you feeling now, Malcolm? What medication are you taking?'

Dr Don Diablo, the chief inquisitor, looked through his notes. His scales changed colour, and his eyes glowed red. The other two interrogators slid their chairs backwards, in a show of respect.

'Last time I saw you in January, you were taking tranquillisers and medication for an inflamed prostate gland. Is that still the case?'

Malcolm stared three feet above Dr Diablo's head.

'Yes. I'm still on tranquillisers and also anti-depressants. I've been taking them for three months.'

'There was some suggestion that your prostate trouble was linked to the stress you've been going through. Is it still giving you trouble?'

It was true that Malcolm had suffered in the past from prostate trouble. The condition had now cleared up, a fact he was going to keep to himself.

'Yes. It's still really painful.'

Miss Simms, a government inspector, who was in her late fifties and feeling left out of the interview, took this opportunity to assert herself. She had little idea of where a prostate gland was, but still felt she should show her concern.

'What exactly are the symptoms you're having?'

Malcolm could not believe his luck. He took the opportunity of waiting a few moments before answering, and glanced at the other two men, already grimacing as they anticipated the reply.

'Do you know where the prostate is, Miss Simms?'

'Isn't it somewhere in your neck?'

'No. It's just here.'

Malcolm leaned back in his chair, lifted both his legs and pointed his finger at the region midway between his scrotum and anus.

'It's here, but the only way you can get at it is via your anus. It's called a DRE – Digital Rectal Examination – and the doctor has to do it with his finger.'

A look of terror appeared on Miss Simm's face.

'There are three main symptoms. One is like having a red-hot needle inserted inside your penis, another is a broken bottle being twisted inside your sphincter, and the third is like being continually kicked in the testicles. The only treatment, but it didn't work for me, is large doses of antibiotics. They just made my foreskin swell, and develop a fungal infection that resembled a cauliflower, as well as making my bottom turn red, like a baboon's.'

Miss Simms turned as purple as the foreskin Malcolm had been describing, and James began shuffling in his chair.

Malcolm continued.

'And then there's the discharge, that forms crusty scabs in my groin.'

Dr Diablo took the opportunity to intervene, as he too was becoming a little nauseous.

'I think we should talk more about your mental state at the moment, if you don't mind. How are you sleeping?'

'Not very well. I keep having nightmares that wake me up in the middle of the night.'

James Watson, Malcolm's third Inquisitor, realising that this was his field, stopped feeling for his prostate, and pretended to make notes with his other hand.

'Can you describe these nightmares. Are they always the same?'

'I'm usually in a classroom, teaching geography. The children are trying to put an old-fashioned dunce's hat on my head, and forcing me into the Wendy House. Then they all start singing, "Postman Pat and his black and white cat". Then, I usually wake up.'

'And how do you feel when you wake up?'

'Well, actually, I sometimes feel quite sexually aroused.'

Miss Simms went white, and it was suggested that she might like to take a break. This suited Malcolm. It would give him a chance to think up more material to persuade the panel he was certifiable.

Miss Simms did not return. She was not feeling well enough to continue, and so the interrogation continued with just the other two. This was going to be the hard and soft approach. The popular method of breaking down even the most hardened criminal.

A dwarf in the corner stoked the fire, and applied grease to the ratchets of the rack.

Dr Don Diablo was studying a file.

'I have here, Malcolm, a report from your head-teacher. It clearly implies that your behaviour before you went off sick was certainly a little bit erratic, to say the least. What we've got to try and determine, is whether that behaviour was conducive with somebody who was quite clearly unable to carry out the duties of a teacher, and in fact still is, or someone who could now return to resume their responsibilities of a deputy head.'

'I don't really know what I did wrong apart from sello-taping the Special Need's group to their chairs. I realise I shouldn't have done it, but they were being stupid with the Plasticine.'

'But the inspector said, when she visited your class, they had spent the entire day playing with Plasticine. It's no wonder that they might have been a little bored, to say the least.'

'They weren't playing with Plasticine, they were involved in constructive learning. I was differentiating within the ability range in the class. They got the Plasticine.'

'But you were supposed to be teaching them capital letters and full stops.'

'I was. They were making them in Plasticine. It reinforces the basic concept. They write the sentence first and then they make it again, in a medium that helps to stimulate the tactile side of the brain.'

'But in the science lesson before that, the rest of the class were involved in some work investigating how certain materials allow electricity to pass through them, and the same slow-learning group were investigating the conductivity properties of Plasticine, which are completely non-existent.'

'No. Plasticine does conduct electricity, if you've got a large enough current.'

'What, like about sixty-thousand volts? Were you happy with their findings?'

'Yes. I thought the lesson was going really well, until they started being silly.'

'Can you tell me how you get the children to test whether a material is a good conductor or not.'

'They have a length of wire, a battery and a light-bulb. If the bulb lights up, then the material conducts electricity.'

'And what did the group with the Plasticine have?'

'The same as the others.'

'But the difference was that their bulbs and batteries were made out of Plasticine as well, which you had got them to make when they should have been involved in their daily Circle Time session, with the rest of the class. I gather that you don't really consider Circle Time that relevant. What I understand you used to do, was to put all the chairs in a circle ten minutes before break, and then put them all back again, before sending them out to play. The idea of Circle Time is to get the children to voice any problems they might be experiencing. Like, for instance, trying to build a light-bulb and a battery out of a lump of Play-Doh.'

Malcolm felt he was beginning to lose the upper hand. It was time to begin crying.

'I loved teaching. It's just that I can't do it anymore,' he wailed. 'I have panic attacks just thinking about driving to school and having to face all that stress. It took over my life. I couldn't even cope with the simple things that I had to do, outside of teaching.'

Dr Don moved his chair backwards, peering at a particular passage in the notes in front of him.

'Then, there's also the matter of the curtains.'

Malcolm could feel the thumbscrews being tightened. He never thought the curtains would be mentioned. He had spent weeks, during his break-time, making blinds for his new house. It became easier to continue making them during the silent reading sessions which followed the afternoon registration. Before he knew it, he had been able to adapt to teaching everything except Physical Education, whilst overlocking his hems.

Unfortunately, someone had squealed just when he thought he had got away with it. His pathetic excuse at trying to persuade his head-teacher that he was making them to try and brighten up his classroom, had not been believed. That was when he realised that he really had to go all out for the nervous breakdown.

The next day, he came to school in his pyjamas and a dressing gown, carrying a teddy bear he had taken from the infant department the day before. He walked into the staff room during the morning briefing, sat down and began sucking his thumb. An hour later, Malcolm was driven home by the other male teacher, who had a certificate in basic first aid, and therefore the most suitable to deal with a psychotic lunatic. Malcolm visited his doctor, and was given a prescription for Valium.

He never went back to school after that. Nobody ever found the skunk plants neatly tucked away behind the mini-beast garden. Luckily, the slugs got them before it was time for Year Three to study the life cycle of the snail. The children did notice that the snails were behaving in rather an erratic manner. They remained very static for long periods of time, before falling off the wall into the nature pond. Their teacher suggested that it might be something to do with global warming. One afternoon, the class wrote letters to their MP voicing their concern. The local paper came round to take a picture of two of the children looking sad with a pile of empty snail shells in their hands.

Malcolm began to sob a little harder.

'I don't really remember anything for about the last two months. Everything's a blur. I don't think I was completely in control.'

'You seemed to be in control of your stitching. Your seams were very straight. The bias binding was attached very professionally, according to one of the female staff.'

James thought that it was about time he had an imput into the evaluation.

'I certainly feel that Malcolm is pre-disposed to stress. He's presented the classic symptoms of an aggravated form of post trauma.'

'Well, if that's your professional opinion, I suppose I shall have to support it.'

Relief washed over Malcolm like a warm wave. He knew from a friend who worked for the Education Authority that Dr Don was shagging his secretary, and it was a relief to know that he was not going to have to resort to blackmail to obtain his pension.

'We shall write to the Pensions Agency and inform them that, in our opinion, you are permanently unfit to resume your teaching post. They will then let you know of their decision. Good afternoon.'

Malcolm got up and left the room. A forked tongue brushed past his ear as he closed the door.

As he left the building, he caught sight of Miss Simms sitting in the waiting room. He bent forward, pointed at his crutch, and said, 'It's like Armageddon up there.'

—·—

Malcolm decided to call into the butcher's on the way home. He fancied tripe, boiled in milk, with beef sausages. There was a mother with a young child in the shop and the little girl was having a conversation with an imaginary friend. He remembered that as a child, he had had an imaginary friend, and possibly now was a good time to re-invent her. She could be his girlfriend. It would keep Nialls off his back, if he thought that Malcolm was back in the dating game. At least she would do anything she was told, and never answer back. He could take her out to dinner that very night, take her home and fuck her mercilessly, any way he wanted. They could watch pornographic films together, and he could feed her large portions of underdone meat.

When he arrived home, Malcolm gave Nialls a ring.

'I thought you might be vaguely interested in the fact that I had my interview today.'

'What, as a professional mourner?'

'About my pension application.'

'Oh yeah. How did it go? Are we going out to celebrate?'

'Well, it looks like I'm going to get it, but I promised to take Gail out tonight if everything went OK.'

'Who's Gail?'

'My girlfriend.'

'You've got a girlfriend?'

'Yes. I met her in the cycle shop when I was buying my bike. She's into cycling too.'

'Oh God! You'll be buying a tandem next, and touring the Norfolk Broads. I can see it now, joint membership of the Youth Hostel Association, and weekends in Derbyshire.'

'Actually, I can't see her on a regular basis. She's an air hostess and does long-haul flights. She's not home very often.'

'Well. You've kept this quiet. How long's it being going on?'

'A few weeks. I didn't tell you because I knew you'd just take the piss. I certainly don't want you meeting her.'

'Why not?'

'Because you'll turn into a large pile of lard, and try and grease your way into sleeping with her. That's why they call you chip-fat Nialls.'

'That's not fair. I've only ever slept with one of your girl-friends, and that was to prove how little she thought of you.'

'That's rubbish. You did it to make a fool of me, and that's why you're not going to meet Gail.'

'I don't want to meet her. Anyway, it'll all end in tears. I bet she's a member of the mile-high club, and as you're ped-dling around the Peak District on a Sunday morning, she'll be experiencing full thrust in the cockpit of a 747, with some co-pilot who works for British Airways.'

'Nothing you can say will affect me in the least. You may as well shut up now. Give me a ring when you hear some-thing definite from Gordonski, or whatever his name hap-pens to be at the moment.'

Malcolm prepared a sumptuous meal of tripe and onions, before sitting down to work on one of his anti-environmental projects. He had two he was working on. One was a board game and the counters were plastic chainsaws. Certain squares resembled rainforests, and when you landed on them, you got to cut down a clearing, and put a herd of cattle on it. He thought he might call the game, *Old McDonald's Farm*, but he wasn't sure whether he could be sued. His other project was a lot more advanced. He had produced a prototype, and was going to take it to the Early Learning Centre, to see if he could get any positive feedback. It consisted of a plastic bag with a picture of a seal on the front. The seal was marked with a coloured dye. Inside the bag there was a balloon, a pair of eyes, two flippers, a bottle of red paint with a pointed nozzle, and a plastic club. The idea was that you filled the balloon with the red paint, blew it up, stuck on the eyes and flippers and then beat it vigorously with the club. It might even be a bigger craze than the Yo-Yo, if it was marketed right. It could also be adapted as a video game.

The following morning Nialls opened his post box. It was built into his garden wall as part of an integral alarm system, with a remote controlled gate and a buzzer-activated telephone, which never worked. Nialls had fallen for the voice on the other end of the telephone, and she was called Chantelle. After she gave him the sales pitch and promised to follow it up with the relevant literature, she found herself on Nialls' mailing list. He had plenty of blank tapes.

There were only two letters. One was from the Bank and the other, post-marked Devon, was from Gordonski. It contained all the details of the Eclipse Festival and a booking slip, so Nialls took it back into his flat to peruse over coffee. He filled in the relevant sections, taking special care over the part that referred to marital status. He could see it was a scam, especially when he read the organiser's name. Anybody called Rebecca Revere-Norton must be suspect. The no men thing was an obvious trick, as couples and single women would be far less likely to cause any hassle, if things were not as they should be. He decided to call himself Nialls Thompson-Fletcher, and requested two bedrooms. If possible, he wanted one with an en-suite, because his partner Frances had a bladder problem. He telephoned Malcolm.

'Hello, Frances. Did you manage to stay dry last night?'

'What the fuck are you on about? You've woken us up.'

'Don't tell me you've got somebody with you.'

'Gail's here with me, and you're interrupting us.'

'I've just telephoned to let you know that I've sent the money for our few days in the country, and you might need to get hold of a colostomy bag.'

'What are you on about?'

'Nothing. I'm just checking that you're still up for it. It sounds like it could really be good fun. Plenty of drum and dream workshops, and nut rissoles by the ton.'

'I'm worried about Gordonski being there. We've only met him briefly. What if he does turn out to be a complete lunatic?'

'Even better, I say. What the fuck does it matter. He'll be no different to all the others. I can't wait.'

'OK. I'll phone you later. Now fuck off. I've got things to do. Gail will be out of the bathroom soon, and I'm feeling like some dirty love.'

Malcolm put the phone down. What was Nialls on about? A colostomy bag? Disability aids always interested him, and he momentarily tried to imagine Gail standing on a Stannah stairlift, wearing surgical stockings.

Gordonski had been working very hard clearing a patch of land to the rear of the house, which was hoped to be a suitable site to plant vegetables. It had not taken him long to realise that Tara and Lynette did not really have much say in the running of Mandalay, as the house was now going to be called. The name had been changed because Rebecca, the chief witch, had had the idea that it would make an ideal name for a haven of tranquillity. The name change certainly pleased Gordonski. He had seen the film and thought it very ironic, considering his own future plans. Although he had been interviewed by all three of the women, it soon became clear that Lynette was just the cook, and Tara nothing more than a glorified receptionist.

Tara and Lynette had been easily persuaded by Rebecca that their enthusiasm and energy was the perfect combination to give the project a positive boost. Their contribution was going to be invaluable to the venture's success.

Money had vaguely been discussed, but they fully understood that at first, they would have to work for little more than their keep. They had no problem with this. Rebecca was a dedicated and compassionate woman whose whole philosophy was about caring for the well-being of the planet.

Rebecca actually had a face and attitude that would have put Cruella de Ville to shame, but helping the less fortunate would have its advantages. It would be costly, but not to her. She had always considered anything New Age an untapped resource, and after leaving her banker husband, began attending a healing group which met every Thursday, in a Kensington basement. The group was led by a priestess called Crystal. Crystal worked in advertising, and had become a white witch after taking too many drugs and having an out-of-body experience. Crystal led Rebecca out of the dark side by putting her in touch with a brilliant lawyer, who got her a large divorce-settlement and the villa in Portugal. All he had had to do was persuade the Judge that the whole experience of her husband's relationship with a rent boy would leave her permanently scarred. As soon as the money was in the bank, she began looking for suitable premises to support a project that would enable her to save the soul of anybody with enough money to pay for the salvation. She would offer workshops involving alternative therapies and, by putting the adverts in the right magazines, could expect to attract a more professional clientele. She would be an alternative Madam, massaging the minds instead of the genitals, and the profits might be just as large.

Rebecca spent most of the time in her room. She was supposedly busy, making preparations for the Festival, but one afternoon, Gordonski discovered her in the walled garden which backed on to the kitchen. He was cutting the bottoms off plastic cider bottles and turning them into slug traps, and it was rapidly reaching the stage that very soon, all the slugs in the neighbourhood would soon have their own individual accommodation. The last thing he wanted anybody to know was that he enjoyed the odd pint or two in the evening, after he had closed his cold frames, and returned to his room in the old stable block.

Rebecca had been working out her current finances and was in a good mood.

'Gordonski. I know I haven't seen you since your interview, but I hope you've settled in.'

'Yes. Fine, thank-you Rebecca. Mandalay is such a spiritual place. The energies are all so positive. Perfect for a retreat which deals with the relief of stress and provides enlightenment.'

Rebecca was immediately suspicious. Gordonski made her feel uneasy.

'I wonder if among your many talents, you might be able to make a sign for the front door?'

'I'm sure I could, Rebecca. What sort of sign did you have in mind? Something like, "Pity All Those Who Enter Here". That's a joke, by the way.'

Rebecca did not see the point of jokes. She never laughed. She often felt pleased, but that was different. That was when she had just got the better of somebody.

'I'd like a sign made in something that looks like driftwood. Do you think you could find something?'

'I'm sure I could. There are some old pallets around by the greenhouses. I could always join them together. What do you want written on it?'

'I'd like a dove painted on it, to represent Peace. With the words, *We Provide The Hands To Catch You When You Fall.*'

'That's a wonderful sentiment, Rebecca. I used to utter that phrase when I began my workshops.'

Rebecca feigned interest. Maybe here was somebody else she could use to her own advantage.

'What workshops did you do? I'm still looking for session leaders for the eclipse week. Maybe you could offer an imput of some sort.'

'I mainly specialised in dreaming.'

'Like interpreting dreams for people?'

'Sort of, it was more assessing the dimensional gateways into the inner mind.'

Rebecca had no remote idea what Gordonski was talking about, and neither did he.

He went off to look for some wood to start making the sign. He resented being asked to save anything combustible, as it meant one less opportunity for a fire. At least the wording of the sign caused him some amusement. It might prove to have a different meaning to what was intended, as at least two of the organisers appeared to have obvious drink problems. And Gordonski was so used to falling over, the provision of any number of hands seemed completely irrelevant.

He found some wood and nailed together a suitably distressed background, on to which he could begin his sign writing. He was not very good at doves, but he did manage a reasonable attempt at a seagull. He felt sure nobody would notice, and if they did he could tell them that doves and seagulls were related. It took a few attempts to get the lettering right, especially the capitals, which began to become a little smudged. An hour later the slogan read, *We Provide The Glands To Catch You When you Ball*, but eventually he completed what he considered a reasonable attempt, and leant it against the potting shed, to dry.

That night Gordonski had a visitor. It was Simon, and he was very distressed. Apparently, Lynette had been testing out the flotation tank and she had become so tightly wedged, that she could not get out. She was becoming agitated because Tara and Rebecca were considering calling the Fire Brigade, and Lynette, becoming tenser by the second, was now firmly stuck. Simon was hoping that Gordonski might be able to help. Gordonski initially thought about suggesting a mild explosive device.

'What about a large sink plunger, Simon, or a harpoon? I can't really tell without assessing the situation myself. I'd better come and have a look.'

'You must hurry, Gordonski. She can't move.'

Gordonski arrived to hear Rebecca screaming. 'Get her out. She's going to fucking ruin it. Can you do anything, Gordonski?'

Lynette was becoming tenser, causing her to stick more firmly. Gordonski fetched a set of step-ladders, and began to put his logical mind into operation. It was not a pretty sight.

'I think I can see a way of getting her out, but it's going to be tricky. Lucky she's wearing a swimming costume.'

'Why? What are you going to do?' sobbed Lynette.

She was beginning to turn blue.

'Simon, can hold her arms and pull one way, whilst somebody else pulls her costume down past her thighs and over her feet. That should give her just enough clearance to get out.'

'You can't do that. I'm not taking my costume off, in front of everybody.'

Gordonski could quite understand her point. He started to make his excuses to leave the room.

'You'll have to do it, Gordonski.'

Rebecca was serious. He was not going to get away with just providing a consultation.

'Tara and I will never be able to move her. She's like a fucking, spouting whale. If she damages that tank, it will come out of her wages. Go on, Gordonski. Do it. Get her out.'

'OK, Simon. I'll get her arms. I'll promise not to look. You can deal with the other end.'

'You make sure you keep your eyes closed,' screamed Lynette, as Gordonski grabbed her.

Tara was looking terrified at the prospect of Lynette's

seventeen-stone being deposited on the floor without a safety net.

'Don't you think we should put something down on the floor first?'

Rebecca turned on her with a face like granite.

'Put something down. She's the one that needs putting down. Let's just call in the Japanese whaling fleet, and they can process her for fucking whale meat. Get her out of my bloody tank before it explodes.'

Lynette slipped her costume off her shoulders, and Gordonski closed his eyes as Simon pulled and he took the strain. The costume came off surprisingly easily, like a magician pulling off a tablecloth. Suddenly she was lying in the tank naked, and Simon was on his back on the floor with Lynette's gusset over his head. Gordonski let go of Lynette's arms, and she clambered out of the tank and fled towards the door, quickly followed by Tara. Lynette would need moral support after her dreadful ordeal.

Rebecca inspected the tank for damage. She was still fuming, and Simon slipped out of the door unnoticed. Gordonski did not go anywhere. He sensed that Rebecca might need calming down and he had healing hands, as well as a bottle of vodka and a bag of strong grass. This could be an opportunity to enlighten her on his Shamanic gifts. It might even be a chance to get the shagging bonnet out.

'I'm sure it'll be alright, Rebecca. Tanks have to be strong and Lynette's weight wouldn't make all that difference. Remember, she would be much lighter in water. It was only her hips that were causing the problem.'

'God, she ought to be living in the everglades, providing amusement for tourists. I'm just surrounded by complete idiots. She's no bloody advert for a wholefood chef. She's built like a bloody barn, and as for Tara, she'll fall apart at the first sign of trouble.'

'Well, there's always Simon.'

'Simon. Anybody who's married to that monstrous lump must be out of their tree.'

Gordonski had all the information he needed. He would at least be able to prove himself indispensable, and now was as good a time as any.

'Do you fancy a drink, Rebecca? I know it's not really allowed, but under the circumstances I think a little drop might do you good. It's been very stressful for you. I could go down to the village if you want, and get something.'

'No need for that. I've got some in my room. You can join me if you like.'

'Well. Maybe just a small one.'

Meanwhile in the kitchen, the staff were unhappy. Simon had made them all a cup of Camomile and Raspberry tea, and they were trying to understand Rebecca's reaction to what had happened. She certainly had not behaved in the manner they would have expected. When she had interviewed them, she had been so calm and considerate. This was not the woman they had met when they answered the advert. Rebecca had made them feel special. She had been interested in their thoughts for running the Festival, and especially Tara's ideas. Rebecca had agreed that it would be definitely acceptable to limit the places on the workshops to married couples or single women only. Single men would be more likely to put up barriers, and Tara had been through so much.

Tara had had her heart broken so many times that she could no longer envisage any sort of a life involving men. She saw them as vultures, awaiting their opportunity to destroy her. She was always left broken and shit-faced at the end, and the sessions in detox, after her failed relationships, were always painful. She was an emotional mess, and when the inability to cope presented itself, she would resort to the bottle. This new project was going to give her the opportunity to find herself again, and working with people that understood her problems might give her the chance to regain her confidence. Unfortunately, those present at Mandalay were already beginning to show flaws, and she was experiencing the feelings of panic that would lead her to drink. She took a gulp of tea, trying to be positive, but tea did not offer the same comfort.

Lynette was pissed off with everything. She had been considered beautiful as a young woman, but after a few broken relationships, had begun to put on weight. Simon was the only man that had been interested in her, when she had ballooned to the elephantine portions she was now, and she really resented him for it. She considered him a spineless wimp because she could dominate him so easily, but Simon allowed her to do it because he knew it made her happy. He also liked big women. He found Lynette's immense rolls of fat a turn on, and the bigger she became, the more he loved her.

His mother had been large. She had once got stuck in the turnstile at a swimming pool, and whereas most children would have been embarrassed, Simon had been proud. It made her shine out from all the other mums who fitted very neatly through. As a boy, Simon had been rewarded for being good, and so he learnt to enjoy doing what he was told. It was a simple philosophy, and he could not see any reason to change it. Unfortunately for Simon, Lynette ordered him about with no thanks, as well as berating him at every opportunity, and this was now beginning to make him miserable. But he still did what he was told. He just kept hoping that it would get better. Only it never did. The more he tried to please her, the more intolerant and irritated she became.

'I just think Rebecca's feeling very stressed at the moment', said Tara. 'She's got a lot to cope with arranging all the courses and everything.'

'I'm sure that's the reason,' answered Simon. 'She certainly is very tense.'

'Simon, you're such an arsehole. She was so rude and you didn't stand up for me at all. She made me look a complete fool and you just stood there, and let her. I'm sure I could have got out on my own, if you'd given me more time. I'm not that big. Anyway, I'm going to bed. I've had enough for one day.'

'I'll come too. Maybe I should rub some Arnica on the bruises, then you might not be so sore in the morning.'

'You're not coming anywhere near me tonight, or you'll find yourself having to rub Arnica onto your bollocks.'

'I just want to look after you, Lynette. Shall I go down to the village and get you some chocolate? It might cheer you up.'

'Yes. That's a good idea. You can get me a Mars Bar, a

packet of Pringles and a can of Fanta, and see if there's anything savoury as well'

Tara was surprised at Lynette's demands, considering she was supposed to be an expert in nutrition, but it also gave her a let-out clause.

'Whilst you're down in the village Simon, could you get me a bottle of Southern Comfort?'

Tara did not even feel the need to make an excuse. It was as if the night's proceedings had allowed them to drop their adopted facades. Maybe none of them were as spiritually enlightened as they thought.

Simon climbed into the old van that had been bought as the centre's runabout, and headed off towards the village.

———

Seaton Staveley was two miles from Mandalay, and the narrow lanes twisted in every direction, until, suddenly rounding a bend, there stood the ancient church. Opposite was the pub, and twenty yards up the road, the village shop. Two elderly sisters, who smelt of Eau De Cologne and stale urine, owned the shop, and had lived in the village all their lives. They had never married, preferring to wait in hope for a Prince who would arrive one day, riding a white horse. They were fans of Val Doonican, and hoped that the Prince would look like him, but he would have to wear more sensible sweaters if he was going to survive the winters in Seaton Staveley. They had spent nearly fifty years running the same shop, but still jumped when the doorbell clanged, and as Simon entered, they peered over the counter at the man who they recognised as belonging to a group of beatniks from the old rectory.

They had heard all sorts of rumours about plans for the house, ranging from a brothel, to a home for the insane and they were suspicious of anybody who came from there. The way things were taking shape at Mandalay, both rumours could be considered as near the truth.

Simon perused the shelves. The shop had been a self-service unit for years, but the owners had never really adjusted to modern approaches to retail selling. They still preferred to take the goods off the shelves themselves. It made them feel less redundant. The smaller of the women was standing on a stool and peeping at Simon from over the till.

'Can we be helping you, young man, but we don't sell Kunzle cakes. We tried it once, but they didn't sell and we stopped stocking them. Were you looking for Kunzle cakes?'

'No. Actually, I was looking for the Mars Bar's, and some Pringles, if you've got any?'

'We've got some pasties that are still alright. They're made in the village, and there aren't any mad cows in them. We haven't got mad cows here. They've got mad cows in Oldthorpe though. Don't buy no pasties there. It's 'cause of the incest. The whole village is full of it. It's the llamas.'

'What llamas?'

'They turn them into jumpers. Put them in a big vat and mash 'em up and make cardigans out of them. I've heard he's thinking of getting some ostriches as well, but he's not going to make jumpers out of those, but they'll all be full of mad cow disease before long. I think he wants ostriches to breed with the llamas, but that'll never work.'

'I'm sure it won't, but have you got any Mars Bar's?'

'No, but we sell Milky Way's. Nearly the same, but they're made on a different planet, but you can't tell the difference.'

'OK. That's fine and what about Pringles?'

'What are they?'

'They're like crisps, but in a round tube.'

'We've got toilet rolls, but you don't get crisps inside of them, unless it's one of those promotional things. Is that what you mean?'

'Not really. Have you got any normal packets of crisps.'

'What those with the small wrapper of salt in them? We haven't been able to get them for years, and we can't be bothered with all those strange flavours, like raspberry ripple and such like.'

'I think you'll find that raspberry ripple is an ice cream flavour.'

'No. We don't sell that either. They did the same thing with that. Who on earth would want salt and vinegar-flavoured ice cream.'

Simon could see that this was going to take forever, and he probably was not going to get anything he wanted, so he settled for a packet of custard creams, a bottle of lemonade and the inter-galactic Milky Way.

As he was leaving, he remembered Tara's Southern Comfort.

'Have you got a licence?'

'We haven't got a car any more. The propeller came off in nineteen fifty-eight, and they couldn't repair it. I think we had one for the dog once, but he be long gone.'

'No. I mean a drinks' licence. I want a bottle of whisky, or something.'

'No. We don't have anything to do with drink. It makes your brain shrink, and then it begins to rattle in your head like a pea in a tin. You'll have to go to the pub. They sell plenty of drink there, but don't tell them that we told you.'

Simon left the shop and headed for the pub. He thought he might have a pint before heading home.

———

The Lamb had not changed in thirty years. The brewery could not see the point of spending money on renovations; as far as they were concerned its days were numbered. The pub's takings never varied except, for a few weeks in the summer, when a few passing tourists came in search of food and a pint. The Lamb never did hot food, but it served mulled wine at Christmas for strangers, who could rely on a cold stare from the landlord. He spent his days putting the world to rights, and he had erected a blackboard above the bar stating his list of rules, and these greeted the weary traveller or visiting Townies looking for genuine hospitality.

The sign was basically a list of do-nots.

NO MOBILE PHONES ALLOWED IN THE BAR.

NO MENTIONING THE LOTTERY.

DON'T ASK FOR DIRECTIONS.

NO CHILDREN OR PETS.

The list went on in great length, and verged on being racist, but it left the visitor under no illusion that they were welcome in any shape or form, unless they happened to live within fifty yards of the pub. The final statement on the hit-list stated the landlord reserved the right to refuse admission to anybody he considered undesirable, especially if they were not suitably dressed.

As Simon entered The Lamb, he was met by stony silence. He did not notice the blackboard, as he approached the bar to ask landlord for a drink. However, there was one thing that overcame the local's hatred of visitors, and that was their nosiness. They knew where Simon was from, and this would give them an opportunity to find out exactly what was going on at the old rectory. The landlord decided to be civil.

'Evening Sir. What will 'e be having?'

'I'd like a half pint of bitter please. Something not too strong. I've got to drive in a minute.'

The landlord picked up the dirtiest glass he could find and poured a beer from a cask kept under the till, out of sight. It was a locally-brewed beer. In fact, it was so local it never left the premises. The landlord brewed it illegally in the basement. When it did leave, it was in the bladders of the few willing to take such an onslaught to their systems, which might render them blind, or at the very least, incontinent. The beer was known by the initiated as *Old Samuel's Brain Fuck*, and the landlord had been making it for years, selling it undercover, to anybody prepared to take a risk. The locals found it especially useful, whenever the truth was required, for it was far superior to any lie detector. There would not be anything they needed to find out, after Simon had downed a couple of pints.

'I've got this 'ere organically-brewed ale. It's not very strong, but it's full of goodness. All our other ales are a bit on the powerful side. You'd best stick with that if you're driving.'

'Well, I may as well have a pint. I haven't got far to go.'

'Where 'e be staying then?'

'I live at Mandalay.'

'Where that be then?'

'Mandalay is the old rectory. We decided to change its name.'

'O you have, have you. Why be that then?'

'It was the new owner's idea. She's called Rebecca, like the name of the book.'

'After a book. That's a bit strange. I suppose she could have called it *Noddy in Toyland*. Now that's a book! Who wrote *Rebecca* then?'

'Daphne Du Maurier.'

The landlord turned and faced the other two men, whose faces looked like they had been set on fire and put out with croquet mallets. They were both well into *Old Samuel's Brain Fuck*. One of them had Rocacea, and his nose had doubled in size. It was covered in red shiny pustules.

'Either of you two heard of Danny Du Morry?'

The one with the enlarged nose said, 'He be a female impersonator. I've seen him on *Blankety-Blank*. He dresses up like a tart with a daft hat on.'

Simon took a swig on his pint. He felt a warm glow spread down his body into his toes.

'No. I think you mean Lily Savage.'

'And who the fuck's Lily Savage, when she's bending over backwards with a pole up her arse?'

'He's a female impersonator on *Blankety-Blank*.'

'What, that cow with the country and western haircut, looks like Dusty Springfield. I thought she was just an ugly woman.'

'No. He's a man. No. I mean she's a man.'

The drink was taking effect, and Simon focused on the pulsating nose.

'God, if you sat with your head out of the car window, you'd get through traffic jams in record time. You could pretend to be a police car.'

Simon's legs went numb. The fascinating speciality of *Old Samuel*, as Simon was about to find out, was that as well as rendering you quadraplegically incapable, it also made you say exactly what you were thinking.

Simon picked up a pork scratching. It did not look as if it was from any animal he had ever encountered, more likely from some prehistoric beast that had originated in a primeval swamp. It was dark green and covered in scorched hair.

Simon was experiencing similar feelings to the ones he

had the day he once took magic mushrooms. The lights in the bar were flashing in colours, and the optics were shimmering. He downed the rest of his glass and passed it to the landlord, for a refill.

He stared at the red glowing nose again. It had grown to even bigger proportions, and was pulsing like the lighthouse at the entrance to Roscoff Harbour.

'Have you ever thought of working for Trinity House? You're absolutely made for the job. They're doing away with all the man-operated lighthouses, but you could be one of the new generation of warning systems. All you'd need to do is sit on a rock and occasionally turn your head out to sea. You'd save them a fortune. Christ, I feel like I'm in a Fellini film.'

Luckily for Simon, any brain cells that had once been present in the local clientele had long since been converted into alcohol, and his logic was not making sense to anybody. As long as his comments remained generally obscure he was safe. Well, he was for now. Simon would never realise what they had in mind for him later, for this young fresh-faced boy from the city.

'Enjoying the drink, young man? How about a refill?'

Simon certainly was enjoying the drink, and the nose now began to resemble a weeping strawberry. The other man passed Simon's glass over to the landlord, who poured out another pint. Simon now concentrated his attention on his questioner, relieved to see that he was every bit as big a freak as the other one seemed. He had enormous ears and long arms, with hands that reached to the floor. He had to use both hands to help guide his glass into his mouth, and as Simon watched him pour his drink down the side of his chin, he began to giggle. It was clear that the man had severe motor skill deprivation, and could benefit from the use of a nosebag.

'Maybe you should use a straw.'

The Orang-utan dribbled and leaned over the table. The 'up-country' boy was not used to drinking and his tongue was getting the better of him, but they had seen it all before and were always prepared to make allowances for first timers.

'What do you mean by that, young man?'

'I don't know. I don't really know what I'm saying. I think I'm going to be sick.'

'Have another drink, then. That'll make you feel better.'

Simon doubted it would, but he was willing to try anything that might possibly return him to reality. He was then violently sick and passed out. He did not remember anything after that, but woke up in the drive at Mandalay in the early hours of the morning. He presumed the locals in the pub had brought him home, and he was grateful. His head was pounding and the rest of his body was numb.

Simon stumbled up the drive, and as his body slowly regained its feeling, he became aware of a warm sensation in the region of his anus, and it felt sore. He supposed it was only to be accepted. God knows what was in that beer, but it was enough to give anybody the runs. But where was that smell of chip fat coming from?

The front door was locked, so he walked around the side of the house towards the stable block, where Gordonski slept. He could not face Lynette. She would be really angry with him now for not coming back earlier, and he fancied a joint. Gordonski had always said come any time.

Simon met Gordonski coming around the side of the house. He was wearing a safety helmet, and carrying a plastic bag with chains spilling out of it.

'What's happened, Gordonski. Is everything OK?'

'Everything, Kool and the Gang, Simon. I've just been giving Rebecca a demonstration of some of the security measures she might need to consider for the Eclipse Festival. She's naïve. I had to get quite cross with her. So, are you alright Simon? Has Lynette recovered? I bet all that weightlessness must make you feel very giddy. At least we managed to bring her back down to earth, without too much hassle.'

'I haven't seen her for ages. Anyway, she won't talk to me. She hasn't had her Mars Bar and Pringles fix. Are you going to bed, Gordonski? I don't half fancy a smoke. I've had a very strange night, and I'm not sure whether I dreamt it or not.'

'No problem, Simon. I've got a bit left. It's not very strong, but it might relax you a bit.'

So for the second time in one night, Simon was forced to put his trust in someone else. But at least Gordonski was not going to take advantage of his altered state.

Simon was again comatose. Gordonski had rolled one of his extra large cones, and Simon had smoked most of it. As he leaned over a chair to pick up a CD, Gordonski noticed a damp patch of grease on the back of Simon's jeans.

'Simon, there appears to be something very strange coming out of your arse.'

Simon reached round, felt the greasy patch and became aware of just how sore he was. Meanwhile Gordonski was taking a closer look.

'It smells like fucking rancid chip fat. What's that doing coming out your fucking ring piece?'

'I don't know, but I'm really in a lot of pain. I think it must have been the beer.'

'What beer?'

'The beer at the pub tonight. I don't really remember, but I got really drunk with some of the locals and sort of blacked out.'

'Well. I think I had better take a look. Drop your trousers.'

It did not take Gordonski long to diagnose the cause of Simon's discomfort. On closer inspection, he saw what was obviously teeth marks on Simons cheeks and the remains of some type of root vegetable, poking out between them.

'Can you see anything that might be causing it?'

Gordonski removed the cause of Simon's pain, and threw it in the bin.

'Yes. It's obviously a reaction to the beer. I would stick to wine if I were you, and… er, change your pub. Were there any locals there tonight, with suede teeth, playing banjos?'

'I don't think so. Why, what do you mean?'

'Or was there anybody who looked like Burt Reynolds, paddling a canoe?'

'No, why?'

'Are you any good at impersonating farm yard animals?'

'No. Why should I be. What's that got to do with anything?'

'Just a thought Simon. Take another blow on that joint and forget it.'

Rebecca climbed off her bed and stood on something sharp. It pressed itself into the bottom of her foot and she winced with the pain. Her mouth was dry and she felt like she had just been run over by a train. There was an empty bottle of Jack Daniels on the floor, and two empty coke wraps in the fireplace. She struggled to put the previous hours into a logical sequence as she tried to discover the cause of her discomfort. It was a press-stud. Then she remembered. Gordonski had searched through her entire underwear draw, selecting items that he felt needed further investigation. He had been particularly interested in the Janet Reger Teddy, as it had a leopard print and appealed to his cave man spirit. He had certainly behaved like a caveman. First he had made her put it on, then take it off, and then he had made her put it on again. Consequently she had become confused, and fuelled by bourbon and coke, had tried to pull it off over her head, sending the poppers flying. A stud had landed in Gordonski's head and it became imbedded like shrapnel. Not that it bothered him. It would be a wonderful story to tell his grandchildren.

Rebecca's floor was now scattered with the entire contents of her wardrobe, most of which had been worn by Gordonski during the course of the evening. She was feeling sick, which was not the best time to find the polaroid's scattered around the bed. They were mostly of Gordonski wearing one of her crêpe cocktail dresses. The front hem was draped seductively over his erect penis, and he was thrashing silent guitar to *Ace of Spades.* The music had been very loud, and he had insisted she took pictures of him as he hung chains off the end of his penis.

She remembered that he had not seemed that sexually interested in her, and she had become annoyed with him.

'Come on you bastard. Stop playing with yourself and give me some attention. You're behaving like a bloody guitar-playing poof,' Rebecca had shouted.

Gordonski was rarely logical, even when straight. The points of his brain were operated by Railtrack, and coupled with large quantities of cocaine and Jack Daniels, made him take the accusation very seriously. He was not going to let this mouthy bitch get the better of him, and apart from everything else, her bedroom was a fucking disgrace. Something was stirring up his subconscious, but fortunately for Rebecca, his brain was not processing clearly, and by the time he had decided to respond to what she had said, he had forgotten the accusation. He had left her alone overwhelmed by the desire to go and tidy his room.

Rebecca was convinced she could make a success of Mandalay. She understood the untapped resource of human frailty, and would be certain of making herself a great deal of money. The eclipse was perfect bait to attract any number of fucked-up people. She was offering a selection of two-day lectures and workshops, culminating in a music festival. Some exclusive accommodation would be provided in the house, and with the camping facilities, she hoped to lure about two hundred people. The music festival was going to be a one-day event, and would hopefully attract even more people. For security reasons, and to avoid a rush of gatecrashers on the day, the name of the headline act was a well-kept secret, but Rebecca had hinted that it would include a one-off reunion of one of the major bands of the Sixties. Only Rebecca knew that despite managing to contact the Dreamers, she was having vast problems locating Freddie.

Getting a licence had been relatively easy, once she had agreed to re-establish the village show in the grounds of Mandalay, after an absence of thirteen years. She had also provided the members of the local council with an opportunity to fleece the punters. They were mostly farmers, and would provide the extra car-parking that would be needed. Everyone knew that farmers were having a lean time.

Organising the workshops had been simple. Crystal, her space cadet friend, had provided the names of numerous, recently-trained Reiki healers and mediums. They needed a venue to launch themselves into the ethers, and were only too willing to put a free imput into a worthy cause.

SOLARISATION

August 9-11th

**A Festival of Light and Rebirth
in the Heart of the Devon countryside.**

Spend three days coming together in the beautiful setting of
Mandalay. Contact your inner self and find peace through
structured workshops, alternative therapies and spiritual
well-being. Join us, and meet some of the leading specialists
in their field, to explore our deep consciousness as we become
in tune with the great God of Heat and Light. Culminating
in a day of music and dance, to celebrate the phenomenon
of the Eclipse. Psychic fayres, ethnic stalls, fireworks and
a gourmet wholefood experience.

**Full-star line-up to be announced later.
3-Day tickets £120 (inclusive of camping).
Entry to Music Festival only – £65.**

For tickets or enquiries, write to
Solarisation Festival, Mandalay,
Seaton Staveley, Devon.
Or telephone 01479332479,
Or visit our website www.solarisation.com.uk

Rebecca knew about PR and had targeted the right magazines. Requests for tickets came flooding in, and her bank
balance was definitely taking the right supplements.

She had hoped to discuss the security arrangements with
Gordonski, but any hope of that had quickly disappeared
up her nose. He had confused her with talk of electric
fences and minefields and somewhere to boil oil. She knew
that there would be some gatecrashers, but as she was still
making a fantastic profit in advance sales, she was not worried. The staff were working on trust, and she would
employ a few of the locals if she needed extra help.
Everything was, as Gordonski said, 'Kool and the Gang'.

CHAPTER EIGHT

•

The night before they were to travel down to Devon, Nialls and Malcolm decided to go for a drink. Nialls had invited Chantelle, thinking that Malcolm could ask his air hostess friend, but Gail was apparently flying somewhere, so could not come. As usual, Nialls took the initiative.

'Let's go check this new bar that's opened in the Lace Market. It's trendy and bound to be full of twats.'

Malcolm found Nialls' obsession with a constant need to find fodder for his humour, tiresome. Always on the look-out for someone to be rude to, Nialls always seemed able to talk himself out of any situation that looked like it might be getting out of hand. Admittedly, Malcolm sometimes found Niall's exploits amusing, but he always went too far.

'Why can't we just go for a drink in the country? It could be training for the next few days, and get us used to rural life.'

Nialls was adamant.

'No. It's got to be *Le Pub Belgique*. They do really good authentic Belgium beer and, anyway, Chantelle likes to drink there.'

'I thought it was just going to be the two of us. You said an early drink. I hope you're not planning anything disgusting for later. If you start getting all greasy round her, I'm going home.'

'I just thought I might meet her for one drink and she might be bringing a friend.'

'Nialls, I'm not interested. I'll just find the whole experience acutely embarrassing. You know I'm no good at talking to women. I clam up. Anyway, once they find out I'm a clapped out ex-teacher they're never interested. I haven't got a flash car and a flat in The Park like you.'

'Well, you can lie. For fuck's sake, tell them we're sharing a flat and your car's being serviced. Tell them anything. What the fuck's it matter.'

'You know I won't feel comfortable with it.'

'OK. We'll only stay a short time. For a couple of drinks,

toilet to acclimatise himself before venturing out to find Nialls. Nialls was talking to Keith the Fly.

'Hey, Malcolm, have you met Keith? Keith, this is Malcolm, my driver. I've just brought him out for a drink. Got to keep the workers happy.'

Nialls had introduced Keith to Malcolm on numerous occasions, but Keith was too spaced to remember. Anyway, Malcolm was not a customer, so he wasn't worth remembering. Keith had his mobile permanently trapped under his chin, waiting for the all-important call. If the drugs did not mash his brain, then the radio waves would.

'Hey great, OK, Driver. Hey, really good. If you ever need anything to keep you awake, give me a call.'

Malcolm did not see the point in putting Keith straight on his job description, and turned to the barman.

'Two pints of strong lager please.'

'We don't sell pints. Only bottles.'

How pretentious thought Malcolm, but it was Niall's treat so what the fuck.

'What you got then?'

'They're all on the board.'

Malcolm looked up at the blackboard. He did not recognise anything, so he went for the most expensive.

'Nialls, I've ordered the drinks. It's seven pounds. I got you a bottle of something brewed with organically-grown hops. It's apparently left to ferment in an oak vat before being given a secondary fermentation, involving freeze-dried molasses and Bulgar wheat. It also tastes like shit. Hope that's all right.'

'Fuck off. Go and clean the car.'

Nialls turned back to talk to Keith.

'So Keith, have you got my order?'

'Yeah, sure Nialls, best quality, guaranteed to get your feet tapping. They're ninety per cent mescaline, and twenty per cent MDMA.'

Maths was not Keith's strongest subject, and Nialls knew from experience that Keith would not object if he was underpaid by a few quid.

'What about the Aznavour. Did you get that?'

'Five grams of the best. One hundred per cent Columbian.'

'OK. That's good, and have you got any of that pure MDMA powder left?'

'Not very much.'

'I only need a bit. Just enough for one night.'

Keith sorted through his pockets and handed Nialls his goody bag, minus a half-gram in weight. Nialls handed Keith the money, minus thirty pounds. They'd both be happy with that.

Nialls went to the toilet and checked the bags. He picked out the powder and put the rest back in his pocket. He needed the powder now. Not for himself, but Malcolm was in need of being perked up, if the evening was going to progress as he hoped.

'Fancy a Tequilla?'

'If you're buying.'

Nialls got the drinks and slipped the powder into Malcolm's glass. Chantelle would be here in a moment, and Malcolm needed to be able to hold a conversation.

Nialls was an expert at judging the most potent mix necessary for almost any situation. The right drug with the correct short, given at closely monitored intervals, usually got the desired results, and the victim was too shit-faced to care.

Nialls now began to do his infamous slalom walk. If they ever made it an Olympic event, Nialls would be up for gold. He cruised around the bar, side-stepping here and leaning there; homing in on whomever he thought might give him a few minutes amusement. He paid particular attention to the wives. It gave him an opportunity to ingratiate himself as their husbands discussed business, and stared at the barmaids' breasts. Malcolm was dragged along by Nialls, and after being introduced, was promptly forgotten. He was left to stand on his own, feeling uncomfortable as the women laughed at Niall's jokes.

Malcolm was beginning to feel weird. He was actually laughing at Niall's jokes, could not stop chewing and his smile was out of control. Suddenly, Nialls spun around to face the door, and dug Malcolm in the ribs.

'Hi, Chantelle! You look fabulous.'

Chantelle was wearing a bat-winged leather jacket and a skirt, barely covering her backside. Her backcombed hair had blonde streaks, and she resembled a backing singer from a New Romantic band. Her white stilettos echoed on the Delebole slate floor as she walked towards them.

'Hello Nialls, sorry I'm late. I couldn't get my tan to go off. This is my friend, Claire.'

'Hello girls! Do you fancy a little drinkypoo?'

Malcolm thought Nialls was sounding more like Leslie Phillips than Leslie Phillips, and the sight of Claire terrified him. She looked like a woman who was more than a match for any man that he could pretend to be.

'This is Malcolm, girls! Not much to look at, but he's got fantastic body temperature.'

The girls giggled. After all, Nialls had a BMW, and a state-of-the-art security system.

'Hi, Malcolm! What do you do for a living?'

Malcolm stared at Claire's shoes. They were red with very high heels, and he was getting a hard-on.

'I'm an architect.'

Malcolm could not believe what he had just said, but somehow it seemed perfectly acceptable. Why shouldn't he be an architect? He had landscaped his garden and briefly studied Le Corbosier at college. He had also spent a day in Barcelona. Of course he was an architect, and a very successful one at that. He had put a very large design imput into the Sydney Olympics, and was presently involved in designing a new palace for the Sultan of Swing somewhere sandy, and what was that music? The piano sounded really good.

'I work for the same firm as Chantelle. I'm a PA. Where do you live?'

'London. I live in London. I've got an apartment in the Docklands, near the Dome. It's very large, and my studio is underneath. I've got a Ferrari. It's red and goes really fast.'

Despite being so animated and spilling most of his drink down his jacket, Malcolm could not believe his new found confidence. Nialls was pleased that he had judged the correct strength of Malcolm's special cocktail.

'Glad to see you're feeling a bit more lively Malcolm. What do you fancy now, going to a club or something?'

'Yeah. Lets go to a club. I feel like dancing. What about you girls, do you fancy coming?'

The girls certainly did, and they called a taxi. Malcolm sat next to Claire, where he spent the entire journey rubbing himself against her leg. He had not felt this good for ages. Claire was really sexy and he wanted to hug her, especially when her skirt pulled itself tightly over her thigh, revealing the outline of a thong. Nialls sat in the front, grinning at Malcolm's antics, as he held Chantelle's hand over the back of the seat.

Once inside the club, Malcolm felt he could detect every single beat of the music, as he twisted and gyrated around the floor, staring seductively into Claire's eyes.

Nialls, however, was beginning to get bored. Things were not going as he had planned. Malcolm was having too good a time, and Claire seemed definitely interested. She had not met many architects before, and Malcolm was putting on a class act. Nialls needed to pull something out of the hat quickly, before everybody became too drunk to care.

'What do you think Claire thinks of Malcolm, Chantelle?' Nialls was stroking her hair.

'She thinks he's really sweet. Has he really got a Ferrari?'

'I haven't a clue. I haven't known him very long.'

'I thought he was a big friend of yours.'

'No. I met him a couple of days ago in out-patients, at the hospital.'

'What were you doing there?'

'I was seeing about my arm. I injured it some time ago. He came out of the Special Clinic and sat next to me. Apparently, he was waiting to see a specialist.'

'What's the Special Clinic?'

'You know, Special Clinic. For special diseases. VD, stuff like that. He'd been given an enormous mountain of tablets. I'm sure that's why he's behaving so hyper, mixing the tablets with the drink. It's bound to make you behave strangely'

'Oh, Nialls, you're so nice. Most men wouldn't have said anything. I really respect you for that.'

'That's not being nice Chantelle. I couldn't have possibly not told you. I think we should get rid of him and go back to my place.'

Chantelle relayed to Claire that Malcolm was apparently

suffering from terminal gonorrhoea, and Claire kicked him hard in the shins, before storming off to find her friends. Malcolm, who was flailing around the dance floor, felt a sharp pain in his leg and opened his eyes to see Nialls and Chantelle disappearing up the stairs, towards the exit. He panicked when he realised that he was on his own, and despite an extensive search could not find Claire anywhere. It dawned on him why he was suddenly feeling flat and anxious, when only a few minutes before he had been on a high. Another Niall's special! He had spiked the drink; no wonder the music sounded really good. All he could do now, was go home and lick his wounds.

When Nialls arrived at his flat, he phoned Malcolm and left a message saying he would pick him up at eight the following morning. Then he clipped the nails of his right hand before joining Chantelle in the bedroom.

Malcolm walked home. His mind was racing and he knew that he would not be able to sleep. He lived in the same part of town he had first moved to as a child, and behind his house were fields, whose furrows led upwards towards a wood known as the Spinney. It was popular with walkers and Malcolm used to go there with his parents on Sundays, after lunch. As a teenager, he went there to drink sweet sherry, talk about sex and play guitar with his friends. The main path led by the side of the cemetery, but recently a new footpath had been constructed with stiles and a kissing gate. The Jewish section of the cemetery backed onto the old path, and it had been a permanent target for vandals, so the council had re-routed the footpath in an attempt to keep people away. The Spinney had been formed on an outcrop of ground facing the city, and from there you could see the distant castle that stood on a promontory of rock, raised above the surrounding land. Malcolm was looking for the place where he had remembered once building a den, and as he rounded a large oak, he stopped to rest. Sitting on a bench called Bill, he could hear the distant sound of trains, as he leaned forward and closed his eyes.

Malcolm had been born at the end of a lane that weaved between a line of Sycamore trees, and ended at a gravel path. The sound of the path was one of his earliest memories, as he lay in bed and heard his father's van coming home at the end of the day.

He lived with his brother and sister in a village on the outskirts of the Vale of Belvoir, pronounced 'Beaver', and his hero was Davy Crocket. The subtleties of language had still to make their mark on Malcolm, when one morning, he set off armed with a Lone Star cap-gun and one of his mother's hairnets. Davy Crocket wore a beaver fur hat, and he did not have one. He imagined that the surrounding countryside was overrun by dam-building rodents, and he was going 'to get me one of those darned critters' for his own. He was not exactly sure what a beaver looked like, but one of Davy Crocket's talents obviously included millinery, so Malcolm thought he could throw the hairnet over the beaver, knock it unconscious with the butt of his cap-gun, and stretch its arse over his head.

—-—

He didn't find a beaver, but he did find a dead rat on the canal bank and tried flattening its tail with a stone. There, his mother found him, sitting in the mud making burglar cakes. She had been frantic with worry, and carried him home for boiled eggs and buttered Marmite soldiers. In the afternoon, she cut off the fur collar from an old coat, and turned it with enviable ease into the best coonskin hat this side of the Redwoods.

The summer before Malcolm was taken to the city to live, he had his first sexual experience. He was six and Alan Holmes was a remedial with a hair lip. The sexual experience was not with Alan Holmes; he was just there spoiling it. But he was two years older than Malcolm, and despite his impediment, was able to lure Janet Timms into the cornfield. She had Titian hair that reminded Malcolm of the Pre-Raphaelite painting that hung in his mother's bedroom. That afternoon she showed them her genitals and Alan had got his penis out. Malcolm had felt very inadequate, but refused to be dictated to by a boy with a facial disfigurement, so he went home for tea.

Janet Timm's father was built like a brick shithouse. His face was bloated red, engorged with drink and rested on a non-existent neck. The day after the experience in the cornfield, Malcolm's father announced during tea that Janet's dad was coming round later that evening, and Malcolm broke out in a sweat. She must have told her dad she was going to have a baby. But he had not done anything. It was all Alan Holme's fault. Malcolm thought they were just going to pick cowslips, and slide off the pigsty roof.

Later that evening her father appeared carrying a scythe and an old hessian sack and Malcolm fled into the outside barn.

So there he was hiding in the darkness not knowing what to do, but he was not going to take the blame for what that remedial freak had done. He braced himself and charged out into the light.

'It won't be my baby, cause it'll have a hair lip', he shouted, at the top of his voice.

Neither his father or Janet Timm's dad seemed remotely interested in his statement, as they were busy chopping up a colony of grass snakes that had made their home in some old packing cases. Well, his father wasn't. He was standing some way off, looking very uncomfortable. He had a phobia about snakes; a man who was a Major in the British Army and landed in France to chase the Bosh all the way to Germany. Good job he hadn't come across any snakes on his way to liberate Paris.

'Major Brown, Sir!'

'What is it corporal?'

'Sir. There's a couple of snakes on the road ahead, and we know how you don't like them very much. What do you want to do?'

'OK. No problem. We'll go via northern Italy.'

—·—

Malcolm's first real taste of sex was at fourteen with a girl called Heather. She kept kissing him by the wall bars in the gym at the Upper School dance, and he touched her breast before depositing the contents of his testicles into his pants. The experience left him feeling cheap and so he decided to enter the church. The next day, Heather phoned to ask him round for tea and Malcolm got his Mum to say that he had just enrolled as a choir boy, and was learning to be a bell ringer, so would be busy for the foreseeable future.

He was sixteen the first time he fell in love. She was called Rosie. She became his first girlfriend, and they held hands in the cinema, kissing in the interval before getting the ice creams.

Malcolm could not believe that someone so lovely wanted to be intimate with him.

They were together for about eight months. She bought him a cigarette case, and he gave her a charm bracelet.

Rosie lived in the country, and three nights a week he spent two hours on the bus, travelling to visit her. They would lie on her bed listening to records holding hands under the covers, as Otis Reading sang *My Girl*.

In February, Rosie contracted tonsillitis. It only seemed a minor inconvenience and one night, as the snow howled outside, they made love. It was their first time and afterwards, listening to the radio, they held each other close. Then Malcolm caught the bus home.

Rosie died that night from septicaemia. He went to the funeral, but he would never remember it. Six weeks later, he received a letter from her parents, returning the bracelet he had given her. It was then Malcolm realised that God was just as big a bastard as everybody else.

—

Malcolm opened his eyes. There was a dog sniffing his leg, and it was beginning to get light. He rubbed his eyes and pushed the dog away. The city was starting to hum, and he needed sleep.

He opened the door and checked his answer phone. He knew that there would be a message from Nialls.

'It's me. It's half-past-three, and I've just dropped Chantelle off. Hot night or what! I'm just going to grab some sleep and I'll be round at about eight. Hope you had a good night. You were certainly going for it when we left.'

Malcolm nearly phoned back, just to tell him to fuck off. Instead, he went into the kitchen and ate some cold black pudding before getting himself to bed.

Nialls arrived at eight-fifteen. They headed out of the city, towards the motorway. For the first ten miles, the road snaked away from the suburbs and into the country. Malcolm felt he was in the cockpit of a DC 10. The drugs and late night were making him paranoid.

'Fucking Hell, Nialls. Slow down, will you. We've got all day.'

Nialls was driving at a steady eighty-five, but the car gripped the road as tightly as Malcolm was holding on to the seat. It glided around the corners with perfect balance, and Nialls was in his element.

'Don't you worry about my driving. This car's engineered to perfection. It sticks to the road like a limpet's arse.'

All that Malcolm was aware of were the white lines in the middle of the road, and the frequency that Nialls was crossing them.

'Watch those fucking lines. They shouldn't be on the left-hand side of the car.'

'I'm in complete control, but talking of lines. Open the glove compartment will you, I want you to pass me something.'

Anything to take his mind off Niall's driving was a welcome distraction, so Malcolm leant over and sprung the catch. Neatly chopped out were two identical lines of cocaine.

'Fuck That! You're not having any of that while we're driving.'

'It's not coke. It's only some pretty weak speed I prepared for the journey, to keep me awake. You don't want me falling asleep do you? I've been up most of the night.'

Nialls licked his finger, reached over, dipped into the white sticky powder and rubbed it into his gums.

Malcolm knew it would be pointless objecting. He closed his eyes and hoped that the motorway was not far off. At least then they would be relatively safe, cruising down the fast lane of the M42.

As they approached the slip road, Nialls suddenly pulled onto the hard shoulder, causing Malcolm to jolt forward. He opened his eyes and wondered how long he had been asleep. Over to the right, in the distance, he recognised a rocky outcrop with a lone building standing at the top.

The Saxon church of Breedon-on-the Hill had been a point of reference for centuries. It allowed travellers to get an accurate bearing, but Malcolm was more used to seeing it as he travelled east up the motorway. Soon after leaving it behind, he knew he would spot a plane taking off from the local airport, and the next exit was the one to lead him the final few miles home.

They had not travelled very far, so why was Nialls stopping? Malcolm got his explanation when the back door opened and a young couple climbed onto the back seat. The last thing Malcolm wanted were other people to share his journey. He had been hoping to sleep his way down to Devon, but Nialls had other ideas. He had administered himself a little pick-me-up and was in definite need of company. Especially if it included an attractive young student, suitably dressed for clubbing in Ibiza.

'So guys, where are you heading? I'm called Nialls and this is Malcolm, but I wouldn't bother with him. He's feeling a bit delicate today, too many medium sherries last night. At University are you? I suppose you're enjoying the long summer holiday. I have students working for me sometimes. I design environmentally friendly apartments. Pass me a cigarette Malcolm, and put some music on. What do you fancy hearing in the back? I think I've got the new Massive Attack with me somewhere, but I think they've lost it a bit since Tricky left.'

The couple in the back glanced at each other and smiled. They had lecturers like this. Thought they were really cool, but were still ten years out of date. Why couldn't they just grow old with dignity?

'That'll be fine. We listen to anything, and thanks for stopping. I'm Kate and this is Andy. We're going to Exeter, but anywhere on the way will do. Now we're on the motorway, it's usually quite easy to pick up lifts.'

Malcolm went through Niall's CD collection and found

Massive Attack. He put it to the bottom of the pile, chose Dire Straights instead and turned up the volume.

'Oh my God, Malcolm! What the fuck's this you've put on?'

'It's your copy of Dire Straights, Nialls. You know you never go anywhere without it.'

'It's not my copy. It belongs to that bloke who works in the next office. He must have left it in the car by mistake.'

'But it's got *Happy Birthday Nialls, this is to replace your vinyl copy that's seen better days, love Mum*, written on it.'

'Don't be so stupid Malcolm, and don't try and be funny. I'd never listen to Dire Straights. They're crap.'

The girl in the back leaned over between the front seats.

'Is that the CD with *Romeo and Juliet* on it, only I really like that track.'

'Well, is it Malcolm? You've got the CD there, for fuck's sake?'

Malcolm read down the list of tracks, but it wasn't there.

'It might be on one of these other CD's you've got Nialls. You've got their *Greatest Hits* here as well.' Nialls leaned over and smashed the eject button, grabbing the CD and stuffing it into the side compartment in the door.

'OK, Malcolm. You choose something if you can find anything you know. Most of your record collection hasn't even been considered worthy of being updated to CD.'

Malcolm put in Massive Attack and leaned back into his seat. He'd enjoyed that, but Nialls was already plotting his revenge.

Kate and Andy were not a couple at the moment. They had been for the previous year, but had decided to keep their relationship platonic for the foreseeable future. Andy still had some unfinished business that was still hanging on from sixth-form, and Kate was going to France for the rest of her holidays with a friend. It did not take Nialls long to recover his composure once he learnt of Kate's and Andy's break-up. She was a single woman and her age was irrelevant to Nialls, who licked his finger and dabbed it into the plastic bag, secreted in his pocket.

Nialls was now demanding Kate's full attention. An imaginary barrier divided the car as he attempted to impress her with his endless charm. Malcolm and Andy may as well have not been in the car, but neither of them really cared anyway. Andy knew that Nialls was making a complete fool of himself, and Malcolm had heard it all before. He was still feeling sick and decided to try and get some sleep. Andy turned up the volume on his headphones to drown out Nialls' unremitting monologue and awful taste in music.

Nialls did not think that it would be difficult to impress Kate. Being a young student, she would certainly lack maturity, but he must not be condescending in any way. He did not want to sound like her father.

Kate was more than confident that she would be able to keep Nialls in order. She just had to appear interested. She had tutors like him, and she was always fending them off. She lived in an isolated village, thirty miles the other side of Exeter, but felt sure she would be able to charm Nialls into taking a little detour, after dropping Andy at the local services.

As they pulled into the car park, Kate mentioned to Nialls that if he didn't mind, she would like to stay with him a little longer. Andy was leaving, but Nialls could drop her off on one of the roads that led onto Dartmoor. It was remote, but she would pick up a lift eventually, and if she didn't, it was only an eight-mile walk to her village.

Malcolm was still feeling ill, and suggested something to eat, as it might make him feel better. They ordered a Chef's Farmhouse-Style All-Day Breakfast, but after one mouthful, Malcolm rushed off to be sick. He left the toilets still feeling dizzy, and returned to the car where he crawled onto the back seat, covered himself in coats and passed out.

Nialls did not miss Malcolm, he was too busy telling Kate about his plans for the future, and how he was now ready to expand into time-share's. When he learnt that Kate was studying advertising, he became very animated and suggested that they must keep in touch. Kate was more immediately concerned that Malcolm had not returned and was preventing them from leaving. She could not envisage her relationship with Nialls, business or otherwise, lasting beyond him dropping her at her front door.

'I wonder where Malcolm is? He seems to have been gone a long time.'

'He's probably soiled himself in the toilet. I'll have a look on the way out.'

'Well, I suppose we'd better be going then, Nialls. You've still got a long way to go.'

Nialls went to look for Malcolm.

Kate watched him go.

'Especially if you're going to do a forty-mile detour first, to take me home.'

After a cursory glance into the bushes Nialls decided that Malcolm must be lost, and would have to find his own way down to Devon. Niall's priorities were in making sure that Kate got home safely and, anyway, Malcolm had tried to make him look a fool earlier, so it would serve him right.

Kate certainly did not have a problem leaving Malcolm behind. It would ensure her a personal chauffeur service, and she needed little persuasion to climb into the front seat.

Nialls was looking forward to a drive across the moors. He could impress Kate even more, and her heated swimming pool sounded really inviting. It was a hot day and a few gin and tonics might lead onto any number of things.

They turned off the road, over a cattle grid, and up the drive that led to Kate's house. It was a farmhouse, and there was a Range Rover parked by a converted stable block. Nialls turned off the engine and sighed the type of sigh that infers you have travelled a long way and have now reached your destination. He turned to Kate for his invitation to stay, but she was already out of the car and pulling her bags off the back seat.

'Cheers, Nialls. Thanks for the lift. You'll be pleased to know that Malcolm's in the back here, but he's looking a bit green. Have a good journey.'

And she was gone. Up the drive and into the house. God, how dare she treat him like this. He had brought her breakfast and driven miles out of his way, and now she was dismissing him like a servant, and Malcolm was throwing up over the back seat. He was not standing for this, but before he could unclip his seatbelt, two overweight Rottweilers bounded out and stood snarling at Niall's door. In a parting act of defiance, he managed to squirt the dogs with his windscreen washers, before skidding back along the drive and onto the road.

Chapter Nine

•

Nobody had seen Rebecca. She was in self-enforced exile, counting the money and making her final plans, but she had appeared briefly to enquire about the catering arrangements. A contact had been made with a local farm, prepared to supply all the necessary produce. Tara and Lynette had been busy planning the menus. It had been a simple act of delegation, but it made the staff feel valued. Rebecca was expert in people management. They could feel as valued as they wanted, as long as they were able to demonstrate unlimited versatility in the preparation of courgettes, potatoes and carrots. Rebecca had contacted some hippie wholefood caterers,who would provide for the campers, so everything was going to plan.

Mandalay had suddenly become alive. A tepee had been erected on the lawn, and Dreaming Pulse, a multi-gendered percussion band, had set up their drums in the house.

By mid-afternoon, things were chaotic. Simon had been sent out to the main gate and was now officially in charge of security. He had never seen so many half-timbered cars and 2CV's. Everybody owned them, apart from the stall-holders and caterers. They were driving grimy white vans that promised all sorts of intestinal discomfort, and sported Mexican moustaches and chewed fingernails. Simon made a mental note to only eat what he had personally prepared for the next few days.

The camping area was rapidly filling up, and rooms were being allocated to the workshop organisers. Rebecca had changed into an Indian printed kaftan, Moroccan sandals and her hair was beaded. She was feeling flustered because everything was being drowned out by the constant ringing of cowbells and wind chimes. Apart from showing a few people to their rooms, Rebecca hoped that she would not have a lot to do. Tara and Lynette were in charge of the catering, and that would either succeed or fail. It didn't matter to her. Her only concern was whether she would have enough money for a holiday in the sun. So far, she had spent very little. Everybody was either paying her for the privilege of being part of the Festival, or working for free. The caterers had been persuaded that it was a worthwhile investment, and everybody else was there for the good of the planet. The music fans were unaware that their day was going to be mainly unplugged, although Rebecca had condescended to hire a mediocre PA system that, reputedly, the Pink Floyd had used on one of their world tours.

By evening, the camping site was overflowing and the house was engulfed in a meditational haze. Chanting and drumming were spiralling from out of the tepee, and mediums were trying to contact their spiritual guides. All the major Egyptian Dynasties would be represented, with the exception of Tutankamun, whose channel healer had been unable to attend, as she was suffering from a severe bout of rheumatism. She had managed to contact by telephone, which due to the nature of her work was the least used method of communication, two friends who specialised in naturistic trans-ethereal consultations. They behaved exactly the same as any other medium, except that they contacted the After Life in the nude, and Mandalay was going to provide them with a perfect opportunity to show off their tans. They had run a cycle shop in Acton before deciding on a more spiritual path. As naturism began to take over their lives, Phil kept having near misses with his Campagnolia gear systems, and his wife, Phillipa, felt more and more reluctant to serve the public wearing clothes. She initially tried to compromise by only wearing a loose fitting nylon work coat, but the static caused her nipples to be constantly erect, and her glowing breasts were putting the customers off. Her doctor first thought that she was suffering from an extreme case of mastitis, before she explained her predicament to him.

One evening, after attending a woman's assertive course at the back of her local health food shop, Phillipa had a calling. She had always considered herself a spiritual person and that evening in the bath, she heard her mother speaking to her. She lay there breathing softly, allowing the lavender bath crystals to lead her into a trance, as she rubbed camomile essence over her nipples.

'Phillipa. Where's my Bovril?'

Phillipa came to with a start.

'You've had your Bovril. Go to sleep.'

Her mother slept in the next room and was bedridden. Suddenly Phillipa became aware of her own mortality, and her future seemed bleak. Was Bovril and a run-out to Southend, weather permitting, all she had to look forward to? She needed to drastically alter her life-style if she was going to tread her true path.

The next day she visited a naturist medium, and after an introductory session, decided to train as a facilitator. Taking her clothes off was a natural progression, and she was naked by the third visit, having contacted a post-nineteenth-century European dictator, and Emily Pankhurst. Being nude seemed to attract more interesting spirits, and she decided there and then to make this her own personal approach in bringing solace to the living. She could hold naked séances. There already was *The Naked Civil Servant* and the *The Naked Chef.* She would be The Naked Medium, as long as her clients only wanted to hold hands.

Phil was happy to support Phillipa in her new venture, and was pleased that, in the future, he might be able to give up the cycle business. At the moment however, Phillipa needed his support, and he could not think of anything more rewarding than the possibilities of surrounding himself with naked women in search of enlightenment.

—

Tara and Lynette were getting on each other's nerves. Their culinary schemes were rapidly deteriorating and they blamed Rebecca, because Rebecca had failed to order the necessary provisions. The proposition was to provide three hot meals a day for the houseguests, allowing them unlimited access to the tea-making facilities. The campers would have to rely on the outside caterers for everything. Breakfast was going to be quite simple. Cereal, egg or baked beans on toast, and tea, but it was the other meals that were causing them concern.

Vegetable soup followed by vegetable bake and vegetables

could be acceptable, if there was a varied mixture of vegetables to work with. Unfortunately, they only had a choice of three, and carrots, potatoes and courgettes did not offer much scope for a varied diet, especially when the same combination was to provide the evening meal as well. They had tried planning a menu leaving out one ingredient at a time, but everything just promised gastronomic blandness. It did not boost their confidence when Rebecca started informing the guests that she had managed to hire a world-renowned French vegetarian chef, and they would be experiencing some wonderful examples of a little known Provence-style of cooking *avec legume au natural.* Tara and Lynette were arguing over which one of them was going to be the French vegetable expert. Lynette could speak a little French, but presumably so could some of the guests, so she would not be able to fool anybody for long. Tara was drunk most of the time, and unable to cope with anything. The ingredient shortage was the last straw. She had gone to see Gordonski and borrowed a bottle of vodka to help steady her nerves. Gordonski knew the whole project was doomed, and was not adverse to it sinking a little deeper before he stepped in to salvage it. In fact, he was very pleased to oblige with anything that could help assist the downward spiral to disaster.

Lynette decided to hit the guests with her *pièce de résistance,* on the first night. Everything might go rapidly downhill after that, but at least they would begin on a high. They had designed a menu containing all the ingredients, in a desperate attempt to stretch the palate of even the most well-travelled vegetarian.

The main course was to be *La Specialite de Provence. Carrot and courgette tart with pomme de terre, á là Gorge du Verdon.* Unfortunately for Tara and Lynette, all their concentration sorting out the main meal meant that they had forgotten to plan the pudding. Their initial attempts to create a good impression were rapidly deserting them, so Simon was despatched to the village to try and get hold of some fruit, preferably on account.

Simon did not like going down to the village, because the last time he had visited it he had contracted some strange anal infection, but he couldn't argue with Rebecca, especially as she had procured the support of Lynette. He decided to call into the local shop to see what the two old sisters had on their shelves. He could not think of anywhere else to try, and there was not much time. He would probably have to try bartering for a tin of fruit cocktail. The village was very busy. There was bunting everywhere to welcome the visitors, and the brewery had suggested to the landlord of The Lamb that he covered up his Welcome Sign with the Union Jack.

Simon entered the shop. As the bell rang, two heads appeared from over the counter. There was a strong smell of stale urine caused by the sister's excitement at the large influx of visitors.

'Hello young sir! Can we offer 'ee anything from our cold section?'

Simon glanced around. There was a recently acquired, rusty cooler unit standing in the corner.

'Please feel free to finger the goods. We've freshly-made sandwiches and local produce and all, an' we haven't had an outbreak of foot and mouth for years.'

'Well. Actually, I was wondering if you had any fruit.'

'Fruit? We might have. There maybe some fruit over in the freshly-made sandwiches and local produce section, if he'd care to have a look.'

Simon reluctantly went over to have a look. There certainly was not any fruit, but they did have a strange selection of sandwiches.

'That be our continental selection.'

A scratched recording of Edith Piaf started up from behind the counter, and Simon noticed that a selection of postcards showing European capitals had been stuck on the walls. He could not see what was particularly continental about the sandwich display, but it was certainly unusual. The halves of all the sandwiches were different. Some were made up of half-brown and -white bread, but the more adventurous were half-sliced bread and half-finger rolls. It was an interesting display and the fillings were stunningly inventive. There had been a serious attempt to diversify from the more common combinations of filling. There was *cheez and paarsnip, spam and rubarbe and sun-dryd tamarto with beetroot*, all wrapped up in greaseproof paper and labelled in felt-tip pen. Simon tried to see if there was any fruit in the cabinet, and as he moved the sandwiches aside, he saw that they were resting on uncooked sausages.

'You can't put uncooked meat with sandwiches. You'll give everybody food poisoning.'

'What's that young man? Are you wanting anything from our continental range?'

'You'll give somebody Salmonella, if you're not careful.'

'We can't give anybody Salmonelly. We tried to get some, but they can't kill them till the Glorious Twelfth, and they think the 'clipse will frighten them and make them all disappear, and that'll be too late for this 'ere festival, if they all swim away the day before.'

'Salmonella's food poisoning. You get it from mixing raw and cooked food.'

'What you're saying, young sir? Salmonellas all poisoned. Like the rabbits, eyes alla bulging and weeping sores. I remember that. Tragic it were. All those little buggers running around in circles, and crashing into trees.'

'Salmonella's a stomach bug. It makes you very sick and you can die from it. It's not an animal. Have you got any fruit or not?'

'Got some prunes. Lots of prunes. Boxes of prunes in the back, but we might be needin' 'em for sandwiches though, like what Johnny Foreigner has with garlic. Prunes an' garlic.'

'No, I don't want any prunes. Apples or bananas, have you any of those?'

'O aye, apples and bananas you be after. Then why didn't he say so?'

'Have you got some then, and maybe a few pears?'

'No. 'Aven't got any of them. He 'ave to go supermarket for 'em up Mulchester. Fifteen mile as the crow barks.'

Simon knew he was now going to have to make a thirty-mile round trip, but if he took his time he could have a few hours peace, and maybe stop for a drink on the way home. He rolled himself a joint. Fifteen miles was a long way and he wanted to enjoy some music on the journey. Two miles out of Seaton Staveley, he rounded a bend narrowly missing a car that was coming in the opposite direction and taking the corner in the middle of the road.

Malcolm closed his eyes and screamed, 'What the fuck are you doing, you crazy bastard?' Nialls, who was steering towards an old van he had encountered on an excursion to the other side of the road, swerved the car around and sneered into his mirror.

'Fucking yoghurt weaver.'

Since leaving Kate, the journey down had thankfully been uneventful. Malcolm was completely oblivious to his abandonment, and Nialls had settled down into cruising mode. It was only when they left the motorway that serious cracks started to appear in Niall's driving. He was finding it difficult to adjust to corners, after cruising at eighty-five for four hours, and this momentary lapse of concentration had not been the first. Malcolm opened the window, leaned over the front seat and increased the volume on the radio.

'Are you alright, Nialls? Do you want to stop and have a coffee or something? I'd quite like a coffee, even if you don't.'

'OK. We need petrol anyway, so look for a garage. There might be a machine, but I'd kill for a beer.'

Nialls guided the car around a hairpin bend, and the tower of Seaton Staveley church appeared in the distance.

'Look, there's a garage up on the right. What's it say? Fucking Hell, Nialls! Hangman's Hill Garage. God, that's a good omen. MOT'S WHILE YOU WAIT. While you wait? For what? Wait to have your throat slit and your children sold into slavery, probably. I bet there's a hunchback somewhere in the back, waiting to dismantle your car and destroy the evidence. He's probably peeping through the grimy windows now, licking his lips and looking forward to releasing all his sexual tension. It'll have been building up inside him for months. There's probably a dungeon underneath the forecourt, full of torture implements capable of ripping you apart.'

The effects of the drugs and the previous night were still in evidence, and he stared at the garage forecourt with apprehension.

'Don't be so bloody stupid. It's a bloody garage for God's sake. They sell petrol and fags and dirty magazines. It's not the hideout for the English fraternity of the Charles Manson gang.'

But Malcolm was not sure, and then he saw the gibbet standing proudly, just to the side of the garage toilets.

'What the fuck's that then?'

'It's probably for the tourists, you prat. They're just cashing in on the name of the place. The only thing that's ever been seen hanging here is the garage owner's cock. It's not even old. Look, you can see it's set in concrete and the rope looks definitely suspect. It's made of blue nylon.'

Malcolm was not convinced, but he eased his vice-like grip on the door handle as Nialls climbed out of the car. His anxiety rapidly returned when he noticed a sign that was above the garage entrance.

THIS IS NOT A SELF-SERVICE GARAGE. PLEASE RING THE BELL LOCATED IN THE OFFICE, IF YOU REQUIRE ASSISTANCE.

'Hang on, Nialls. It might be a trick.'

'What do you think's going to happen? Do you think a trap door's going to open up when I ring the bell, and I'm going to fall into a vat of acid? It's a bloody garage.'

Malcolm gripped the handle again as Nialls opened the door and went into the building. He emerged a few minutes later, with a Gene Vincent look-alike, carrying two cups of coffee.

'Malcolm, this is Wayne. He's into Country and Western, and Triumph motorbikes.'

Despite being a Sixties throwback, Wayne looked reasonably normal, so Malcolm got out of the car, stretched himself and walked over to Nialls, who handed him his cup of coffee.

'Wayne says that there's been lots of strange people heading into Seaton Staveley over the last couple of days, but he's resisted the temptation to eat anybody.'

'Nialls, shut up! He doesn't look like the sort who can take a joke.'

Malcolm nervously glanced across at Wayne, who was now staring at him. He placed the nozzle of the hose into the petrol tank and winked. Malcolm pretended he hadn't seen, and turned to Nialls.

'He just winked at me, for fuck's sake.'

'Now you're just being completely stupid. Why should he be interested in you, when I'm sure he could quench his insatiable sexual appetite with any number of the local remedials?'

Wayne was now rubbing his crotch, and slowly moving the nozzle in and out of the petrol tank.

'He's doing it again. He fucking fancies me. Don't you go anywhere. I don't want to be left alone with him.'

'God! You're a twat, Malcolm.'

'Don't leave me alone, Nialls. He might drag me into the garage and rape me.'

'I won't leave you. Look, if you feel that worried, get back in the car and lock the door. Actually, I think he is looking at you a little strangely. Is that a bulge in his trousers?'

Malcolm edged back to the car door. He had to pass close to Wayne, who withdrew the nozzle slowly again, before replacing it into the tank as Malcolm slunk past.

'If you wanna see my Bonneville, I don't mind taking you for a ride. I got a spare helmet.'

Malcolm certainly wasn't interested in Wayne's helmet, spare or otherwise. He climbed into the car, slamming the door and locking it behind him. As they drove off, Wayne waved and blew a kiss.

'Did you see that? He just blew a kiss at me. How can you say that he doesn't fancy me?'

'Oh, he fancies you alright. He wanted to know where we were going. He thinks he might come along and check the music out, especially if you're going to be there. I told him you weren't in a relationship at the moment.'

'You bastard Nialls. If he comes near me I'll swing for him, and it's just another big joke to you. Any chance for a laugh.'

But what was more amusing to Nialls was that it was one of the best ten pounds he had ever spent. Another good laugh at Malcolm's expense and, hopefully, Wayne might be about to climb towards his first steps to stage stardom.

———

Manderlay was now ready to receive guests. Most of the campers had arrived, and Gordonski had been instructed to paint one of the stable blocks which were going to provide the toilet facilities. Extra water was needed all over the site, and he had already dug a series of trenches that criss-crossed the entire area, and they now contained lengths of alkathene pipe. He had also put in some lengths of wire. Adapting an old crash helmet he had found behind some discarded sacks into a First-World War infantry helmet, Gordonski was now Sapper Corporal Thompson, with a mission to lay down minefields under cover of darkness. He would play his mouth organ through twilight and into the night, before crawling over the trench sides and disappearing into No-Mans Land to sink the charges.

Gordonski had also been attempting to improve his dressmaking skills. He had not been instructed to wear anything special, but he wanted to create an outfit that was in keeping with the forthcoming Festival. Merlin had seemed a suitable theme, and he was now the proud owner of a purple cloak and pointed hat, covered in gold stars. The seams matched exactly, and he was very pleased with his efforts.

He dialled Nialls.

'Hello, Gordonski. How's it going?'

'Ayup, Traat. Where are you?'

'Not far away. We thought we might stay in the village tonight. Can you get away and join us for a few beers?'

'Probably.'

'Is there anywhere to stay?'

'There's the local pub. On the left just after the shop, near the church.'

'What's going on down there? Is everything happening, are all the beautiful people there yet?'

'A bus load of drummers have just arrived and they can't get their wigwam up, to face in the right direction – or something fucking stupid. They're saying that the energy is wrong, because there's a wall in the way. I just want to blow the bastards up.'

'You could blow the wall up for them. They'd like that, and you could get a little practice in.'

'That's a good idea, just a small explosion to wet the appetite for later.'

'Gordonski. I'm joking.'

'I know you are. Anyway Nialls, I prefer to be known as Gordonski de Lesseps now.'

'What do you mean?'

'Gordonski de Lesseps, after Ferdinand, on account of my engineering skills. This place is all going to pieces, everybody's all over the place. It needs a firm hand and I'm going to provide it. We need a tight ship and I'm Captain Bligh.'

'Fucking hell, I thought you were Gordonski de Lesseps.'

'I am. Gordonski de Lesseps-Bligh.'

'OK, Gordonski. Anything you say. I'll speak to you later, as long as you haven't been set adrift in a lifeboat.'

'Kool and the Gang, mon traat.'

Gordonski returned to his workbench. He had spent the previous few hours adding to his firework collection and it was going to be spectacular. After all, pyrotechnics were his main contribution to mankind. Ever since he had blown up a neighbour's pigeon loft, he had fought a continuous battle with his conscience. To blow things up or not to blow things up was his constant dilemma, and his conscience was loosing.

Not that Gordonski was putting himself through mental turmoil. If things needed to be blown up, so be it. It was as simple as that. He did not need a political cause. Just a severe psychological imbalance and a dependency on drugs and alcohol, plus a very vivid imagination. More than enough. The fine line between producing a pretty visual effect, and an explosion capable of blowing up a house, were just a few minor adjustments of a very simple recipe. Adding a bit more of this and a little less of that was the thrill, and Gordonski was beginning to find the thrill incapable of resisting. This was his final solution, the culmination of his master plan.

Gordonski decided to write a list. It would help him to prioritise. He reached into his draw for his pencils. He had the entire range from 5H to 5B, and he always bought them unsharpened. He chose the HB. It was a compromise and he slowly whittled away the end with his twenty-four-piece Swiss army knife. The conical shape at the tip needed to be exact. It had to be perfect, otherwise there was no point, and no point meant no list.

One hour later, and the list had not progressed beyond the date. Gordonski could not decide what his priorities were and he'd spilt cider over the paper. The margin was wrong, and the handwriting was not neat enough, so he decided to phone Nialls again.

'Hello, Traats. Are you nearly here? You should be by my calculations.'

'We're just coming into the village now. I can see the church. Where did you say the pub was?'

'You can't miss it. It'll have a village idiot standing outside. He might even be falling over. They do it for the tourists. If he's got a bucket, be careful.'

'Why?'

'It's a village idiot trick. You go into the pub and he follows you in a few minutes later with his bucket all bent, and says that you have just backed over it in your car. You give him the money for a new one and offer to buy him a drink. He's been practising in preparation for the visitors. It's expected to improve the rural economy by millions.'

'Are you coming down to meet us?'

'Yes. Later. I'm just making a list.'

'Never mind a list. You're missing valuable drinking time.'

Gordonski sharpened his pencil again and wrote 'go and meet Nialls and Malcolm', before adjusting his cloak and heading out of the door. He was desperate to try some of the local beer they brewed, and felt he had a score to settle on Simon's behalf, who was still having problems walking. He went to look for Rebecca. He had not seen her properly since their torrid night together, and he was feeling bitter about how she had treated him. He could not remember anything clearly about the night, but he knew that for some reason, she had been contemptuous of his advances and he had felt rejected.

He found Rebecca in the kitchen, shouting at Lynette.

'Where's that fucking useless husband of yours. He only went to get a bit of fruit. I wasn't expecting anything too exotic, just a few apples and bananas. No mangoes or paw-paws or anything too taxing, and where's fucking Tara? You're supposed to be serving dinner in two hours.'

Tara was in the pantry sorting the vegetables, and having

a quick slug on a bottle of vodka. The thought of providing the evening meal was terrifying her, and she could hardly stand. Lynette was prepared to forgive her a mild indiscretion. She might need an ally, and a drunken one was better than nothing. She was also becoming increasingly more irritated with Rebecca's attitude, and her changing moods.

'She's in the cold store. It's not going to take that long. It's only bloody vegetables.'

'Listen, if we're going to keep these lunatics here for the duration, we've at least got to start by creating a good impression.'

Tara appeared from the pantry carrying a box of courgettes and deposited them with a bang on the prep table.

'Well, everything had better be ready. Our whole reputation is resting on your shoulders. If we don't get this right, it could screw up the whole three days.'

'Perhaps you'd like to stay and give us a hand.'

'No. I've got far too much to do. I'm still waiting for guests to arrive.'

The guests she was referring to were just driving into the village and about to enjoy their first pint at The Lamb. They would not be arriving for some time.

Gordonski caught Rebecca leaving the kitchen.

'I'm sorry to bother you Rebecca, but we're going to need some disinfectant and I think I'd better go down to the village to get some. Do you think you could let me have some money?'

'What do we need disinfectant for?'

'The toilets.'

'What's wrong with the toilets?'

'They're beginning to smell, and in my capacity as environmental health officer for the site, I'm advising you that we should be taking some basic precautions.'

'Who says you're the environmental officer?'

'I thought I'd better volunteer when the man from the council came to inspect the sanitation this afternoon.'

'When was that? Has he gone?'

'He was very pleased. It did help that I'm conversant with local government procedures, but he did point out that we should have adequate disinfectant, in case it was needed.'

but I've got to go, because I've arranged to meet Keith the Fly.'

'Yeah, well there's definitely something else on the agenda, if you're planning to meet him.'

'I've just ordered a few comestibles for the trip. If we need to sample them tonight, it can't do any harm. We need to know what to expect.'

Keith the Fly was dealer to the stars, and could get anything at a price. He provided an exclusive service to the city's professionals, and could be spotted any Friday night cruising in his black Golf through The Park, as he made drops to solicitors or dentists. His clients only snorted through fifty-pound notes, and the police left him alone.

Nialls parked his car outside *Le Pub Belgique* and the suited necks inside the bar strained to get a better look, to see who was going to climb out from behind the dark tinted windows. Malcolm adjusted the collar of his Marco Polo jacket, and eased himself out of the car. Most of his clothes were cheap. Unable to afford designer labels often, he did own one or two, and he saved these for trips out with Nialls. Nialls owned nothing but *Paul Smith* and only ate chilled Gourmet Meals for One from Marks and Spencer.

Nialls zapped the central locking, and adjusted his Raybans.

'God. There they all are, boring each other to death.'

Nialls pushed the door open and entered the bar. The sounds of voices and laughter filtered through into the street.

'I really hate this pub, Nialls. It's full of monied trendies. I really don't want to stay long.'

Nialls was already inside, pushing himself towards the bar.

La Pub Belgique was no different to any number of bars that littered the old Lace Market. The menu was written in French and overpriced, and once a year they would compete with all the other establishments to get the first batch of *Beaujolais Nouveau*. The waitresses would dress up as French tarts, and the owner would wear a beret and watch the customers getting very drunk.

Malcolm felt uneasy in trendy bars, so he went to the

'How much do you think you'll need?'

'About fifty quid.'

—··—

Gordonski climbed the fence that surrounded the grounds and joined the footpath that led down to the village. He was looking forward to a gentle stroll and felt that he looked particularly impressive in his new outfit. He broke off a branch from a tree to use as a staff, and the herd of heifers grazing in a nearby field were certainly impressed. As he approached them, they gathered around him, but a wave of his wand brought them into line, and they now stretched out in a column behind him as he headed across the field.

Gordonski could see the school from the path. It led down the hill and around the edge of the school playing field and out into the village, beside the church.

The head-teacher was playing rounders with her middle infants class when she first noticed who she thought was the farmer, driving his cows down the hill. It was a bit early in the day for milking, and the farmer was wearing a pointed hat and a purple cloak.

She shouted to a young boy who was waiting to bat, and was stuffing grass down the neck of one of his team-mates.

'Gareth. Is that your dad up there?'

She hoped it wasn't.

Gareth looked up the hill, and screamed with surprise and latent pride. The rest of the class quickly followed suit. It was not every day that your friend's dad let it slip that he was a closet Harry Potter, on a secret mission from Hogwoits. Being six, and with heads full of dragons, their excitement was too much to control, and the entire class ran towards the fence that divided the school from the farmer's field. Gordonski was overwhelmed at the extent of his welcome. He climbed the stile and waved his wand at the head-teacher, trying to usher the children back into school.

CHAPTER TEN

•

Nialls eased his car into a space between two Morris Travellers, and checked out the village idiot, who was fiddling with something behind the church wall. Malcolm was nervously studying the rear-view mirror in case they had been followed, and he was half expecting to hear the unmistakable sound of a throbbing four-stroke, being driven by a camp petrol pump attendant come into view. There was a group of people sitting on the pavement outside the pub, and Nialls placed them in the Old Hippie category. They had been observing Nialls intently, from the moment they had heard his un-environmentally friendly gas-guzzler enter the village. He ought to have known better than to pollute the world with something so ostentatious, and to make matters worse, he had managed to park it right in between their Morris Traveller's.

Nialls got out of the car, threw the end of his cigarette into the gutter, and started to count to five under his breath. He only got to three before somebody spoke.

'Excuse me.'

Nialls ignored him.

'Excuse me. Would you mind picking that up?'

Nialls still did not react.

'That cigarette that you've just dropped on the floor. Would you mind picking it up, please. Only it's such a pretty village and it's a shame to spoil it.'

'Are you talking to me?'

'Yes. Please pick up that cigarette and put it in a bin.'

'I would if there were any bins about, but there aren't any. Can you see a bin?'

'Well no, but you could always put it in the ashtray in your car.'

'I'm not leaving it in my car. It'll make it smell foul. There's nothing worse than a car smelling of stale tobacco. It's disgusting. Anyway, I thought that you might want it to make one of your reefers, or is this just a ploy to get me to buy one of your magazines?'

'What do you mean? I'm not selling magazines.'

'Aren't you? I thought you were selling the *Big Issue*, or something. Isn't that what you homeless people do, sell the *Big Issue*, and beg on street corners?'

'I'm not homeless. I'll have you know I'm a lecturer in North American studies and my wife's a specialist in colonic irrigation. We're here to attend a seminar in the village.'

Nialls turned his attention to the wife.

'God. I had a friend who had that done. He got a prolapsed arse, and couldn't have sex for weeks. Can you sell me any dope?'

'You're deliberately changing the subject.'

'How on earth can anybody take a degree in North American studies? There's nothing to study except car factories, which is pretty fucking boring. But at least it's not as boring as it was when all those Indians lived there. At least they've all fucked off. I suppose they weren't any good at making cars. I bet when they were working there, you'd sit down for a tea break and suddenly find the top of your head missing. You couldn't develop a very varied CV, if you're into North American Studies. There's not much call for buffalo hunting and scalping at the moment.'

'You're being deliberately provocative and I'm not listening. Are you going to pick that cigarette up or not?'

'What will you do if I don't?'

'I shall be forced to pick it up myself.'

'God, that's really terrifying. So if I don't pick it up you will. Is that right?'

'I'll have to. I'll have no other option. I can't let it stay on the pavement.'

'Look. I haven't cleaned my car this week and it's filthy. Will you clean that for me, if I refuse to do it?'

'Of course I won't.'

'Why not. It's the same thing. Look, I'll tell you what. I'll pick up the cigarette instead of you, and in return you can clean my car. It's called bartering. You should know all about that, what with you studying North America.'

'Don't be so ridiculous.'

'If you're prepared to pick up my cigarette, why did you bother to ask me to do it?'

'Because I thought you should have the chance to see that you shouldn't have dropped it, in the first place.'

Nialls banged on the car window and beckoned Malcolm to follow him into the pub. As Malcolm was about to step onto the pavement Nialls turned and said, 'Oh Malcolm, pick that cigarette-end up will you, that those fucking hippies have thrown away. I can't get them to, and my back's aching after all that driving.'

Malcolm was impressed. Normally Nialls did not give a toss about the environment.

—·—

'Good afternoon sirs, and what would you be wanting to drink?'

The landlord of The Lamb winked at the scattering of locals that were sitting in the bar. Up until now, the odd visitors that had come in for a drink were what the landlord classed as hippies. He thought that hippies had died out years ago, back in the Sixties, and been replaced by punks. But he must be mistaken, judging by what he had been observing over the last couple of days. He had never been into hippies or punks, or in fact any of the major fashion statements over the last fifty years. He still wore the same style of clothes that he always had, ever since he had been taken to his first farmer's market, when he was fourteen. His trousers might have got wider and narrower as the years went on, but they were always corduroy and brown. He did once succumb to an olive-green pair, when he first met his wife-to-be, but once all that silly shennanigans was over and they had tied the knot, he reverted back to brown. He had one suit and it was black, and he had only worn it the once, and that was when his father was buried. His father had been the landlord before him, and he had stepped backwards one to many times, when the trapdoor leading to the cellar was open. He broke wind before breaking his neck, or it could have been the other way around. It did not really matter, as the result was still the same. It all happened so fast, and the local GP pronounced the father dead, and very heavily soiled.

'Two pints of strong lager please.'

'We don't do lager on draught. There's not much call for it. We have got a few bottles of Kalibur, but they might be a bit strong.'

Malcolm turned his back to the bar and whispered to Nialls.

'But isn't Kalibur non-alcoholic?'

'Just leave it to me. OK. We'll have two bottles of Kalibur, and can you put a large whisky in them please.'

Malcolm was more confused.

'What's the point in putting whisky in a non-alcoholic beer?'

'Shut the fuck up, will you. Can't you see that he's trying to take the piss?'

'He might not know that it's non-alcoholic.'

''Course he knows, he's a barman isn't he. Don't be such a twat.'

Malcolm and Nialls picked up their drinks and sat down opposite two men in cloth caps. One had a large red nose and the other, extremely long arms. They were both drinking a cloudy liquid that would have looked more suitably at home in a witch's cauldron. Nialls thought that he might give the brew a try, if the Kalibur did not come up to scratch.

'Alright?'

Nialls had taken a drink and was concentrating on the engorged nose. The engorged nose chose to ignore him.

'Obviously not then. Sellafield round here, is it?'

'Nialls, don't go there. You don't know what they might be capable of, I'm sure the one on the left's got blood down his jacket.'

'He has. He's probably been eating the other one's nose,' and then he raised his voice slightly. 'It's a dreadful thing, radiation poisoning. Sometimes it takes generations to mutate, but other times, it can be almost instantaneous.'

Malcolm dug him in the ribs. Today could be the day his luck ran out.

'Hi, are you local? It's a lovely village. I really like the church. Is it Norman?'

Malcolm had attempted to take over the conversation, but Nialls was behaving like a dog with a bone.

'As far as I know, there are two main courses of physical disfigurement. One of them is radiation, and the other's hereditary, usually due to incest. With the absence of any nuclear processing plant, I guess it has to be incest.'

'Please Nialls, shut up. It's not funny. If you don't shut up, I'm leaving.'

'OK. I'll shut up, but go and get some more drinks. I want to try what they're drinking. Get me a pint of that.'

Malcolm approached the bar, and was aware that the man with the long arms was following him.

'Can I have two pints of whatever they're drinking, please?'

Malcolm indicated to the landlord the glass that had been placed on the bar beside him. It was attached to a long bony hand, and its fingers were the same length.

'Is it good, the beer? It looks pretty strong to me. Is it brewed locally?'

'What the fuck's your mate saying about insects. Is he trying to take the piss?'

'No, he wasn't saying anything, honestly. Can I get you and your friend a drink?'

'Well, he better not be taking the piss. Me and my sister will have a pint of special then, and some scratchings.'

'What about your other friend? Does he want a drink as well?'

'What other friend? I'll only be here with my sister, nobody else.'

Malcolm shivered. The engorged nose was a woman. He resisted the temptation to turn around, and hoped to God Nialls would not notice.

He paid for the drinks, and carried them back to his table, sneaking a sideways glance on the way. He could not see how she could be a woman; she was almost sporting a full beard, but he was able to make out a tell-tale bulge, underneath her tank top.

Nialls took his drink.

'What did that mutant want? He looked like he was giving you a bit of a hard time.'

'No, he was alright. He was telling me about the church. He was quite interesting.'

'Well, I'll tell you something really interesting.'

'What's that then?'

'Rudolph's a fucking woman. She's just been for a piss and she went to the ladies.'

'Don't be so stupid. You must be mistaken.'

'And she's wearing slingbacks.'

Malcolm gazed down at the floor under their table. The secret was out, and he began to panic again.

'Well, if I were you, I'd forget anything that you might be thinking of saying. I was lying. The one with the long arms wasn't talking about the church. He was getting very heavy about what you had been saying.'

'Do you think they're married? Can you imagine what the children must look like?'

'They're not married. They're brother and sister so they won't have any children.'

'I wouldn't count on it. Maybe the village idiot belongs to them.'

'Anyway Nialls, I'm warning you – any more – and I'm leaving.'

'I don't think you will. I think you'd better stick to me as closely as possible.'

'Why? What are you talking about?'

'Look who's just come in.'

Wayne walked over to the pool table, took off his leather jacket and threw it over a chair. He was wearing a black T-shirt, with *Gene Vincent and his Blue Caps* written on the front, in silver glitter. He gave Malcolm a wink, as he searched for a suitable cue.

'Either of you two fancy a game, then?'

'I'm not playing, Nialls. You can if you want, but I'm not going to. You're better than me anyway.'

'Look, you're only putting off the inevitable. If it's Winner Stays On, you'll be playing him next game.'

'But you're good, you might beat him. You could stay on all night, if you really tried.'

'I could do, but I've a feeling that I'm going to be beaten quite convincingly. I can feel Wayne's urgency eating away at my confidence.'

Malcolm pretended not to take an interest in the game

but as expected, when it looked like Nialls was going to win, he deliberately miscued and potted the black.

Once again, Nialls had manipulated the situation to his own advantage and at Malcolm's expense. But Nialls had not finished yet. Malcolm thought that he could just loose quickly and leave. He could lock himself in the car, and wait for Nialls to get bored. But Nialls was far from being bored. He was having a great time. The beer tasted good, and the fun had only just started.

'Do you two fancy playing doubles?'

Nialls had walked over to the bar, and was addressing his new friend with the extra-terrestrial arms.

'We might do, why not. I'll get my cue.'

The barman reached up above the bar and handed the man his cue. Nialls estimated that it was easily twice the length of his; but then his arms were twice the length of his as well.

'Anyway. I'm Nialls and this is Malcolm.'

Nialls resisted the temptation to shake his hand. He would have probably had to go outside the pub, and stand in the middle of the road to do that.

'Oh, and this is Wayne. But you probably know him, he works at the local garage.'

'I be called Seth and this be Chastity. Shall I break?'

Malcolm lit up another cigarette. He was now completely surrounded, playing pool with a gay biker and two in-breeds. He was in a play that was missing the script, and it was being directed by Nialls, whose least concern was winning an award.

Seth picked up the chalk, and rubbed it on the end of his cue. The end had disappeared up into the stratosphere, amongst the horse brasses, and a light dusting of blue chalk began to float to the ground as he studied the form.

The beer was now affecting Nialls' and Malcolm's judgement, especially Malcolm, who was beginning to loose his inhibitions and enjoy himself. Nialls was continuing to become more obnoxious.

'So Seth, have you got any children?'

Seth had just taken his shot, and was leaning on the wall.

'No. I haven't got any children. I'm not married.'

'I thought Chastity was your wife?'

'No, she's my sister.'

'So you haven't got any children, then?'

'Of course I haven't got any children. I've just said I'm not married.'

'Well, you might have had a child, a good-looking man like you. I bet you've had your fair share.'

'I'm not be interested in women. They're a waste of time as far as I can tell.'

'Animals, then?'

'What?'

'Animals?'

'What do 'e mean by that?'

'Have you got any animals? Lots of people who don't have children, have animals instead. I bet you've got an odd pig or two in your back garden. Something to play with when you're feeling lonely, or do you play with your sister instead?'

'I don't play with anybody.'

'Just yourself then, but it must be difficult with arms like that?'

Seth was trying to remember if any woman had ever paid him any attention, and his brain had not caught up with whatever it was that Nialls was implying.

Malcolm was having a fantastic time, as he leaned over the table to take his shot. He was squinting down at the ball and having trouble gripping his cue.

'Good job we're not playing snooker, or Wayne would be wanting to pot the brown at this moment.'

—

'Ayup, Traats. I think you're just about to get hit with the bucket sting. The village idiot was eying up your car when I walked in. Mine's a pint. Did you bring the weed killer?'

Gordonski approached the pool table, and one of the low beams knocked his hat off.

'Hello Gordonski. No, sorry — forgot. I expected you to be wearing a kaftan rather than looking like Merlin the Magnificent. I can recommend this local brew. It's got a real kick to it.'

'Never mind, Traat. I think I've got enough stock to keep me busy, and I'll try the beer.'

Malcolm had completely missed his shot and as he turned, he stepped on Wayne's foot.

'Sorry Big Boy.'

It was now Wayne's turn to become uneasy.

'So what's happening, Gordonski?'

'It's a disaster, everything's falling apart. The energies wrong and the Devil's in our midst.'

'Been on the cider have you?'

'Yes, but everything is certainly not Kool and the Gang down on the farm. But don't fear, all is not lost. Merlin, the slayer of evil, will be there to save the day when all the hippies have fucked everything up.'

'I'm sure he will. That's you then, is it?'

'Yes. Merlin is biding his time until needed, and the way things are going it's not going to be long.'

'I'm sure it won't be, Gordonski. Have we got somewhere to stay?'

'No problem, Traat. You've got the best room in the house, sorted it myself.'

Nialls thought that Gordonski's state of mind had definitely deteriorated since their last meeting. But Gordonski considered himself extremely focused, possibly better than he had in his entire life. The village idiot made his pitch, and was given short shrift from Nialls, but was promised a pound if he cleaned his car.

———

Simon had found his visit to the supermarket most invigorating. It had not taken him long to re-adjust to the buzz of a large town, and he had taken the opportunity to treat himself to some Kentucky Fried Chicken. He had bought his bargain bucket, and scurried back to the van because he did not want to be spotted by anyone, in case Lynette found out. He was supposed to be a committed vegetarian, but he could not resist the taste of the skin, and wished that he had been granted the secret of the seven different herbs and spices.

At least he had bought the fruit, and now all he had to do was stop off at the garage. He knew from a previous visit that it had a great selection of porn, and there was nothing to stop him having ten minutes quality time, indulging in one of his personal hobbies on the way back.

———

Simon parked next to the church, and thought about what he should do. As he was late and going to get a bollocking, he thought he might as well go to the pub. At least he would be pissed when it was administered. He saw Gordonski drinking at the pool table with two men.

'Hi, Gordonski. Why are you dressed like a wizard?'

'Because, Simon, that's what I am.'

Niall's impressions of Mandalay, as relayed by Gordonski, soon persuaded him that they should get there as soon as possible, and not stay in the pub for the night. Besides, the landlord was being far from friendly, especially after Malcolm had ripped the felt on the pool table, trying to impress Wayne with a double-cushion shot, holding the cue behind his back. They were becoming increasingly boister-ous and as they got louder, the more the Landlord turned up the volume of the jukebox. Wayne had left, because Malcolm had begun to pay him more attention, and the joke had started to backfire. He was considered a bit of a stud, and it would not do anything for his reputation if it got out that he had been propositioned by a Townie poof, with a sports car.

Seth and Chastity were jiving in the corner. Chastity was all of five-foot, even in her slingbacks, and looked like she was being suspended from a crane, as she pirouetted under-neath Seth's gangling frame.

Eventually they all fell out of the pub, and walked towards Simon's van, which was parked next to the village shop. There was a woman with a baby in a pram, and as they started to cross the road, she looked at Nialls and shouted,

'Bigger shoes?'

Nialls span round to Gordonski.

'What the fuck did she say?'

'I don't know Traat. It sounded like "bigger shoes", to me.'

'Bigger shoes?'

'She did say "bigger shoes", Traat.'

'There's nothing wrong with my shoes. What the fuck do I want bigger ones for?'

The woman rolled her eyes.

'No bigger shoes?'

'I don't know what the fuck you're on about. There's absolutely nothing wrong with my shoes. They fit me perfectly well, and I don't want any bigger ones, thank you.'

Malcolm glanced down at what she was holding in her arms.

'She's not saying bigger shoes you twat, she's saying *Big Issue*. She's selling *Big Issue*'s. Oh, for God's sake! Is this Earth?'

'Well, I knew somebody would be, but she'd stand more of a chance selling me a new pair of shoes.'

Malcolm gave her a pound, and they piled into the van and headed towards Mandalay.

———

Mandalay had ceased to be a rectory some period after the First World War, when the population had dwindled in the surrounding villages, and the church was closed. The conflict had led to household's being more concerned with worldly pursuits, and it was not the church that was going to put food on the table. By the time the flock had recovered enough to embrace religion again, the house had been sold to an industrialist, who had had the vision to adapt his factories to the production of munitions. He built an extra wing on the house, and added a stable block around the side. It soon became one of the largest houses in the area, employing staff from the local village. The grounds were then landscaped by an architect, and a small lake constructed and stocked with fish for the benefit of the guests, who used to visit for weekends. There was an avenue of trees, leading from the derelict gatehouse, and these followed the slow curve of the drive that ended in front of the main door. There had once been two columns at the gate entrance, with majestic hunting dogs facing each other over steel gates.

The dogs were now leaning outside the front door with broken bases, and the gates were overgrown with ivy and thrown in a ditch. The house had been sold again in the Sixties to pay for death duties, and was bought by the drummer of one of the first super groups. He had a swimming pool installed, and converted the stables into a recording studio. He was rarely in residence, but allowed the local children to use the pool when he was away, and when the church approached him with an idea to revive the local fête, he even provided the marquee. He retired to the States, and the house slowly degenerated, allowing Rebecca to eventually buy it at a very reasonable price. He would probably be very pleased if he could see the house now, on one of the hottest days of the year, as banners flew in the wind and brightly coloured tents filled every available space. It would have reminded him of The Isle of White Festival, when he headlined there in 1969.

The bank of the lake was overgrown with weeds, but Gordonski had managed to clear an area around the boathouse, and some of the campers were swimming in the murky waters towards an island. A Welsh flag had been stuck in the middle, and there was some good-humoured international rivalry going on between them and the English contingent on the shore, as they threw mud at each other. Neither party had noticed the lengths of wire stretching across the water, or the freshly covered holes.

There were lots of areas in the garden overgrown with ivy, and children were discovering the pathways and old statues that had been left unnoticed for years. Like their parents, they had no problem losing their inhibitions and had formed themselves into a lost tribe, as they prowled the woods looking for adventure. They did not realise the relevance of the lengths of flex they kept finding, and why it disappeared into the ground every few meters. They were enjoying their games too much to investigate further, and instead, had made a camp in a grotto they had unearthed in some rocks, behind the lake. If they had discovered the grotto earlier in the day, they would have found the flex rolled neatly onto cardboard drums, standing next to a metal box with a skull and crossbones painted on its lid. Gordonski had hidden it there the previous night, before returning at daybreak with an assorted selection of Pringles crisps boxes, which he had buried in the ground.

But for now, the house was saturated with incense and well-being. The weather was hot, and everybody was truly chilled out. Chartered surveyors from Daventry, and social workers from Exeter were sharing anecdotes worthy of Woodstock. Cars had been parked in circles around the tents, and everybody had found their sacred space, as long as it was not near the sanitation block. Nothing was worse than camping near the toilet facilities, especially after the first day, and when the weather was hot. There is green and green, and those who chose to be close to the toilets would regret it by the second day.

The lecturer in North American studies was particularly interested in the configuration of wigwams that surrounded the house. He thought that their choice of scaffolding poles and bin liners, as building materials, needed further investigation, and he decided to go and talk to them about it later.

Some of the visitors had experienced the Sixties, and the ethos had never quite deserted them. They still had the potential to be anarchists, and had deliberately ignored Gordonski's camping plan. Neat rows of tents were not for them. They were on a three-day freefall. Sex and drugs and listening to Meat Loaf on their children's Walkman's. In fact, they were so laid back, some were dropping their inhibitions and saying 'Fuck' in front of their children.

The lecturer in North American Studies thought that he had better check the pressure in his tyres. He might forget later, as he intended to get a little spaced. He had always been practical. That's why he had searched the adverts until he had found a Morris Traveller. They were real cars, properly built and well engineered. Unfortunately, the year he purchased coincided with the Ministry of Transport clamping down on fuel emissions, and he had to spend a fortune getting it through its MOT. It was about as environmentally friendly as an oil slick, but it had real cedar wood on the side, a wood that was now rare, due to mass de-forestation.

He opened the back doors and found the gauge, enclosed in a leather case.

'Hey, er, excuse me but, er, have you got any skins?'

There was a man standing over his shoulder, and he was wearing the same sandals and sweater as the lecturer in North American Studies.

'Hi, I'm Neville. I'm camping over there. Only I seem to have come away without any papers.'

The lecturer had no skins, but he also did not want to loose a potential friend.

'I think I might have some in the glove compartment, but if I have they will be king-sized. Will they do?'

'Yeah, that would be really far-out. You can join me for a spliff, if you like. I've got some resin, but it's not very strong. It's not like it was in the old days.'

'Oh, I know. I can remember when you could buy a half for four quid. It would last you weeks, and it was real laughing gas. You know what I mean? And there was such a choice then, *Lebanese Gold, Nepalese Temple Balls, Paki Black*. God, they wouldn't be able to call it that now, would they, *Paki Black*?'

'Well, I always refused to buy it. I thought it was a politically incorrect name, even in the Sixties. It's a bit more acceptable now, because you can say "black".'

'Yes. I suppose then, it should have been Pakistani Coloured. But you're not supposed to say "coloured" now, are you?'

'Pakistani Coloured would have been alright. Anyway, it was good dope. It used to give you a really good high. I read *Lord of the Rings* on it.

'Shame you can't buy it today, now we know what to call it, without offending anybody.'

Neville reached into his pocket, got out a pipe and filled it with tobacco.

'Is that *Clan*? I haven't seen that for years. Do you mind if I have a bit?'

'Course you can. Do you smoke a pipe?'

'Sometimes. I've got one in the car.'

They both took a draw on their pipes, and thought about how radical they had been back in the Sixties. Thank God they had never lost their ideals.

'So, do you fancy a smoke then, if we can get some papers?'

'No Thanks. I'd better not. I've got to check the oil and tyres, and I'll be wanted back for tea in a minute.'

'That's a point. I said I'd peg the tent down properly. I'd better do that before I forget. Maybe later then.'

'Yeah, far out. Let's meet up for a five skinner after tea. We could get really blasted, and go and check the wigwams out.'

—·—

Dinner was being served and the Vichyssoise was going down well. Simon had still not appeared with any fruit, but Rebecca had managed to borrow a catering tin of apples, from one of the stalls which were selling crêpes. Everybody was getting to know each other, appearing friendly, whilst checking out the opposition. Apart from the gaggle of healers, mediums and the drum workshop, there was a varied selection of alternative therapies represented. There was a retired post-mistress, who specialised in Fen Shui, and an Indian Head Masseuse from Bromsgrove. The post-mistress was a devout Christian, and had arranged the flowers in her church for years. It was her intention to bring peace and harmony to the home, by demonstrating her floral displays. They had bonded instantly, and were going to share the conservatory for their workshops, next to a middle-aged man with a burgeoning midrift and a ponytail. He was called Dolphin, and his specialist subject was Tantric sex. Dolphin was with his wife, who he had met in the Far East, as he was travelling through Thailand, on his way to Vietnam. Stellana was approaching the menopause, and had fancied Dolphin the moment he had walked in the bar. He had actually stopped on the Khao San Road to pick up a lady-boy for the night, but there were none available, so he had settled for Stellana instead. They had got married in the Phillipines on their way home, after attending a two-day introduction to Tantric sex, run by a Swede called Klaus. It had been very enlightening for both of them, although Stellana had difficulties with the final session; this required them to sit above a mirror and study their genitals. Dolphin had found it hard to balance and look over his waistline at the same time, but he had been pleased to see that the wart contracted in Amsterdam had finally cleared up. They were only fledglings in the art of Tantric sex, and had decided to concentrate on a less intimate approach at the beginning, although they did have a selection of rubber sarongs on sale, for the more adventurous.

Phil and Phillipa were completely naked. It had only been a matter of minutes before they had stripped off. If they were going to promote their right not to wear clothes, it had to be from the very beginning. Luckily, the soup was at a moderate temperature.

Rebecca felt that she should say a few words between courses and so, before the desert appeared, she prepared to welcome her guests.

'Hello everybody, and welcome to Mandalay. The warmth of my feelings to you can only be matched by the sunshine. We have gathered in our midst, for the next two days, a group of people who have been hand-picked for their integrity and expertise. All professionals in their field, offering help and support to all. I am convinced that everyone will leave this place at the end truly enlightened, and able to continue on their spiritual path, to wherever it leads them.

'Before I go, I would like to leave you with a story taught to me in an Asram in Northern India by a Sufi Elder. It is the story of the Mulla Nasrudin, Sufi mystic, Chief of the Dervishes, and Master of the Hidden Treasure.

'Nasrudin gave his wife some meat to cook for guests. When the meal arrived, there was no meat. She had eaten it.

'Nasrudin said, "Where is the meat?" and she replied, "The cat ate it all, all five pounds of it."

'Nasrudin put the cat on some scales. It weighed five pounds.

'"If this is the cat," said Nasrudin, "where is the meat? If, on the other hand, this is the meat, then where is the cat?"

'Enjoy.'

Rebecca floated out of the room and the assembled devotees applauded, despite not understanding a word of what she had just said. Dolphin returned to eyeing up the girl with the dreads, who played the drums, and lived in the wigwam, which was erected in the grounds, belonging to a woman, who lived in the house that Jack built.

PART THREE

CHAPTER ELEVEN

.

Rebecca had retired to her room for a much-needed shot of Jack Daniels. She lay back on her Regency-style chaise longue, covered with a cheap throw bought from IKEA. The chest-of-drawers and wardrobe had never been intended to live together, but an enterprising antique dealer with a flair for 'cut and shunt', had constructed something that to the untrained eye, resembled a matching George III boudoir set. Velvet curtains, bleached by the sun, hung on bamboo window poles that strained under the weight. There was a reproduction Jardinière in the corner, but the cracked bowl contained only cigarette ends, and the odd wet-wipe. Rebecca had painted the room, but already the cream ceiling was beginning to turn brown with nicotine, and damp was appearing again, below the window sills.

She had just taken a swig on the bottle when she heard the sound of gravel being churned up on the drive outside. Simon was weaving the van towards the house, and Gordonski was hanging out of the window shouting abuse at the campers. Stones were flying out from under the wheels and bouncing off tents as the van skidded to a halt, in front of the main entrance.

Rebecca groaned, before standing up and going to the window. God, Simon was useless. He couldn't be relied on to do anything. Luckily for him, dinner had gone well, but she still felt the need to shout at him, very loudly, so she ran down the back stairs and out onto the drive.

'Where have you two been? You should have been back hours ago. Did you get the disinfectant, Gordonski? The toilets are stinking'

The back doors of the van were kicked open, and a man wearing a leather-flying jacket climbed out onto the grass verge. Rebecca thought that he was handsome, and his clothes suggested that he was probably in possession of a substantial bank account.

She momentarily forgot about Simon, and turned her attention to the rest of the passengers. There was only one other, and he was unloading the luggage and looked far less interesting.

Nialls was running his fingers through his hair as he walked towards Rebecca, in an attempt to disguise his rapidly receding hairline.

'Hello. You must be Rebecca. I've heard so much about you. I'm called Nialls. Do you own all this?'

His head performed a three-hundred-and-sixty-degree rotation, as he tried to evaluate the saleable price of the house and grounds.

'Yes. It all belongs to me.'

Rebecca was conducting a survey of her own, and there was a temporary silence as they mutually assessed each other's potential. It was an instantaneous attraction, and they both recognised it immediately. But it was not just physical. They each smelt financial gain and fully appreciated that this meeting could develop into a far greater spiritual experience.

Nialls instantly began oozing charm, and Rebecca became the willing sponge. She loved to be flattered, and he loved to dish it out. Neither of them meant it, but that did not matter. They could feed off each other for as long as it was necessary. Nialls was aware of the real challenge, for Rebecca was not going to be easy. It would take more than a public school charm to win her over, and Rebecca knew that she was more than a match for anything he could secrete out of his pores. Nialls, in fact, might be perfect for her over the next few days, if things got tough, and both of them could smell money, an aphrodisiac far stronger, and more essential, than any oils from the east.

Rebecca's nostrils flared as she fiddled with the buttons of her blouse.

'Have you booked? Only we are quite full.'

'Yes. Nialls Thompson–Fletcher, I booked some time ago. A single room, and one for my friend, Francis.'

'Oh! Yes. We've been waiting for you, but we were expecting you to be with your wife, called Frances? You requested separate rooms. I even bought a rubber sheet for your wife's problem.'

'Well, there must have been some mistake. I'm here with

my friend, and he's definitely a man. He'll certainly need the rubber sheet though, so that won't be wasted.'

'It's just that we made a rule that we weren't going to have any single men on the Workshop.'

'Well, I'm sure that you can make an exception in my case, Rebecca.'

Nialls leaned over and whispered into her ear.

'Do you fancy a line? It's a hundred per cent Columbian. Uncut. No glucose. It's even got the kite mark embossed on it.'

'Simon, show Nialls and his friend to their rooms will you, and then get that fruit into the kitchen.'

Gordonski emerged from the van and looked around. He was even more troubled. All the tents were in the wrong place, campers were walking on the grass that he had only just seeded, and lengths of wire were sticking up above the surface.

'Fucking Hippies.'

'Gordonski, help Simon with Niall's bags and for God's sake, don't you think you should get changed?'

'No. I fucking don't. I've got far more important business to attend to, and I certainly don't need to get changed.'

Gordonski threw his cloak over his shoulder and pulled his hat down onto his head, before marching off into the direction of the stable block. The next time he appeared, he would be in the initial stages of meltdown.

Simon carried Niall's bags upstairs. They were matching and in embossed leather, made by Burberry, and Rebecca thought how expensive they looked.

Malcolm carried his own. They were plastic, from Asda and bought on special offer. A free holdall with every suit-case; destination Costa Del Sol, courtesy of EasyJet.

'If you'd like to join me for a drink when you've settled in, Nialls, I'm in the rooms at the top of the stairs.'

'I certainly would, Rebecca. I've got half-a-dozen bottles of a particularly good *Fitou* with me. I'll bring a couple. See you in a minute.'

Simon opened the door for Nialls, and put his bags down. The camaraderie in The Lamb was forgotten and Simon felt like a hotel porter, only this time he was not going to be offered a tip.

'I might see you later then, Nialls?'

'I doubt it, Simon. Maybe you could show Malcolm round or something.'

'Why? Where are you going to be?'

Malcolm had followed them into the room, but he already knew the answer.

'I suppose you're going to be spending the evening with Rebecca. Well, fuck off then.'

'Now then Frances, don't be like that. We don't want you getting excited and soiling yourself.'

Malcolm went to find his own room. Nialls would not be changing his mind, and spiritual enlightenment was not going to be one of his priorities during the next few days. This was because Nialls had met a woman, and for the time being, that was that, unless of course he met another woman, which was more than likely. Rebecca was only really to be the springboard for some depravity. Nialls had already noticed the woman in a green boiler suit and red hair.

Malcolm's room was small, and distinctly in need of a makeover. The bed in the corner had come from an army warehouse, and the wardrobe had been covered in Fablon, sometime back in the Sixties. The walls were painted purple and the lampshade was constructed of paper cups, stuck together to form a sphere. It had been made by the child of the previous owner, and Rebecca had kept it as an example of Retro Art. Malcolm lay on the bed and considered his options. He could go and have a look round, or he could go straight back to the village and carry on getting drunk. He decided on a compromise. He would go and find Gordonski, see what he was up to, and then go back to the pub.

He wandered out into the late afternoon sunlight. There was a light breeze and badly-painted banners nailed to roofing battens, were flapping in time to drum beats drifting out of an Indian tepee. The flags, made out of old sheets, were covered in painted symbols. Gordonski had based the designs on cave paintings and had used some old emulsion he had found in one of the sheds, but the colours were already beginning to wash out. Malcolm looked up at his bedroom. Like the rest of the house, all the windows were in a sad state of neglect and streaked with grime. There had been an attempt to fill the rotten sashes before hurriedly covering them over, and the bushes underneath the windows were covered in white paint. A ladder had been abandoned beside a length of broken guttering.

—

Gordonski was painting mousetraps. He had noticed droppings at the back of his cutlery draw, and needed to do something immediately. He hated the thought of mice. They were dirty vermin and had to be exterminated. He had decided to paint the traps because they were a little drab, and he had chosen a red and yellow chevron pattern. The colours worked well with the rest of the room, and by using masking tape, the lines were immaculate and straight. He finished the last one, reached for the box of Pringles on the sideboard and emptied the contents under the sink. He was laying a trail to attract the mice before he put the traps down. He also needed the Pringles' box for one of his fireworks, as they made an excellent container. Gordonski had collected quite a few. In fact, this was the last one. The others were neatly packed, in a box under the table, waiting to be connected to batteries.

'Hi, Gordonski. Can I come in? Do you fancy a beer or something?'

Malcolm could see Gordonski was engrossed in something. He appeared to be cramming wires into a Pringles packet.

'And what might something be?'

'I don't know. I've just left Nialls chatting Rebecca up, so he'll be out of action for the rest of the evening.'

'I might fancy something if it involved starting a fire. That would be quite good.'

'What's the matter, Gordonski? You seem a bit troubled? What's that you're doing?'

'That's a Wizzbang, Malcolm. It's a fucking big Wizzbang, and soon I'm going to light it, but not yet. I'm not ready yet. There's still such a lot to do.'

'What do you mean, it's a Wizzbang? Is that a firework?'

Malcolm glanced around the walls and could see wires hanging on hooks, connected to terminals.

'What are all those wires for, Gordonski?'

'They're for Wizzbangs too. Won't be long now. Have you never tried to make fireworks, Malcolm? It's very easy. You just need a few wires, some basic chemicals, a container and that's it. Kool and the Gang.'

Gordonski was sounding more weird than usual, and what was he doing with those red and yellow mousetraps? The room was immaculate. Even the empty cider bottles were stacked in neat rows, waiting to be discarded.

'OK. So what are you really doing? And what are those mousetraps for?'

'They're for mice. I'm going to take the mice out – fucking dirty rodents.'

'Look Gordonski, you're sounding really fucking weird. Can't you just talk normal for once?'

'I'm not called Gordonski. My name's Rob, Belfast Rob.'

'I'm going, Gordonski. I don't know what to believe.'

Gordonski began to laugh.

'They're fireworks, Malcolm. Just simple, pretty fireworks.'

'What are?'

'These. They're fireworks – very benign. I thought we might let them off on the final night. Just a small display to end with. I've cleared it with Rebecca, and she thinks it's a really good idea.'

'Yeah. It sounds fantastic, just as long as you know what you're doing.'

Malcolm only possessed a rudimentary knowledge of electronics, but it was enough to know that Gordonski was not just an amateur radio enthusiast. It was the configuration of wires and where they were going to be connected, that was giving him the most concern. He remembered the first time they had seen him, standing in a fire, holding onto a flaming cross and blowing burning lighter fuel out of his mouth.

Malcolm decided to skip Gordonski and head down to the village. Whatever he was up too, it could be ignored for the time being, and Malcolm was still feeling a bit muddled.

The bar of The Lamb was empty. Malcolm was immediately aware of the state of neglect. The horse brasses on the beams looked like they had never been cleaned, and their lack of lustre reflected the general demeanour of its owner. The afternoon shift had gone home to milk the cows, and the jukebox was now playing a more contemporary selection of music. It was after six, and the landlord had started on large whiskies. He always waited until he heard the opening bars to the Six o'clock News, before he pressed his glass against the optic that was mounted on the wall, away from all the rest. This was his special bottle, and where he was not averse to adding a bit of water to the others, this one always remained completely pure.

He had put up with the previous six hours, standing behind the bar being tetchy, and by six o'clock he was feeling flat. Now he could start drinking, and be even more miserable, until it was time to finally bolt the door for another day.

'Can I have a pint please, but not that beer we had earlier. Just a pint of Otter, and are you doing food?'

As a special dispensation for the expected influx of visitors, the landlord had decided to do basic meals, and with the help of his mother had come up with a selection of bar snacks. They were going surprisingly well. He handed Malcolm a menu, printed on the back of a faded Mother's Day card, covered in sticky plastic.

'What's the Stable Lad's Platter?'

The landlord's mother had spent hours doing her research, pouring over back copies of the Women's Institute magazine.

'I don't know. I'll find out. Mother, what's Stable Lad's Platter?'

Mother appeared from a back room, wearing a floral housecoat and carrying a soup ladle.

'Stable Lad's Platter. That's bread and cheese with a bit of salad. It's very tasty. It comes with authentic Branston pickle, and a choice of brown or white bread.'

'It's a bit like a Ploughman's then?'

'He says, "Is it a bit like a Ploughman's?"'

'I don't rightly know. What's a Ploughman's like?'

The barman turned to Malcolm.

'What's a Ploughman's like?'

Malcolm decided that he did not want it, whatever it was. He really wanted something hot.

'What about Neptune's Fish Pie (Sea Style). What sort of fish is it?'

'What sort of fish is in the fish pie, Mother?'

'It says on the menu.'

Malcolm had not noticed the writing underneath. It read, 'a sumptuous mixture of locally-caught white fish in a white wine sauce, topped with puff pastry'.

'It says that it's made with locally-caught fish.'

'That's right.'

'But we're nowhere the sea. It's about fifty miles away. How can it be locally caught?'

'He says, how can it be locally caught, Mother? He says the sea's miles away.'

'That's what it said in the magazine I copied it from, and that had been copied straight from a book by Nick Stein, and he's got his own fish and chip shop.'

'Yes. But he lives by the sea, so his fish would be locally caught. Where did you get your's from?'

'Iceland, and you can't get more local than that. It's in Mulchester and that's only about half-an-hour's bus journey, and shorter still if you get a lift.'

'OK. I'll have the fish pie. I'll be sitting over there, if that's alright?'

'Don't forget your ticket. I'll shout your number out when it's ready.'

The Landlord handed Malcolm a cloakroom ticket.

As he was the only person in the bar at the time Malcolm did not see the point of a ticket, but he took it anyway.

He went and sat over by the jukebox. There was a local paper on the table, and he started to read the front page. The headline said, FIVE-LEGGED SHEEP BORN ON LOCAL FARM. He decided not to go there, and instead began to scrutinise the classified's on the Announcement Page. It was littered with photographs of anybody who had reached an age, which gave their families the pretext to send in the most embarrassing baby picture they could find.

'Good Evening Miss, and what can I be getting for you?'

Malcolm put the paper back down on the table, and strained to hear over the music. He was intrigued. He had not seen anybody in the pub, as yet, that you could be certain was female. This must be a very special occasion for the Landlord to be so definite, without first demanding to see a birth certificate.

'I'll have a pint of cider please. I can't seem to get a signal on my mobile. Is it always like that?'

'I don't know, Miss. I've never been asked before, but there's a gentleman over there with one. He might be able to help you.'

Malcolm looked around and realised the barman was talking about him. He had recently bought a Pay As You Go mobile, and it was still making him feel a bit self-conscious. Nialls was continually telling him how un-cool it was to have to buy vouchers. He had not actually had to buy that many, but he still kept it continually turned on, just in case. He stood up and went to the jukebox, and chose five songs that were part of a Seventies compilation album. Eton Rifles began to play and he strained his neck around the pillar. She was sat on a bar-stool, drinking her pint, and Malcolm thought she was very beautiful.

The immediate attraction he felt was very unusual for Malcolm, because recently he had not met anybody he had remotely fancied, unless it was chemically induced. He grabbed his phone and checked the signal, before returning to look at his paper, trying to concentrate.

'Number One's Fish Pie, Sea-Style.'

'Yes please. Over here.'

The landlord sauntered over and placed it on the table.

'Bon Soir. We do have a wine list if you'd like to see it'

'No, thank you, I'm fine.'

Malcolm began to eat. It was very good, and he was not aware of her approaching his table until he heard her voice.

'Hello. I'm sorry to bother you, but I see you've got a mobile, only mine's not working, and I was wondering whether it was faulty or something?'

'It's probably the network. You can try mine if you like.'

'No. That's very nice of you. I just wanted to check if I had any messages. I can always use the phone in the bar, but I'll join you if I can. Would you like a drink?'

'Yes please. Thank you. Thank you very much. I'll have a pint of beer, please. Thank you very much.'

Malcolm always overdid the gratitude when he was feeling nervous, and he had to stop himself saying thank you again, as she walked towards the bar. He was even more impressed when she returned, carrying the two drinks. Not only was she beautiful, but she drank pints. He had not met a woman that drank pints since his college days. All the women he seemed to meet drank stupidly-named trendy drinks that cost a fortune.

'Thanks for letting me join you. I really need a pint. It's been a long day and I seem to have been on the road for hours. My name's Sophie, by the way.'

'Hi. I'm Malcolm.'

'I know. The barman told me, something about a ripped pool table?'

'Yeah, I had a bit of an accident.'

'Do you live here?'

'No. I'm down for a few days. There's an Eclipse Festival being held near here.'

'That's what I'm here for. I've been asked to write an article on it, for one of the colour supplements.'

'Are you a journalist then?'

'Yes, I try to be. I'm doing freelance work at the moment. It's a bit thin on the ground, so I grab what I can. What do you do?'

This was the question that Malcolm always dreaded. Once he would have had an audience in stitches, regaling them with stories of his personal commitment to educational malpractice, and sedentary teaching techniques. But not any more. Now he was a boring fucker, according to Nialls. In loosing his confidence, he had also lost his ability to communicate and had become tongue-tied and clumsy, especially when talking to women. Their eyes would glaze over after a couple of minutes, as he tried to sound interesting. He didn't blame them. He even bored himself most of the time. He had lost the spark he had once possessed, and that's why he had been relying on Nialls for support, but Nialls had just succeeded in helping to erode any self-esteem Malcolm had been left able to cling on to. Maybe Sophie would help him to emerge out of this cocoon-like state, to calm him. She was certainly far better looking than a bottle of Valium.

'I was a teacher, but I gave it up, and now I'm just trying to work out what I want to do next.'

'God, I don't blame you giving it up. It must be one of the most thankless jobs in the world. I thought about being one once, but I came to my senses in time. Everybody's always slagging teachers off, making out that it's all holidays. It's almost as if they believe that teachers can take time off when they want.'

'I used to say that I needed the long holidays to spend all the money I earned. That usually pissed them off even more.'

'I bet it did. Malcolm's a nice name.'

'It's actually my second name. My first name's Colin, but somewhere, when I was a baby, it sort of got changed around. I don't think my father liked it very much.'

'Colin's a good name as well. My brother's called Colin. It's Scottish isn't it?'

'It's actually from the name of a Gaelic folk character called Colin Tampon, it means lusty youth.'

'So you're named after a sanitary towel then?'

'I suppose I am. If I ever become an angel, I'll be Colin Tampon with wings.'

'It's the pads that have wings, but I get the point.'

This was it! Not only did this woman drink pints but she also had a sense of humour, and there is no greater aphrodisiac than that.

Malcolm wanted to lean over and kiss her, and suggest that they watched *It's A Wonderful Life* together. He had never even watched the film with his wife. He always cried when the bell rang on the Christmas tree and the Angel got his wings.

The birds continued to sing in his ears, and the tide kept crashing against the shore.

'Where are you from, Sophie?'

'I'm from Herefordshire. My parents run a stud farm.'

'I've always wanted to visit Herefordshire. My mother was based there during the war and it sounds a beautiful place.'

'It is. The colours are magnificent in the autumn, but the winters tend to be quite long. We've got some arable land we let to the local farmer, but my parents' main love are the horses. We've won a few awards over the years.'

'So they manage to make a living, then?'

'Yes, but they do have some hair-brained ideas sometimes. They tried to open a Gypsy museum once, but it was a complete disaster.'

'How did that work?'

'They got a few old caravans, the old horse-drawn ones, and put them on display and had a little farm for the children. It all went belly-up, and they lost quite a bit of money.'

'It's also a coincidence you live in Herefordshire. My favourite book's based there.'

'Well, here's another one then. So is mine.'

'OK… Well, this book of mine involves twins. How about yours?'

Sophie was carrying a rucksack. She reached inside, got out a notepad and tore off two sheets, before handing Malcolm a pen.

'Write down the name of the book, but don't show me.'

They wrote on the pieces of paper and passed them back to each other. Sophie opened her's first, and leaned over and touched his hand.

'It's 'The Vision' isn't it? You want to know where 'The Vision' is. I know. I've been there. I found it.'

Malcolm placed her piece of paper on the table, and covered it with his hands. He knew he did not have to look at it, but nothing was going to prevent him from reacting to the most powerful act of sensual intimacy he had ever experienced. He took his hands away, smoothed out the paper in front of him and read:

On The Black Hill.

'Fuck. I don't believe it. *On The Black Hill.* Fuck me.'

Sophie smiled, touched his hand again and thought that she probably might.

Nialls put his cases on the bed and began to unpack. First his clothes, which took seconds, and then his cosmetic bag, which took considerably longer. He never travelled without a full range of facial products, and he arranged them neatly on the dressing table, before chopping himself a line on his travel mirror. He was famous for his lines. Chopped and arranged in perfect furrows, using his platinum Mastercard. He ran himself a bath, and laid his *Paul Smith* jeans neatly on the bed. He preferred to shower, because a bath dried out his skin, but he was well prepared with an adequate range of oils to rejuvenate his scales. After bathing, he trimmed his stubble which was always kept at a precise length, before filing his nails. Tonight, he paid particular attention to his right hand before choosing two bottles of wine, and heading off to find Rebecca.

Rebecca was also preparing herself. She had not had good sex for ages. Gordonski had been a complete waste of time, and before that, it had been with the estate agent who had shown her around Mandalay. She had only done it with him because she had wanted to find out what offer she was going to have to come up with, and he was supposedly sworn to secrecy.

Being an estate agent, he was not going to tell her the complete truth – that a dilapidated grade-two listed building had not received much interest at all. He took her from behind on the mezzanine floor, hoping that she would not notice the dry rot in the skirting boards.

Rebecca knew that a night with Nialls was going to involve snorting drugs, and therefore she took the precaution of hiding anything that could be used for bondage purposes. She had been with cocaine users before, and she was not into playing Dungeons and Dragons tonight. One of her lovers had once turned up, wired out of his skull, carrying a box of disposable rubber gloves, and a varied selection of vegetables. He had arranged them in some sort of order, known only to him, on her duvet before she had sent him packing, to look for an appropriate card in one of the local telephone boxes.

Nialls knocked, and without waiting for a reply, opened the door.

'Hello, Rebecca. You look fabulous. Have you got any glasses?'

Rebecca handed him two Dartington crystal glasses that she had saved from her marriage.

'Nice glasses, Rebecca. You can always tell good Dartington, they're so resonant.'

Nialls held one of the glasses up to the light and flicked it with his finger. It immediately shattered.

'God Rebecca! They can't be real Dartington. They're probably made in the Far East. They can copy anything over there. Anyway, never mind, can't be helped. I'll just drink out of the bottle. So how's it going then? Is everything running smoothly? It looks a very impressive set up.'

'Yes. Everything's going really well, despite the staff being crap, but I suppose you only get what you pay for. So what do you do for a living, Nialls?'

'I'm in property. Spending most of my time developing loft apartments at the moment. Can't spend it fast enough. You've got lovely cheekbones, Rebecca. Have you got any East European blood in you?'

'Yes. I have actually. My grandfather was a count. He owned some land north of Prague, but it was sold years ago and the money invested. Mandalay's just a hobby, really. An opportunity to bring spiritual well-being to those who are searching.'

'That's very philanthropic of you. Are you searching for anything in particular? Apart from somewhere to go on holiday.'

Nialls had noticed the holiday brochures piled up on Rebecca's bed.

'I did think I might go away for a few days. It's been very tiring organizing the Festival.'

'Not planning to do a runner or anything else like that then?'

'No, of course not.'

Nialls had dealt with all types of people through the years and Rebecca was about as genuine as he was, and he was as genuine as Rebecca's Dartington glass.

'Do you fancy a bit of a pick-me-up?'

'Well, if you're twisting my arm.'

Nialls chopped out two large ones, and she managed to take one, and half of the other, before taking a breath.

'Steady on Rebecca. There's plenty more. No need to hurry. We've got all night.'

But Rebecca did not want it to take all night. She wanted a quick hit, chemically and sexually. She still had not decided where she was going to go on her summer break, and she needed time to plan. Nialls was handsome, but she'd had plenty of good-looking men. There would be plenty more wherever she decided to go. She was in a fast and furious mood, no long seduction necessary. She did not want *Cosmopolitan* sex. She wanted it hard and she wanted it now.

Unfortunately for Rebecca, she was going to be in for a long wait. Nialls could only perform at his speed. There was only one species in the world whose seduction technique was slower than Nialls, and that was a breed of retarded tortoise. He knew he was going to have to act, but at least he had three days. Even that was pushing it. Not that Rebecca did not enjoy being pursued with flowers and trips to the ballet, but that was with men that she saw some kind of future with. This was different. Nialls was just an egotistical Bob the Builder with a coke habit, but she was sure that he could still give her a good time.

Rebecca leaned over to get the bottle of wine, allowing her breasts to brush against the side of his head. Nialls felt distinctly uncomfortable. What was she doing? He hadn't even had time to suggest making her a tape.

———

'Actually, I've got a small confession.'

Sophie was rolling a cigarette and licking the edge of the Rizla.

'I noticed you when I walked in. I even gave you a second glance, believe it or not. It's interesting that you were playing The Jam. Paul Weller's got a great voice. It reminds me of taking my GCSE's. I spent more time listening to them than revising.'

'You didn't do very well then?'

'No. Not really. But it was enough.'

'So you went to university?'

'Yes. I did eventually, but I took some time out first. I can't say I really enjoyed student life. They were all too busy being radical. Spending their money in London, marching for larger grants.'

'So you were a bit of a swot then?'

'No. I still managed to have a good time. I even stood for Social Secretary, but got beaten. After that I took on editing the university magazine.'

'Did you get a good pass?'

'I got a First, which I put to good use by working in Burger King.'

'So then what?'

'Well, I was quickly promoted to counter assistant, and got friendly with the sub-editor at the local evening paper who used to come in. He suggested that I might like to submit some articles about the local music venues. Apparently none of the existing staff were under forty. So I became a part-time reporter.'

'Did you stay there long?'

'Long enough. I decided I wanted to travel, and thought that I should visit Goa before it began to resemble Margate.'

'And did you?'

'Yes. I managed to get some work writing articles for *Rough Guides*, and I finished up with a great tan and a dose of amoebic dysentery.'

'Then what?'

'That's it really. I spent a couple of years temping, before helping to run a community music festival in Bristol, and concentrating on my freelance writing. So Malcolm, why do you like *On The Black Hill*?'

'It's just a brilliant story. It must be special, because I didn't read anything for two years, but that was the book that got me reading again.'

'So why didn't you read anything?'

'I went through a bad time. My marriage ended and I was screwed up.'

Malcolm went to get more beers, and Sophie watched him as he stood at the bar. He knew his music, made her laugh and was good company. Like him, she had also had a long spell in the wilderness.

The Landlord was slumped up against the optics.

'Two pints please, and one for yourself.'

'Six-fifty and mine's a whisky,' and then he followed up, after a few seconds, with a belated, 'Thank you.'

'No trouble, and please tell your mother the fish pie was excellent.'

'Was it?'

'Yeah. Of all the fish pies I've ever tasted that was one of them. No really, it was very good.'

The Landlord turned and shouted at the kitchen door.

'He says the fish pie was alright.'

The Landlord's mother did not hear him because she'd had trouble converting Fahrenheit to Centigrade, and was busy scraping next day's Lasagne from the oven floor.

'So what's your article going to be about? As far as I can tell, things certainly seem to be a bit dodgy at Mandalay if the choice of employees is anything to go by?'

Malcolm had returned with the drinks. He was really enjoying himself. Sophie was interesting, attentive and he could not stop staring at her. She had quickly restored his faith in something.

As he sat down, she focused her eyes on his, meeting them somewhere in the space above the table, directly above the beer mat, advertising a lager brewed in the Midlands with an authentic taste of Bavaria.

'It's just a general article, really. I'm not looking for anything contentious. I'm not an investigative journalist, but I'd like to look around for a bit before telling anybody who I am.'

'Sounds like investigative journalism to me. Have you got a hidden video camera in your shoulder bag?'

'Why? Do you think I'll need one?'

'Well, I've not been here long but I've already seen a couple of highly suspect characters, two naked healers for a start. It would certainly be worth catching their set.'

'So what exactly are you here for then? Are you searching for spiritual enlightenment?'

'I was once, but now I'm not too sure. I came because

Nialls persuaded me too. Although I'm actually finding it increasingly hard to admit that he could persuade me to do anything, but that was before today.'

'Why. What's happened today?'

'Quite a lot already, and I still haven't had my pudding.'

'So who's Nialls and why should he have the power to persuade you to do anything?'

'He's an old friend. I've known him since school, and recently I've come to rely on him a little too much.'

'So he knows all your inner secrets then?'

'Yes, I suppose he does really.'

'Well, you'd better tell me everything before he does. I think an in-depth interview is certainly on the cards. We'd better take a couple of bottles up to my room, if you're going to be persuaded to tell me all your secrets. And these are on me.'

She handed Malcolm a twenty-pound note before walking towards the stairs.

Malcolm took a deep breath. Was this it? Very soon, he was going to be alone with a beautiful journalist, but how far was she prepared to go with her investigations? Was he an archaeologist about to be taken to the lost continent, to a land that had certainly been forgotten? And more importantly, did he have his magnifying glass?

CHAPTER TWELVE

•

Rebecca was becoming very impatient. For all his smooth-
ness and sophistication, Nialls was turning out to be a complete letdown. They had drunk the wine and taken the
drugs, but he was still showing no inclination in making a
move. Instead, he had spent the entire evening flattering her
looks and praising her commitments to world peace, and
she had spent the passing hours pretending to believe him.
But now, she was bored. If he liked and respected her half as
much as he was saying, she should have been barely able to
walk by now.

'For God's sake Nialls, have you got a problem or don't
you fancy me? You've been droning on for ages about my
beautiful eyes and wonderful figure.'

'Oh, you have Rebecca! You're fantastic.'

'Well, I'm getting really bored. If you don't start something soon, I'll have to go and find Gordonski.'

Nialls gripped his right thumb firmly with his fingers
before pushing it deep into his pocket. It wasn't going anywhere and it certainly was not going to be pressed. Used
to taking the leading roll, his thumb had taken the hump, in
fact, and was not going to come out to play again, unless it
was allowed to take the initiative.

'No need to rush things, Rebecca. Why don't you have a
little more coke? Or maybe I should just go.'

'If I have any more drugs, the only thing I'll be wanting is
Rehab. Can't you just get on with it?'

Nialls thought about looking for the woman in the dungarees, or even trying to find Malcolm – he would be in his
room, sulking. Anything would be better than this. He
glanced around the walls of Rebecca's room, playing for time.
There were some photographs of her standing with a group
of musicians, and Nialls needed to make conversation fast.

'Is that George Harrison you're standing with there?'

'Yes. I used to go to his parties all the time. So what?
Come on Nialls, lets dance.'

Rebecca was swaying to the music of *Spanish Steps* and

had undone her hair, which now hung down over her shoulders. Nialls never danced. He did not see the point, but tonight things were different. Anything that could delay the inevitable should be encouraged, and dancing might give him time to catch his breath, collect his thoughts and take charge again.

'OK. But do have another line, please.'

Nialls stood up and faced her. She had her eyes closed, and her head was rolling backwards. Nialls made sure that his hands were pushed firmly into his pockets, as Rebecca surged forward, clamping her hands around his shoulders and jamming her knee between his thighs.

'Come on, Nialls, show me what you can do.'

This was Niall's cue to pull out all the stops. As far as he was concerned, it was far too early for any form of physical contact, so he broke away and went freeform. He was solid gone and in the groove, and anything else that he needed to be to get out of Rebecca's clutches.

Rebecca felt her hands being pushed away, and she opened her eyes and started to laugh.

'God, Nialls! You're such a twat.'

What she saw was pure pantomime. Nialls out of control and dancing completely out of time, gyrating like a lunatic to one of the most laid-back tunes of all time.

'Fuck, Nialls, you don't dance like that to Van Morrison. You don't dance like that to anything, unless you've been given a lethal dose of volts after walking the green mile.'

'No. I'm really getting into this, Rebecca. Put it on again.'

But Rebecca was still laughing.

'For God's sake stop it, or I'm going to need some incontinence pads. Come on Nialls, fucking boogie! You're so far ahead you're beautiful!' she shrieked.

Rebecca had stitch from laughing, and sat down to ease the pain.

She poured herself another glass of wine, and fiddled with the zip on her skirt. It eased the discomfort in her side, and helped her to prepare for what she hoped might follow.

'Well, you look a lot more relaxed, Nialls. It's a bit of a pathetic attempt to try and impress me into bed by dancing like a lunatic, but you deserve full marks for trying.'

Nialls did not care what he looked like as long as it was taking her mind off sex. He would keep it up all night if he had to. Maybe, he could laugh her into submission. Initially he had felt self-conscious dancing like an idiot, but it had stopped Rebecca in her tracks. He was taking control again, and nothing turned Nialls on more than when he was in control. He may have had to make a temporary fool of himself, but it was a small price to pay to gain the upper hand.

'Come on, Rebecca. Don't stop. I'm enjoying myself. I'm really starting to feel the energy between us. It's really pulsing.'

Nialls was aware of the systolic beat of his heart, somewhere around the nail of his right thumb, as he approached Rebecca with a sneer on his lips. Suddenly, he was on the floor in front of her and her skirt was round her waist, as his thumb parted the elastic at the top of her left leg.

Nialls preferred the left leg approach. It gave him the right amount of purchase, and he could use his other arm for added support. Rebecca had been taken completely by surprise and the force of the onslaught caused her to slip forward. Nialls found that resistance was practically negligible.

'Nialls, at least give me the privilege to gasp in anticipation.'

Not that Rebecca wanted to put up any resistance. She had been waiting for something to happen all night, but this was not going to be what she had expected. Rebecca was about to experience Nialls' basic rotating-thumb technique, and Nialls was convinced she would soon be putty in his hands. He had been using this method for years, and it never failed if the circumstances were right. It was especially effective when drugs and alcohol were combined, as it cut through any loss of feeling, made worse by over-stimulation. He had always prided himself on a quick result, and this time he needed to prove himself, even if everything was happening quicker than he would have liked. With a bit of luck, he could be bathed and down the pub long before closing time. He might even have time to try out his technique on somebody else before the end of the evening.

But like Nialls, Rebecca was also a well-seasoned campaigner, and she had her own ideas about how things should progress.

'Nialls. I really appreciate this and everything, but after all a thumb is only a thumb, and it can only do so much. I'm afraid you're going to have to do a bit better.'

This was not what Nialls wanted to hear. He increased the pressure in an attempt to win her over.

Rebecca reached down for the zip on his trousers.

'Come on, let's see what you've really got.'

He was losing control again, and in a last desperate bid to regain the initiative, he decided to attempt his rarely performed undulating snake technique. It was a difficult manoeuvre, and required great concentration. He had only had to resort to it once before, when for some inexplicable reason, the basic rotation method was failing and the usherette was rapidly approaching with the ice creams.

The undulating snake allowed his arm to continue the twisting movement of his thumb, and then reverse the action from his elbow back along his arm, so that his thumb performed a figure eight, resulting in immediate orgasm.

There was no doubt that Rebecca wanted one of those, and Nialls had found the spot, but she was not going to be satisfied.

'Nialls. I want more. I don't want foreplay. I want sex now. Penetration, for fuck's sake!'

She launched herself at his trouser buckle, knocking him backwards onto the floor.

'Come on, Nialls, I don't want that anymore. Just do it.'

She managed to get his trousers down to his ankles in one pull but he grabbed the top of his underpants, and there was no way that he was going to let go of those. He hung onto the waistband with both hands.

'Stop it, Rebecca! This isn't right. You're being too forceful.'

'Of course I'm being fucking forceful! I'm fed up waiting. It's like trying to shag a three-toe'd sloth.'

'I've never had any complaints before. Women usually have a fantastic time. I'm not used to behaving like a performing seal. I can see that this isn't going to work. I'd better go.'

'You can't fucking do it, can you? You might have been able to satisfy a few stupid women with your bloody finger, but I'm a real woman. You're so full of shit. Bore me senseless for two hours, and then try and finger me to sleep. God, it's better than a fucking lullaby. How many women have you put into a comatose state with that? If you spent as much time concentrating on getting a hard-on as you do spouting off nonsense, you'd be sensational.'

Nialls did not know how to reply. He was out of his depth and needed to escape, to be allowed to retreat and lick his wounds. He pulled up his trousers and rushed for the door.

The staff were cleaning up after the evening meal when Gordonski appeared, carrying a bottle of vodka.

'Here you are, Traats. A little pick-me-up, after all your hard work.'

He sat down in front of the Aga and began perusing a wiring diagram. He had been asked to look at the broken microwave, and it was now on the floor in front of him.

The wiring diagram was not for the microwave, but for a basic explosive device that required a timer switch. He had already worked out that the mechanism from the oven was far too intricate; but it gave him the opportunity to check the clockwork egg-timer he had noticed on the shelf earlier, in case there was anything wrong with that. Fortunately there was. He discovered that it was completely useless, and may as well be put to another use. Lynette was surprised as she had only just been using it, but Gordonski was the handyman.

'What about the microwave, Gordonski? Are you going to be able to fix that?'

'I'm not sure yet. I may have to take it down to my shed to have a closer look. You have to be careful with microwaves. They give off radiation.'

'Have you checked the fuse, Gordonski?'

Simon was trying to appear helpful. He was still in everybody's bad books because of the fruit episode, especially Lynnette's.

'Don't be so stupid, Simon. The fuse is the first thing to be looked at. Gordonski's bound to have checked that.'

Simon mouthed 'Bollocks' at her from behind the safety

of the kitchen cupboard, as he put the plates away on the shelves.

But Gordonski had not checked the fuse. He was not bothered in the slightest about the microwave. All he wanted was the egg-timer, but he still allowed Simon to carry it down to the potting shed for him. It was going to be a long night, and if it was only the fuse, he could use it to heat his cocoa.

'You know, Traat, you shouldn't let her talk to you like that.'

'I know, but with luck I'm only going to have to put up with her for a little longer.'

'That Simon, is very good news. There's an incinerator round the back with her name on it, if you're interested. Feel free.'

Gordonski went around the back of the shed and lifted up a piece of plywood. He dragged out an assortment of ropes, some large pulleys and an old toilet seat. He carried it back to his shed and laid it on the table. He began searching through a pile of papers, until he found a page out of an old yachting magazine. It gave simple instructions on how to tie knots and splice rope. He attached four pieces of rope to the corners of an old window frame, and then spliced the other ends together around a shackle, which he linked onto the bottom of a wooden pulley. He then nailed the toilet seat to the window frame, and tried it out for size. It was perfect. He manhandled everything onto a wheelbarrow and set out in the direction of the old icehouse. The building was derelict, but Gordonski managed to lash one end of the rope to part of the old roof-frame. From where he stood, he had an uninterrupted view of the clock tower, and he now began pushing his load slowly towards it, allowing the rope to trail out along the ground behind him. It was going to be a long night, and this was only one of the tasks he needed to complete before daylight.

—

Sophie reached for Malcolm's hand as he followed her into the room.

'So what do you want to know about me, Sophie?'

'Not a lot at this moment in time. I know your tastes in music and literature, so I think that will do for now. Do you fancy opening the wine?'

Malcolm had been partially drunk for most of the day and now alone in the room with her, he was glad of it.

Sophie smiled.

'I know you're a bit nervous Malcolm, but don't worry. I'll be gentle with you.'

'Nervous, Sophie. Me? Well, possibly a little bit, maybe.'

Then the moment happened. It was quite sudden and managed to take them both by surprise. It was like waking up in the morning and not being able to recall the moment immediately before you fell asleep. One second, they were talking and the next, embracing, but they would never remember exactly what was being said the moment before that first kiss. The kiss that tipped them over the edge, and onto the bed, that had once been slept in by some famous highwayman, or so the landlord would have them believe.

'So tell me about Nialls. I'm fascinated. He's obviously featured quite large in your life?'

Sophie and Malcolm were lying on the bed and comparing their pasts.

Sophie apparently had not had a serious relationship for two years, and that had been with a musician. He had only loved her when he was touring, and she found out that he had been constantly unfaithful. She decided the time was right to give him back his twelve-inch selection of punk anthems. The promised recording contract never materialised, and she heard that he had found work on a cruise liner, touring the Norwegian fjords playing hits from the Eighties.

'Nialls is sort of my oldest friend. I have this love-hate relationship with him. We've had some really good times together, but it's only recently, after my marriage split up, that I've seen him a lot. My wife didn't like him very much.'

'Is he married?'

'No. He has been, three times, but he doesn't really like women. In fact, he doesn't really like anybody very much.'

'But he likes you.'

'Yes, but recently he seems to have taken me over. I've been an excellent foil. I don't blame him.'

'I find that difficult to believe. That you're the sort of man who can be manipulated by somebody else.'

'Well, perhaps a little, but I've realised for some time that things have got to change between us.'

'I can't wait to meet him. He seems to be a very interesting character. Where's he tonight? I'd have thought he would have wanted to be with you, from what you've been saying.'

'He probably would have been, but something better came up. Nialls can only be bothered with someone until something better comes up, and that usually involves a woman.'

'But I thought he didn't like women very much.'

'He doesn't, but he needs to keep convincing himself.'

'So who is it this time?'

'The organizer of the Festival. He'll love you. Nothing would give him a greater thrill than for you to fancy him. He's bound to do all he can to embarrass me.'

——

Nialls was keeping a low profile. Rebecca was completely out of her mind rejecting the Undulating Snake, and she was most certainly a lesbian. If it had been some big butch dyke doing it to her, she would have been in heaven. That's what goes, with trying to please somebody who lives on a funny farm with a load of hippies. There was always that woman with the dungarees, but he must be careful, the last thing he wanted was a repeat of tonight. And where was Malcolm when you needed him? Maybe he was with Gordonski.

Nialls found Gordonski dressed in his purple ensemble, sitting in the camping area. He had been pushing a large sack in a wheelbarrow and had slipped, as one of the guide ropes became entangled around his ankles. He had tripped over his cloak, upset the wheelbarrow and tipped everything out. The sack was on the ground, with all its contents spilled out over the grass.

'What we need is a fucking war and I'm the man to start it. Any man disagree? No. Then fuck off then.'

Nialls bent over Gordonski as he sat adjusting his hat.

'I see you still look like something from a Tolkein story. What the fuck's all this? What do you want packets of Pringles for?'

Gordonski jumped to attention, and saluted, dropping an egg-timer at Niall's feet.

'Bon Soir et ca va, mon traat, c'est le piéce de résistance et le côup de grâce. Allons! Allons!'

'Fucking hell, Gordonski. Now you're a French wizard, and what the hell have you got an egg-timer for?'

'To be exact with my calculations. There isn't much time.'

Gordonski placed everything back in his sack, and marched across the lawn towards the clock tower. The clock had not worked for years, but that did not mean that it had out-lived its usefulness. Nialls decided not to follow. Whatever Gordonski was up to, he seemingly had everything under control.

He could hear the sound of drums beating from somewhere around the other side of the house. One drum was beating a sequence, and then others were copying it, accompanied by the sound of didgeridoos and chanting. Suddenly the sweet smell of cannabis reached his nostrils, and he decided this could be just what the doctor ordered.

He approached the tepee from the side, and picked up a set of bongos that were lying on the floor. There were about thirty people sat around in a circle. They varied in age from early twenties to mid-fifties, and Nialls noticed the lecturer in North American Studies over at the other side of the campfire. He was sat next to another man, and they were both smoking pipes. Nialls started to strike his drum, dancing his way around the outside of the group and sitting down behind them.

In front of the tepee entrance was a younger man dressed in an Indian headdress, carrying a boomerang. He was chanting as he hopped up and down, and raised the boomerang up above his head.

'Hold the spirit of Chief Sitting Bull amongst us. He comes from his home where the buffalo roam.'

Nialls lifted his head and shouted, 'Where the deer and the antelope play.'

Everybody considered this an appropriate response because they all solemnly repeated in unison, 'Where the deer and the antelope play.'

The lecturer in North American Studies stuffed some more skunk down the end of his pipe, and his friend raised his rainstick into the air and waved it.

The aborigine from North Dakota dropped his boomerang and picked up a small drum. He shouted, 'Do as I do, and we'll talk to the spirits of the warriors that have gone before.'

He struck his drum once, and waited for everybody to copy him. Everybody did in perfect time, except Nialls, who deliberately waited a few seconds before hitting his. This succeeded in confusing everybody, because half the group thought that this was the leader hitting his drum again. They all banged once more, in unison.

The aborigine was not impressed.

'No. We must be as one, if the Great Eagle God is going to fly across the sky and give us his blessing.'

He hit his drum again. One hard resonant bang filled the air and once more, everybody followed suit. Two seconds later, Nialls gave his own individual response and more than half of the drummers did likewise. The didgeridoos and the rainsticks were feeling left out, and so they started to do their own thing, causing even more confusion.

'Listen to me. I am the leader. You must follow me. It's not that difficult. It's only one beat.'

Nialls shouted, 'Bollocks!'

The teacher glared over in Nialls' direction, but he bobbed down behind the lecturer in North American Studies.

'You with the pipe. If you don't start taking this seriously, you'll have to swap your drum for a rainstick. There are plenty of other people waiting to have a go.'

Everybody turned and stared at the lecturer in North American Studies. He turned and stared at his friend, who was taking a long draw on his pipe.

'Maybe you'd like to come and lead the group, if you think you can do any better.'

This was Nialls' cue. He decided to take full responsibility and stood up.

'Yeah, sure. Why not.'

Nialls made his way to the front and snatched Sir's drums, before elbowing him out of the way and back into the tepee entrance. He wacked it hard with his fist once, and then twice. Initially, everybody was a bit startled by the sudden increase of tempo, but they soon got into the swing, imitating him perfectly. Nialls followed that with three sets of three and a little flourish.

'Everybody say: Yeah.'

Everybody did.

'Everybody say: Yeah, Yeah.'

Everybody did that as well.

'Everybody shout: Arseholes.'

Not such a good response this time.

'Everybody shout: Fuck, bollocks, wank and pull your foreskin over your head.'

Nialls did not wait for a response to that, but launched into an avant-garde drum solo that lasted a good five minutes. It was an up-tempo set, with a hint of Latin influence, and extra emphasis on the upbeat. When he had finished, there was a complete stunned silence.

Nialls got out his cigarette lighter, struck it, held it above his head and walked off.

'Thank you and Goodnight.'

Somebody coughed, and Nialls heard the strains of *Kumbaya* being sung somewhere, off in the distance.

He decided to call it a night. As he walked back up the drive, a red Golf convertible sped past him, causing him to step into the ditch. It was already beginning to smell, as the state of the toilets in the stable block had forced some of the clientele to go native, and he kicked some paper off his shoe as he climbed back up onto the drive. The car had stopped in front of the main door, and Nialls watched as a stunning woman with long brown hair climbed out and started to undo the hood. Nialls immediately spotted Malcolm sitting in the passenger seat. He was drinking from a bottle of wine, and the girl walked around to his side of the car and took the bottle from him. He had obviously said something amusing because the girl started to laugh, and then gave Malcolm a long lingering kiss as he pulled her back onto the seat. What the fuck could she be doing with Malcolm? Maybe it was a long-lost sister or an old friend, but they were definitely kissing.

Nialls quickened his step but before he could reach them, Malcolm was out of the car and the girl was speeding back down the drive towards Nialls, who deliberately stepped out so she would have to stop.

'Hello. I'm Nialls. I must say you've got the most beautiful eyes.'

Sophie smiled.

'I thought you must be. See you tomorrow, Nialls. Bye.'

She put her foot hard down on the accelerator, and showered Nialls in gravel as she tore off down the drive.

—·—

Malcolm knew that Nialls would be beside himself. Presumably his evening had not gone entirely to plan, otherwise he would not have been wandering around the grounds so late at night.

Whatever the case, Malcolm was not interested in what had happened to Nialls. He had had a great evening, and although he knew there was no way Nialls could ruin it for him, he was not even going to give him the chance of trying. Sophie was coming round early, and they were going to explore Mandalay together. Malcolm scurried into the house and up the stairs. He was going to lock himself in his room and pretend to be asleep, if Nialls decided to come calling.

'Come on, Malcolm. Let me in. I know you're there.'

Nialls was banging on Malcolm's door and becoming agitated.

'You can't escape. Who was that woman? Whoever she was, she's certainly too good for you. When can I meet her?'

Malcolm remained silent. He had felt his confidence return in leaps and bounds over the last few hours, and it would take far more than Nialls and his Kryptonite wit to wear him down.

'Well, fuck you then. I bet she only kissed you because she felt sorry for you.'

Rebecca was stuffing money into a battered shoulder bag. She had been cashing cheques for some time, and felt vulnerable with all the money in her bedroom. She had spent most of one day deliberating over where she could hide it, and had decided on the old clock tower. Nobody went there. She had found a couple of loose floorboards that would provide a more than adequate hiding place. She slipped down the back staircase, out through the conservatory, and into the vegetable garden. The door to the clock tower had been locked. It had not taken her long to find the key on the enormous ring which she had been presented with, when she had bought the house. What she did not know was that there was also a spare key, in the bottom of the old metal watering can, that was lying outside the door. It had been there for years and had been used by the gardeners who ate their lunch in the clock tower, during the days when the house entertained. Gordonski had found the key completely by accident. He had been looking for odd lengths of lead piping, but came across the watering can overgrown by weeds and thought that it might prove useful. It did not take him long to find out what door the key fitted and the discovery saved him the effort of forcing the lock. He had already decided that the clock tower was going to be perfect for his future plans.

Rebecca unlocked the door and climbed up the stairs to the first floor. She lifted the loose boards and pushed the bag between the joists. If she had lifted a few more, she would have found more bags, containing cardboard tubes with electrical wires sticking out from them, and a sack stuffed full of rope.

She locked the door behind her and picked her way through the nettles, back to the path. She had no reason to think that she wasn't alone.

Gordonski sat back against the wall of the old lean-to green house. It had once been used for growing carnations, but now the white-washed glass was piled up in a corner, and the old door was hanging on a solitary hinge. He was counting stars, as he watched Rebecca disappear into the darkness.

'There's only one thing worse than a hippie, and that's a fucking hippie.'

Nialls drew the curtains and squinted at the sunlight. Outside he could see oversized women in pink tights performing some type of morning ritual in the middle of the lawn.

Apart from the yoga class and a couple cycling naked around the garden, there were exponents of Tai Chi, and a group wearing white vests, performing star jumps to a tape of military marching tunes. He opened the window and shouted, 'I am not a number. I am a free man,' but as no oversized-weather balloons or men in striped blazers driving Mini-Mokes appeared, he closed the window again.

Malcolm was excited at the prospect of seeing Sophie again, but he was also apprehensive about how Nialls was going to respond to his newfound confidence.

'What do you want?'

Malcolm had entered Nialls' room. He was drying his hair and admiring himself in the mirror.

'I've come to see if you fancy breakfast.'

'It's just that I gathered from your behaviour last night that you were happy without my company. Going off and leaving me like that. Call yourself a fucking friend!'

'Everything didn't work out with Rebecca then. I presumed that you were there for the duration. Did she get tired of you?'

'No. She turned out to be a bloody lesbian.'

'You weren't the one to change her then. To put her back on the straight and narrow?'

'Actually she was desperate, but I wasn't going to take advantage of her at a weak moment. She'd have probably regretted it today, and it could have caused all sorts of bad feeling. Anyway, who was that woman you were with?'

'That was Sophie, and you'll meet her this morning. She's a journalist and she's here to write an article on the Festival. I met her yesterday in the pub and we sort of hit it off. I'm really happy.'

'I wouldn't be if I were you. You'll know it'll all end in tears. She's too upmarket for you. You're out of your depth with a woman like that. She needs somebody with money and charm, who appreciates the finer things in life.'

'Somebody like you then?'

'Well, let's face it, you wouldn't be able to keep up with her.'

'Nialls, you can say what you like, but she's not going to be interested in you. She's far too intelligent, and I'd hate you to make a fool of yourself.'

'We'll see. When's she coming?'

'I'm meeting her at nine. She's coming for breakfast. That's why I've called for you. She'll be here in a minute.'

Nialls reached for his bottle of toiletries, and chose a expensive bottle of cologne.

'Nialls, you're wasting your time. You're going to make a prat of yourself.'

Sophie was already in the dining room when they arrived. Malcolm walked over to her, and she stood up and gave him a kiss.

'Sorry. I'm a bit early, but I just couldn't sleep. It's a wonderful day. Good morning, Nialls.'

'I should get rid of him, Sophie. Nip it in the bud now before it's too late. He's pathetic; not the sort of person you could feel confident with in an emergency.'

Nialls stepped in front of Malcolm, and sat down next to Sophie.

'Off you go, Malcolm. I'll have a cup of coffee and a croissant, and what would you like, Sophie?'

'A cup of weak tea please. Would you like some help Malcolm?'

'No, that's fine. You may as well get it over with, but watch his chip fat onslaught of charm. He'll be sliding under the table by the time I get back.'

Nialls turned and stared straight into Sophie's eyes.

'Have you ever been to Tuscany?'

'No. I'd rather visit Sicily, if I was given the choice.'

'Do you prefer opera or ballet?'

'Do you know. Nialls, I couldn't really choose, but I'd love to have seen Fonteyn dance with Nureyev.'

'I did many times. I had a season ticket.'

'Well, that surprises me Nialls. I wouldn't have thought you were old enough. I do love opera as well, though. My favourite singer is definitely Gallicurchi.'

'Oh yes, he's wonderful. I saw him to. He had wonderful pitch.'

'You're certainly older than you look Nialls, and she certainly did have a wonderful voice.'

Nialls ignored his mistake and moved on quickly.

'That's a fantastic car you've got. What model is it?'

'It's just an old Golf. It belonged to my father, so I got it cheap.'

'I've got a BMW, top of the range. Malcolm's just bought a second-hand mountain bike. He's been off touring the Peak District. He's not very good with women. They don't generally hang around for more than a few seconds.'

'Well, I don't think I'll be one of those. I think he's really interesting. Just what I'm looking for.'

Once again, Nialls was beginning to feel out of his depth. He never mixed with women like this, and if he did meet them accidentally, he would quickly pass them by. The experience with Rebecca had unnerved him, and he still did not feel in complete control. He was stuck in a madhouse with a load of forceful women, who wouldn't recognise a real man if he appeared out of the sun with both thumbs blazing.

Malcolm returned with the breakfast and sat down.

'So how are you two getting on? Managed to find something to talk about?'

'Did you have to come back so soon, Malcolm?'

'Why Nialls? Have you been putting Sophie straight about my secret perversions and sordid past?'

'Not at all. She's obviously going through some kind of

trauma at the moment, and for some reason you seem to be helping her. I'm sure she'll come to her senses soon. Anyway, I'm going back to my room now. There's a Tantric sex workshop at ten, and I want to check it out. I suppose you two lovebirds will be walking arm-in-arm through the grounds for the rest of the day, stopping to make the occasional daisy chain. I'll see you later.'

Nialls stood up and flounced out of the dining room. He met Rebecca, who was coming down the stairs.

'Morning, Tom! How are you this morning? Sleep well? Not on anything too hard I hope?'

The sarcasm was wasted on Nialls.

'Morning, Rebecca. I hope you had a pleasant time after I left. Did you manage to get in touch with the local women's hockey team, or were they already booked?'

'Yes. I did actually. I went off and found Gordonski and we had a great time.'

Rebecca was lying, but Nialls still felt resentment welling up inside. That was about her level; a psychopath dressed as fucking Merlin.

'Well, you might have got him to reverse the spell before you left him. I thought it was only supposed to work with a Prince, but I guess in these days of equality it's only fair.'

Nialls made a croaking sound and started to hop up the stairs, on all fours.

———

Nialls lay on the bed and stared at the ceiling. He listened to Malcolm and Sophie returning, and it aggravated the bitterness he was already feeling. What was he doing here? Was he being led by some ultimate force? A force that was hell-bent on teaching him a lesson. Maybe there was something in all this spiritual stuff, and he would go home a changed man: cut his personal profits by a third, and donate the difference to charity. Maybe he needed to show more compassion. Perhaps there was something he had to learn. As he concentrated on the possibilities, he watched a spider trying to gain a foothold on the curtain rail as it constructed its web. He found himself willing it on, giving it encouragement as it fought for a foothold on a dusty ledge, but kept slipping at the last moment, only to start the process all over again. A gust of air blew through the curtains, and the spider made an extra super arachnid attempt that enabled it to settle at last on the top of the rail, and there it rested for a brief moment before continuing its task.

Nialls gave a sigh of relief and considered his own destiny. Maybe he should be more lenient with his emotions and learn to achieve through personal growth, rather than through the exploitation of others. Could the spider be giving him a sign? A gentle push in a new direction that would make his life more fulfilling. He never really had to struggle for anything. Everything just fell into place – and why not? Fuck them all. He rolled a property magazine into a handy-sized tube, before leaning over and smashing the spider against the wall.

Malcolm and Sophie heard the thud, and then the sound of Nialls' door being slammed shut. They both sat absolutely still listening to Nialls' footsteps, as he approached the room.

Nialls tried the door. He would never have considered knocking first. That would not give him the chance of achieving maximum embarrassment.

'Come on. Unlock the door. I heard you come back. You're not here to waste time. Come to this workshop with me. I promise I'll behave myself. Malcolm, come on, think of somebody other than yourself for a change.'

But Malcolm and Sophie were not going anywhere. They sat there, listening to Nialls telling them all the things that he had done for Malcolm in the past, before finally giving the door a hard kick and walking off.

Dolphin and Stellana were badly rehearsed and not prepared for the day ahead. They had woken early and put up
a selection of New Age posters around the walls, as well as
displaying statues of the god Shiva, showing him involved
in various stages of congress with the goddess Shakti. These
were for sale at highly-inflated prices. They were wearing
matching shell-suits, and Dolphin had tied his receding hair
into a ponytail. His round glasses were pink and fastened
together with sellotape. Dolphin was fingering a set of love
balls. They were part of a batch he had bought from a
recently closed-down sex shop, along with some boxes of
dodgy vibrators, but the vibrators were hidden under the
table, as they made him feel uncomfortable.

'Do you think we should throw in a free set of these with
every statue? It might help us to shift them faster?'

'Do what you want. You normally do.'

Stellana was feeling under the weather. She had not had
much sleep, and Dolphin was beginning to irritate her.

'Maybe you should try and get rid of those vibrators as
well.'

'What, before you've had the chance to personally try
them all out?'

Dolphin was also feeling irritated and knew that she was
trying to annoy him. She had been doing it a lot recently, and
he was rapidly losing interest in anything she did or said.

At first everything had been wonderful. Their initial
meeting in Thailand was positively euphoric. High on grass,
as they walked hand in hand through Bangkok and beyond,
diving into crystal pools and riding on elephants was a long
way from reality. Coming home had not seemed too bad at
first. They burned incense, looked at the photographs and
practised their Tantric techniques, but they had been taught
by a master with a chiselled jaw, who was no longer around
to give Dolphin the boot up the backside he needed.

'Well, what do you expect me to do? You've conveniently
forgotten everything you learnt.'

'Let's face it. There's not a lot that that Germanic ponce could teach anybody.'

'Well, at least he taught you what a clitoris was.'

Dolphin had never felt relaxed with the concept of the clitoris. He was convinced that it was part of a myth started by Alex Comfort, in the Sixties. His father had never mentioned the clitoris to him, so they could not have existed in his day. Obviously his mother had got on perfectly well without one, so why should they have suddenly appeared on women born after the war. Unless it was due to some kind of deformity, brought about by nuclear testing.

'Look. I don't want to talk about this now. Just pass me the tapes.'

Stellana threw a box at him from across the room. It contained a selection of tapes used for relaxation and a special boxed set of 4 CDs, which were supposed to introduce the listener to the intricate language of dolphins.

Dolphin had a deep empathy with dolphins. He had always loved fish. He came from Weston-super-Mare, and was constantly visiting the seafront aquarium. When he became spiritually re-born, it seemed only fitting that he should take the name Dolphin, and stop eating tuna fish.

Just before ten o'clock, a trickle of people began to appear. Dolphin put his palms up to face them and welcomed them with a broad smile.

'Please come in and sit down.'

They looked around at the posters, and then at the mats that had been spread over the floor. They were a cross section of ages and most were couples, the single men seemed mostly in their forties, with beer bellies. The lecturer in North American Studies had decided that the day ahead might prove more fruitful to him if he left his wife behind. Anyway, she was cross with him for coming back stoned the night before.

Stellana walked forward and stood in front of Dolphin, who was forced to take a step backwards.

'Welcome to you all. Maybe we should begin by introducing ourselves to everybody. I'm Stellana, and I'm going to be leading the workshop this morning.'

Nialls gave her the once over. She was getting on a bit and

her straggly hair, pushed up on the top, had been recently dyed. There were still streaks of the stuff around her neck. He wasn't very impressed.

'Oh, and… er, I'm Dolphin, and I shall be leading the workshop as well.'

Most of the group were trying to avoid eye contact with each other, but Nialls had no such problem. He had already spotted the only single woman in the group. It was the red headed girl that he had noticed the night before, but today she was dressed in denim shorts, and Nialls thought that she had a wonderful bottom when he had followed her into the room.

Dolphin adjusted his scrotum and stood up.

'Welcome. Can I just ask if anyone has ever been part of a Tantric workshop before?'

There were a few mumblings, but no definite answers. Dolphin breathed a sigh of relief.

'It's just that it's useful to know before we start, so that we can all begin from the same space. Today, we're going to introduce you to a method to awaken all your senses, in order to allow your being to reach its full sexual potential. You don't have to worry. Nothing's going to get too steamy. That's for you to follow up in the privacy of your own space, and at a later date. I am prepared to take on some personal tuition, if anyone feels the need.'

Dolphin glanced at the tight denim bottom, but the bottom was staring at Stellana, who looked far more interesting to her, if the need for any follow up work occurred.

Nialls had positioned himself next to the lecturer in North American Studies, and he leaned over and whispered in his ear.

'Can we get our nobs out now?'

'Oh no, not you again! Will you please go and sit somewhere else.'

'Look, I'm really sorry that we got off to a bad start. I'd had a long drive and I was really stressed. My name's Nialls. I'm sure we can start again. We can both help each other out a little here. I bet you're feeling as self-conscious as I am. What's your name?'

'It's Trevor, actually, but if you start getting abusive I'm going to move away. I really want to get into this session this morning. I think it could be a really valuable exercise.'

Dolphin clapped his hands and bowed, and Stellana started to hand out blindfolds. Nialls began to get interested and wondered where the handcuffs were, but none were forthcoming, so he stopped shuffling across the floor towards the girl in the shorts, and placed his over his head.

'This first session is called The Awakening. We're going to stimulate some of your senses. I'd like you to all put your blindfolds on tightly, and lie back on your mats.'

Nialls could hear Dolphin and Stellana arguing with each other, and the sound of an audiotape being re-wound. Suddenly, the room was filled with the deafening sound of wind chimes, and Dolphin shouted at Stellana to turn it down. The sounds went faint, and the group had to strain their ears to detect anything at all. It seemed to be the sound of the sea breaking on the shore, but Nialls could not be sure at first, until he heard somebody on the tape say, 'Keep between the yellow and red flags please', which rather spoiled the ambiance. Then followed what could only be the cries of whales, underneath the arctic wastes, signalling by sonar.

After a few minutes, the breathing in the room became deeper and everybody began to relax, as their limbs became heavier.

Nialls was getting bored and when someone at the back involuntarily broke wind, he started to giggle. This set off the rest of the room, and Nialls reached over and tapped Trevor on the head, who was somewhere in the region of the Galapogos Islands. He had started to make noises in his throat and was moving his legs from side to side.

'Come on Trevor. Time to beach yourself.'

'I was really enjoying that. It was really relaxing.'

Nialls reached out and felt his flipper.

'You're better out of it, Trevor. I was just about to detect the dull hum of the Japanese whaling fleet. You'd be skinned and tinned if you'd stayed out there much longer.'

But Trevor did not want to be back on dry land. He wanted to stay where he was, out in the depths of the deepest oceans, swimming with the gentlest creatures on earth.

He did not want to return to his mundane life on dry land, surrounded by argumentative middle-class students who thought they knew it all, the endless marking of exam papers, and his nagging wife.

Dolphin felt it was time to move on, and the tape was turned off.

'Now. I would like you to all relax and await the next experience of the morning. This will involve your sense of smell.'

Nialls said very quietly, 'We've already experienced that, and it smelt like Leeds.'

Dolphin raised his voice.

'Can we please try and concentrate. I want you all to try and re-discover your sense of smell. I'm going to come around with a selection of evocative aromas, and as well as being healed by sound, you will now be healed by smell.'

When they had been out in the Far East learning their craft, Klaus, the teacher, had tempted their senses with aromas of spices and oils. He had mixed them freshly, rolling them together on a turtle shell, and asked Stellana to rub them on his torso, to experience them continually changing as his body temperature rose and fell. Dolphin had not been present at this session, but was down in the local village buying souvenirs.

'I want you to try and return to the state of relaxation you were in a minute ago.'

Dolphin had opened a jar of strawberry jam, and Stellana was unwrapping a tablet of Tesco's peach soap.

'We're going to come amongst you holding various exotic smells under your noses, and we want to know how it makes you feel. First, just take in the aromas and relax into them.'

They walked around waving the objects under noses, and the soap reminded Nialls of his Auntie, and how she was still unfortunately as fit as a fiddle at ninety-eight.

Once again, the group had sunk into semi-consciousness and Trevor was floating on a hallucinogenic cloud of contentment. His sense of smell told him he was back in his childhood, drinking dandelion, burdock and picnicking on the gated roads that he used to visit on Sundays. He did not want to be back in reality, worrying about the future. He certainly did not want to be stuck with a woman who bored him stupid. He would not be feeling sensual and warm if she was lying next to him, but the woman over in the corner with the big breasts was another matter, and she had noticed Trevor. She had spent the last few minutes closing in on his space. She had also been single for too long.

Once again the session was brought to an abrupt halt, as Dolphin clapped his hands and asked them to open their eyes.

'We are now going to come around and place wonderful delicacies on your tongue, to enrich your sensations of taste.'

Stellana went to a table and cut up an orange into segments. She walked up and down the lines, placing a piece in everybody's mouth. There was no sandalwood, vanilla pods or fresh mango to pass by ecstatic noses and mouths. Stellana had gone to the supermarket for her sense stimulants, and had got a Buy One, Get One Free offer on a string bag of Outspan oranges.

Nevertheless, to Trevor it tasted nothing like he had ever experienced before. It was not just a piece of orange, but a subtle concoction of mind-numbing power that had him drooling from the corner of his mouth. He could taste ginger and loganberries and exotic fruits he had never even heard of.

'Trevor. Wipe your mouth will you. Oral incontinence is not a pretty sight.'

Nialls was determined not to allow Trevor any enjoyment. He reached over and wiped Trevor's mouth with a paper handkerchief. But momentarily at least, Nialls was not going to have any effect on Trevor's well-being.

It was now Stellana's turn to take centre stage.

'I would like you all to listen very carefully. We will now progress to the touching part of the exercise.'

Eight middle-aged men immediately began to slide their middle-aged backsides towards the denim shorts. They surrounded her like a herd of rampant wildebeest. She found herself trapped between a penis candle and Dolphin, who had decided to participate personally in this part of the session.

'Spread out your fingertips to the person next to you.'

Peeping through blindfolds, eight men waved their arms in the direction of the shorts, like a randy octopus trying to connect.

'Explore these fingers with your sense of touch.'

Like escaping prey, the shorts managed to avoid the approaching attack and headed in the direction of Stellana, whom she hoped might come swimming by. Stellana, seeing her predicament, leapt into the salty depths to save her, and they were soon rubbing fins and blowing bubbles at each other. The men, in order to avoid acute embarrassment, began to explore each other's tentacles. Nialls, who had been biding his time, was sitting alone and waving his thumbs in the air, like a benevolent sea anemone. His main concern was how to block the way of the woman with the huge breasts, so that she could not link up with Trevor. Dolphin sensing failure, decided to call an end to the proceedings.

'I would like you all to remove your blindfolds and face the front. I think we should have a fifteen-minute break now. There's green tea available and maybe you could check out the sales stand, whilst you discuss your experiences informally amongst yourselves.'

Trevor still had not returned to reality, so Nialls waved a digestive biscuit in front of his nose and gave him a shake.

'Come on, Trevor, pull yourself together. I think you've got an admirer.'

'Nialls, leave me alone. That was a really meaningful experience. I felt like I was communicating with whales. They were asking me for help, and I was swimming amongst them and leading them to safety.'

'Don't be such a prat, Trevor. You've been taking to many drugs.'

'You're not going to take any of this seriously. I'm going to go and work on my own.'

Trevor walked off and began talking to one of the older women who was handling one of the sculptures, trying to work out whose limbs belonged to whom. Nialls went into his jacket pocket and brought out a hip flask, which he carried for such occasions. He tipped half the contents into the mug. It was white and cracked, and was decorated with the signs of the zodiac.

'OK Everybody! Are we ready to start again? I want you to find a space, and sit there with a member of the opposite sex, preferably not your partner. Kneel and face each other.'

'Hello. I'm Belinda. I'm actually bi-sexual but I hope you don't mind. What's your friend's name?'

Nialls had been thinking about going. His retreat was now blocked by a fifty-something school's crossing operative, wearing an enormous white T-shirt, displaying the Yin and Yang symbol and a pair of skin-tight black leggings. She hoped that Nialls and Trevor were close friends.

'It's Trevor actually, and I'm sure he fancies you.'

But before Nialls could tell her more, he was interrupted by Dolphin, eager to continue.

'Right. Listen to me carefully. The woman gives out energy from her heart, and the man receives it through his heart. The man gives out his energy through his sex, and the women receives it through her sex, thus creating a Tantric circle.

'Using your breathing, I want the woman to breath out and project the energy, by directing it with her hand from her heart, to her partner's mouth. The man breathes in to receive it, and then breathes out, directing it back from his sexual organs to the woman, who receives it via her Sex. Thus the circle is completed.'

Nialls stood up and began to fiddle with his genitals.

'Sorry, Belinda. Only I've got to try and adjust them so that they're pointing in the right direction.'

Trevor shuffled uncomfortably. He had found himself sitting in front of the woman in the denim shorts, and he felt sure that Nialls was going to single him out for ridicule.

'Nialls! Why don't you leave, if you're going to be stupid? You've done nothing but take the piss since you arrived. I for one am getting really fed up with you.'

'Fuck off. I'm only trying to be considerate. We've got to do this thing properly'

Nialls sat down continuing to adjust himself.

'I hope your leggings haven't got any Teflon in them, Belinda, otherwise you might not get the full benefit.'

Trevor turned round and mouthed, 'Fuck Off', at Nialls, who pouted his lips and blew him a kiss.

The exercise began The only sound that could be heard was gentle breathing, apart from a little bit of moaning and the odd squelching noise, that Nialls kept making with his mouth, at inappropriate times.

Nialls' interruptions were having an effect on the group's karma, so Dolphin asked everybody to sit and face him.

He was sitting in a lotus position at the front and he had taken out his pigtail.

'For this next session, we're going to continue exploring masculine and feminine energy. You're going to walk around the room and celebrate your gender. I want you to make eye contact with everybody in turn in the room, and say, "I am a man, if you are a man, and I am a woman, if you are a woman." Say this to both the men, and the women.'

This was perfect for Nialls.

'What if I'm not sure?'

'Sorry?'

'What if I'm not sure? One of the reasons I've come here is to explore my sexuality. I was thinking of coming out, but I'm still not sure. So what do I say?'

Dolphin had not taken the advanced course, so he was not quite sure how to respond.

'Just say what feels right. Go with your inner feelings. It is only half the truth anyway, because inside every man there is a woman, and inside every woman, there is a man. It is our interface with other people that determines whether we show predominantly our male or female sides. So all of you can say either, I am a man, or I am a woman, because we are all both. Whether you feel predominantly man or woman, shout it out with confidence. Be seductive, or weak, or strong; say it in any way that seems suitable.'

Dolphin suddenly leapt up and launched himself out into the room shouting, 'I am a man!,' at the top of his voice.

This jump-started everybody into action, and for the next five minutes, the whole room strutted proudly or bowed sheepishly, declaring their sexuality. Nialls once more decided to focus his attention on Trevor, and instead of moving freely around the room, kept screaming 'I am a man!', or 'I am a woman!', at him at every opportunity. This was the last straw for Trevor, who completely in tune with his masculine side, swung a punch at the side of Nialls' head, and knocked him flying. This was the type of reaction that Nialls had been hoping for. He picked up a rainstick and poked Trevor in the stomach, who fell over into the box of vibrators, setting off the demonstration-model which began to whir round the floor.

Stellana attempted to calm things down and put on the whale tape again. Trevor had forgotten his earlier empathies, and grabbing one of Dolphin's symbolic paintings of Tantric love, smashed it into Nialls' head. Seeing his livelihood being destroyed, Dolphin ended the argument by hitting both Nialls and Trevor with his hessian shoulder bag. It was not until Belinda stepped in, standing between them and forcing them apart by grabbing their hair, that they calmed down enough to allow Stellana to announce the end of the workshop. There would be an advanced plenary session the following day, if anybody was interested. The room emptied, and Belinda let go of Nialls, but kept a firm hold of Trevor, whom she dragged off to the sweat lodge for some extra-curricular activity.

Nialls thought he'd had a very successful workshop. He was now Tantrically Balanced. He might even try for another session with Rebecca before he went home. She might be more receptive, now that he had got a certificate.

—·—

Nialls decided to get some fresh air before he went for his lunch. He had left his car at the pub the previous day, and he needed to fetch it. Most of the morning sessions had finished and The Tiny Tea Tent and Whole Food Café were busy, spilling their customers out onto the grass. There was a clearing in the wooded area, to the back of the house, where the storms had pulled out most of the long established trees, and this had seemed the ideal place to establish the sweat lodge. Nialls skirted around the outside, and found the path that led down behind the stage and out to the pond. As he passed it, he caught a glimpse of Trevor being daubed in some earthy-coloured dye by Belinda, before being dragged naked into a half stone and half tented contraption, full of smoke and Indian chanting. When Trevor emerged, he would be completely reborn, and with Belinda for added support, would try and explain to his wife his need to rediscover himself. She would be very understanding, before driving home alone and changing the locks. The divorce papers would, and did, follow shortly.

It did not take Nialls long to formulate a pretty accurate assessment of Rebecca's promotional skills, when it came to putting on live music. He could not see any evidence of equipment, or the infrastructure that was capable of dealing with any substantial musical event. There was a very primitive stage, and the hospitality tent had been borrowed from the local Scout-troup. There were no changing rooms, or major toilet facilities except one Portaloo, situated in a clump of bushes. Despite her adequate planning with the rest of the venture, Rebecca had obviously decided not to waste time on even a moderate cover-up, which suggested to Nialls she was not being completely honest about the Grand Finale.

———

Sophie and Malcolm had spent the morning together in Malcolm's bedroom.

'Well, this isn't going to gain me any awards for in-depth investigative journalism.'

Sophie was sitting on the bed, brushing her hair.

'I think we should go and grab some lunch and then have a bit of a sniff around.'

'That's alright by me. I'm starving.'

Malcolm would not have objected to anything. The sun was shining brightly, and he had spent the morning with Sophie. He couldn't hope for more than this. He stood at the window with a towel around his waist, watching the visitors outside queuing for food at the various stalls. He leaned forward holding on to the window-sill, and took a deep breath as the aromas of crêpes and felafels wafted past his nostrils. A group of children were dashing in and out of the trees, and one of them was having a problem managing a balloon, as well as eating an ice cream. Stumbling, he let go of the balloon, and it floated up through the trees, past the clock tower and into the sky. Malcolm waited for the inevitable scream, but the boy just waved it goodbye, before turning around and chasing after a group of older boys. They were attempting to skateboard on the gravel drive, narrowly avoiding Nialls, who had just returned from the village.

'Come on. Open the fucking door.'

Nialls had seen Malcolm at the window, and felt the least he could do was to disturb him, especially as he appeared to be having such a good time.

'Hello Nialls. There's no point in asking if you've been behaving yourself, judging by that big bruise on the side of your head. Who did that?'

'Some poof hit me with his shoulder bag because I talked in his lesson. It's quite clear what you two have been doing all morning. Is she bored with you now?'

Sophie appeared from behind the door, and leaned over Malcolm's shoulder.

'Hello, Nialls. Had a good morning?'

'Alright, I suppose. At least I haven't been wasting my time like you two. You've obviously just got out of the bath. I'm going for lunch. You can join me if you want.'

'We'd love to. You're not miffed, are you Nialls?'

'No. Why should I be?'

'Well, possibly because your friend is having a good time for once. We're really happy. I'm sure Malcolm would like you to be happy for him. Come on Nialls, give us a smile.'

'Fuck off. I'm going for something to eat. Come if you want. I don't really care, either way.'

Sophie was right. He was miffed, but he was not going to admit it. What Nialls was desperately trying to come to terms with was that he was feeling jealous. Only, it would be acceptable if it was Malcolm he was feeling jealous of, but it wasn't. Nialls shivered, and gripped the handrail of the staircase. It was not Malcolm. It was Sophie, and he did not want to feel this way. It reminded him of prep school, and his experiences with the younger boys. Maybe he was refusing to admit to the obvious. He tried to put the image of

Malcolm in his towel and his tangly wet hair out of his mind.

—

The dining room was noisy, with everybody discussing the morning's events. One table was reserved for the tutors, but was empty except for Dolphin and Stellana, who were seated at opposite ends, staring into their vegetable soup. Behind the counter, Tara attempted to carry a large pan of something from the cooker to the serving hatch, but only managed to get halfway before turning back. She put it down on the work surface, allowing Simon to take up the challenge on her behalf. She reached for the bottle that she now kept permanently under the sink.

'I hope Nialls is alright. Only he seems a bit down in the mouth. Maybe we should ask him to join us this afternoon?'

Sophie had placed her bag on the chair next to Nialls, and had joined Malcolm at the serving hatch.

'I don't mind. I think he's given up trying to discredit me, but you never know with Nialls. He's liable to change without warning, but yeah, he can come with us this afternoon, if he wants to. I'll ask him.'

'So where are you two love birds off to, and what makes you think that I would be remotely interested in coming along?'

'Well, this afternoon Nialls, we're going to be visiting a medium who contacts the dead, naked.'

'Are the dead naked as well?'

'The medium puts herself into a trance in the nude. I don't know about the spirits.'

'I hope she takes on physical attributions as well. You know how I like large women.'

'I don't know Nialls. She might do, but she might have a problem projecting them through the ethereal layer if they're too big.'

Sophie got out her tape recorder.

'Can I interview you, Nialls?'

They were interrupted by Rebecca. She was red-faced, and very flustered.

'Nialls. Look, I'm sorry to bother you but I need a favour. Do you think you could give me a hand with something?'

Sophie switched her tape recorder on.

'Hello. I'm Sophie. Are you the organiser? I write for a magazine and I was hoping to interview you.'

'What magazine? You're not from *Hello*, are you? Have you a photographer with you. Only, I demand the right to see any pictures before they're used. What sort of fee are you offering?'

'Actually we're not offering any fee. I thought you might be grateful for the publicity.'

'Listen darling, if you're not offering money, I'm not interested. Why should I be? What's in it for me?'

'Some sort of gratification that your philanthropic activities have been brought to the consciousness of a larger audience?'

'Fuck that! I'm not interested.'

'OK, but presumably you don't mind if I have a look round.'

'Not at all, but I don't want you writing anything. Listen Nialls, are you going to help me or not?'

Nialls did not feel inclined to help. Rebecca looked rough. Her skirt was too short, and her fake tan was streaky. It was failing to cover up the tell-tale signs of scarring, left after the removal of varicose veins.

'I might be prepared to help you Rebecca. What's the problem?'

'It's the flotation tank. There's something wrong with it. I can't get the water to go in.'

'Well, that'll require some form of consultancy fee. I am practically a constructional engineer.'

Rebecca regretted her behaviour the night before. She could not find Gordonski. Simon was useless, and she was in a fix.

'Look, I'm really sorry about last night Nialls. I was feeling tense and to be quite honest, nervous. Most of the men I've been with lately have been pretty pathetic, and you just took me by surprise. I should have given you time. I realise that now. I was really sorry after you left – completely sexually unfulfilled. I'd be really grateful.'

'Well, that's better. Maybe you should ask my opinion on a few other things. Sometimes a man's perspective can be useful.'

Rebecca thought Nialls' perspective on things was about as useful as his dick, but she was not going to tell him that. She could save that pleasure for later.

'Of course, Nialls. I'd be grateful of any help you can give me.'

She gave his hand a squeeze.

'Oh Nialls, you're so in control. I was so stupid to behave like I did last night.'

•

Phil and Phil had amassed quite a reputation, even before their opening session. Phil had manifested himself naked at breakfast, causing quiet consternation as everybody tucked into tea and toast, and Lynette had requested that he cover himself up. With a concession to conformity, he had condescended to wear a thong, but only during mealtimes.

Thus their first session was over-subscribed, and when Malcolm and Sophie arrived, a buzz of excited expectancy was permeating the room, as the lucky few waited for it to begin.

Phil was going to specialise in the reading of anal auras. He had commandeered the photocopier and had run off some prints of his naked backside. He was purporting to be able to gain an insight into the future, by reading the lines.

'Good afternoon to you all. I'm Phil and this is my husband Phil. I'm a medium.'

'And he's definitely a large.'

Nialls had entered the room, and had not been able to resist an opportunity. He was flanked by two elderly women wearing fox fur stoles, and carrying alligator skin handbags. Each stole was made up of two complete foxes, and the heads hung down either side the women's necks and over their shoulders. It was a bad choice of accessory for the venue, but the women were oblivious to modern thinking regarding the wearing of animal products. Nialls had found them wandering around outside. They told him he looked like Val Doonican, and that was good enough for him. They had closed their shop up early for the afternoon, and as they didn't go out very often, had decided to make a real effort by dressing up in their Sunday best. Their identical minx pillbox hats were adorned with assorted Bird of Paradise feathers, and their gloves made of finest chamois leather. The room contained a large percentage of animal right activists.

'Sorry. Don't mind us. We'll just sit at the back.'

Nialls had his arms linked in theirs, and he sat down

between them. Phil and Phil had now stripped off their bathrobes and had their eyes closed, so for now, any concerns regarding the old women's dress would have to be put on hold.

'Firstly, by using guided imagery as a tool to unleash our consciousness, we are going to travel together on a journey of discovery.'

Thirty pairs of eyes focused in between Phil's legs.

'I would like you all to sit down in a circle and hold hands.'

'Come on girls!'

Nialls helped the two sisters to arrange themselves neatly on the floor.

'What have we got to do, dear? Are we going to levitate, like that wonderful Paul Daniels?'

'Paul Daniels? Is he here? I like Paul Daniels.'

'Come on ladies, you've got to be very quiet, and listen carefully and do what you're told.'

Phil continued.

'I want you to close your eyes and imagine a big white light in front of you. This is your protection. Take it with you on your journey.'

'But we've only just got here. I haven't had my tea and biscuits yet.'

Phil came over to Nialls.

'Could you ask them to keep quiet please, otherwise we can't carry on.'

'You ask them.'

Nialls was feeling protective towards his two new friends and thought that they should be given the chance to speak for themselves.

'Could you please be quiet, please?'

They both looked up at him simultaneously.

'Are you going to make us disappear now? Oh, look he's not wearing any pants. I can knit you some out of dishcloths if you want, dear. Like we did in the war. You can't fight the Germans without any pants on. Is Paul Daniels coming soon, with his lovely daughter Debbie?'

'Could you be a little quieter please?'

Phil returned to his wife's side, and she continued.

'I want you to imagine that you're walking through a wood along a path, and it stretches into the distance.'

One of the sisters burst into song,

'I… I… It's the name of the game, and I want to play the ga… ame with you.'

'Cuddly toy and a fondue set. Can I make the marzipan flowers now? He's a lovely dancer. I remember when he used to be on *Sunday Night at the London Palladium*.'

To prevent the onslaught of octogenarian anarchy, Nialls stood the two sisters up and led them to the door. He didn't want to completely wreck the session, not yet anyway, so he steered them in the direction of Fen Shui flower-arranging. They went home giggling at the end of the afternoon, after trying some of the special fudge cake from one of the stalls.

The two Phil's slipped back into role, and the journey continued.

'You are walking along the path and you come to a gate. Is it made of wood or metal? How are you going to get past the gate? Are you going to leap over it, or approach it cautiously? Will it open easily or will it need all your strength to force past it. You might decide that the gate needs painting. If it does, will you give it two coats of undercoat and one coat of gloss, or will you just rub it down and paint it with a nice stain. If it's metal, you'll obviously have to use a suitable primer. Will you choose a smooth or textured Hammerite finish? How will you open the tin of paint? Can you use a coin, or will you need to use something like a screwdriver, to get greater leverage? It might be fitted with those little clips that you sometimes get on them.

'Anyway, you've come to this gate. Is it wide or is it narrow? Is it a five-barred gate or is it one of those that are planks of wood joined together, and have those funny black fittings that are all shiny?'

'Japanned. It's called Japanned, when they're all shiny.'

Phil was feeling a bit like a spare part at a séance, and had decided it was time he put an imput into the proceedings.

'And you put them on stable doors, but you wouldn't have a stable door in the middle of a wood, anyway.'

'I didn't say a door. I said a gate.'

'Yes, but you said a gate that had fixings on it, like a stable door. You don't want to confuse everybody. Do you mean a door or a gate?'

'A gate. I definitely mean a gate.'

'OK. Just as long as we can be sure.'

'A garden gate's sometimes like a door.'

Nialls thought that he might just throw that one in to see if he could get a reaction.

'There's a gate in the garden wall here that's more like a door,' he continued, 'and it's got a pane of glass in it.'

This signalled the floodgates to open, and the introductory meeting of the Debating Society began.

'That's definitely not a gate. If it's got glass in it, it must be a door. Gates don't have panels in them.'

Nialls' neighbour had let go of his hand and decided to speak against the motion. Whatever the motion was.

'My gate's got a letterbox in it and that's not a door. It's definitely a gate because I got it from a garden centre.'

Malcolm decided it was time to waste his opinion on the subject.

'Yes, but was the gate bought with the letterbox as an integral part of it, or did you add it later?'

'What difference does that make?'

'Well, it sets a new precedent.'

'What's that then?'

'What starts off as a basic gate can become something else. At the very least, it widens the parameters of simple definition. The basic differences between a gate and a door are a bit of a grey area to say the least.'

Sophie thought that she might add a couple of her own views. 'What I think Malcolm's trying to say is that a gate has an ability to sit on the fence, if you'll pardon the pun. It can also be a door.'

'A bit like a trans-sexual.'

Phil had been keeping her eyes shut, in an attempt to keep the flow of consciousness running smoothly. She raised her voice a couple of octaves.

'We have now left the gate behind, and in the distance we can now see a lake.'

'But I want to do my gate. I've bought the paint and everything.'

Nialls was trying to keep the red herring swimming, but Malcolm shuffled forward and kicked him on the shin.

The brief introductory session of guided imagery intended to bond the group together had had the opposite effect. By the time they had left the lake behind and got to the supermarket, via the castle, and met the wise old sage waiting to present them with gifts, an hour had passed.

Malcolm had definite problems keeping up with the journey, and had spent the entire time visualising the privet bush that grew outside his front door. Nialls continued to ask questions at every opportunity, and the flow had been lost time and time again, as he steered the group off at tangents. Phil had hoped to give the group time to talk about their journeys and to compare notes, but there was not any time left, so after they finally arrived at Safeways, before paying the ferryman, she quickly led them into the next session.

Phil went behind a screen and brought out a driftwood chair, decorated with symbols and laurel leaves. He had picked them from the garden that morning. Phil sat down, closed her eyes, opened her mouth and began to rotate her head.

'I have a message for someone here.'

Nialls inhaled loudly.

'Is it for me?'

'I don't know. Do you know somebody on the other side, with a name that begins with A?'

'Is it a man with dark hair?'

'Yes.'

'Has he a side-parting and is wearing a suit?'

'He could be. He's definitely wearing trousers and a jacket, but I can't see if they're matching. He's shrouded in the ethereal layer.'

'Is he carrying an old leather suitcase with stickers on it?'

'Yes, I do believe he is.'

'He's not called Alan, is he?'

'Yes, he is. It's Alan. Do you want the message?'

'Not really. I don't know anybody called Alan. I don't know anybody who fits that description, apart from a second-hand car salesman who tried to sell me a dodgy car last year. He had an old briefcase, but it didn't have any stickers on it.'

A man at the back wearing a cowbell, started waving his arms about.

'I know somebody called Alan who is on the other side. He worked in a Gentlemen's outfitters, and was always smartly turned out. Can you see if he's got a tape measure around his neck? Only, the Alan I knew always had a tape around his neck, and he had lovely slender fingers.'

Phil started to rotate her head in the opposite direction. Her nails dug into the side of the chair, and she lifted herself off the seat and stared at Alan's friend.

'He says that you've got nothing to fear. Everything is going to be all right, and you're going to have a happy life. Will you take the message, dear?'

The man began to weep uncontrollably.

'Don't worry. Sometimes messages from the other side can make us feel very emotional.'

'Ask him how he intends me to have a happy life, considering my wife's just left me and taken the children. after she informed me that neither of them were mine anyway. The solicitor said that she'll be entitled to almost the entire value of the house, and I'll still probably have to pay her vast amounts of maintenance. I only came because I thought I might find a little peace, and instead I've got some dead twat, who's also probably shagged my wife, telling me everything's fine.'

Malcolm and Sophie felt that it was time for them to leave. They opened the French windows, and slipped out into the garden. As they closed the door, they heard Nialls shouting something about telling Alan to fuck off, if all he could do was upset people and that he was probably a bastard when he was alive anyway.

———

That evening, as it was the eve of the Eclipse, Simon had organised a little entertainment after dinner in the hall. Everybody was invited, and if anyone could play an instrument or recite a poem, even better. There was a full house, and Phil and Phil had come in the hope that they might be asked to do some impromptu readings.

Dolphin was there on his own, brooding in the corner. His constant bickering with Stellana had led them past the point of no return. Dolphin had secretly loaded the van with anything of any value, and he would be gone before the evening was over. He could not wait to get away, but as a subtle gesture, he had left the box of vibrators for Stellana as a leaving present. He had tried approaching life from a philosophical angle, but it had not worked for him. But at least everything had not been wasted. He had made some good contacts, and thought that he could branch out and maybe get the franchise on one of the Private shops in the West Midlands. What Dolphin did not know was that Stellana had guessed that he might be up to something, and had watched him load up the van. She waited for him to get settled at the concert before picking up the vibrators, and driving away with the girl with red hair and green dungarees. Dolphin was left to catch the bus in the morning, and slid dejectedly out of the door of Mandalay, before anyone was up.

One family had become so inspired by the evening's events that they had been working on a short play, acted out entirely in mime. It depicted the eclipse, and how it temporarily affects the eco-system and nocturnal animals.

Two children scurried onto the impromptu stage area. They were dressed in black bin-liners, wearing paper masks. One resembled a fox and the other a badger. By the inventive use of mime, they were supposed to act out the individual nocturnal habits, but because they were embarrassed, they just stood still, shuffling from foot to foot. A woman appeared dressed in an enormous yellow jumper. She made an arc in the air with her arms, supposed to represent the sun coming out. Immediately, imaginary animals lay down and fell asleep. A man dressed in a polo-neck jumper ran on, and threw a piece of black plastic over the woman. The animals woke up and ran around in circles, acting confusedly and bumping into each other. There followed a short burst of sibling rivalry, each trying to upstage the other by demonstrating their tap-dancing skills, until the fox sent the badger flying into the tea urn. The Sun then slowly pealed off her bin-liner, and the animals lay down and fell asleep again.

It was a wonderful performance and during the applause, one of the children ran off, returned with a bunch of cow parsley, and presented it to the Sun who continued to radiate well into the interval.

Rebecca had decided to put in an appearance. It might be a good public relations move. In a magnanimous gesture to the staff, she had given them all the night off. This was on the strict understanding that they attended the evening soirée, to project a unilateral front. The stress of providing a meal had once again taken its toll on Tara, and she had been drunk by five o'clock, leaving Lynette and Simon to muddle through as best they could. Either they had not noticed, or everybody was too polite to mention, that all the meals were beginning to taste the same. At least the sweet varied. It was a banana for dinner, where it had been an apple for lunch. Tomorrow they might even get a choice. Rebecca had asked Nialls to accompany her to the concert. She did not want to go on her own, and he was the obvious choice. She had given his self-esteem a little stroke at the right moment, and he was feeling in control again. He was prepared to forgive her for her previously outrageous behaviour, as she sat opposite him stroking his hand. She was happy to accept his forgiveness for as long as it could be useful to her. She might need to make a fast escape and he had suitable transport, plus a seemingly endless supply of drugs.

Gordonski had not turned up to the concert. He had stumbled into the kitchen some time during dinner and begun ranting on about the un-hygienic conditions. They had left him scrubbing the kitchen floor, after first taking off his cloak and placing it neatly on a hanger. He then set about polishing all the pans and wiping all the glasses. When he was completely satisfied, he turned his attentions to the net curtains, which he removed and put to soak in a bucket. He could not believe how everybody had let their standards slip.

The concert finished around nine and before everybody

dispersed, Rebecca was asked to clarify the arrangements for the following day. She made her way to the front of the hall and clapped her hands.

'Tomorrow, we are going to celebrate one of the most stunningly natural-occurring phenomenon in the universe, the total eclipse of the sun. I'd like everybody to assemble at 10:30 in the morning on the main lawn, in front of the stage where, I gather, we are going to be taught a primitive aboriginal chant in preparation. Can I remind everybody of the dangers of looking directly at the sun? I do have a supply of special glasses that filter out the harmful rays. They're from the States, endorsed by NASA, and work out at twenty pounds a pair.'

Her voice deepened.

'A wise man was sitting talking with a friend as dusk fell.

' "Light a candle," his friend said, "because it is dark now. There is one just by your left side."

' "How can I tell my left from my right, in the dark?" asked the wise man.'

Her voice returned to its original tone.

'I hope you are all fulfilling your journey with us at Mandalay, and remember that tomorrow is the beginning of the rest of your lives. Enjoy.'

'Come on, Nialls. Let's go and get hammered.'

They left the hall and climbed up the stairs to Rebecca's bedroom. Nialls called into his room for supplies. It was going to be a long night, and Rebecca was feeling edgy at the prospects of the next day looming large after all this time. She had not decided what she was going to do if everything did start to spiral out of control. At the moment, Nialls seemed to be her best bet, she just needed to allow him to feel in charge. Rebecca knew that he was vulnerable, despite his ability to put up a smokescreen, and whatever the hold was he had over Malcolm, it had seriously diminished over the last twenty-four hours. He was in need of a new friend and Rebecca was prepared to ask him round for tea.

Nialls was certainly feeling vulnerable. His isolation had deepened the more Malcolm gained control. He was trying to deal with his confusion. Part of him wanted to tell Malcolm how he felt, but he could not even admit to himself how much he needed him. Instead he would pursue the easiest path, which was to get completely slaughtered.

Nialls walked into Rebecca's bedroom, followed by Malcolm and Sophie.

'I thought I'd ask these two to join us for a bit, to see if they're able to give anybody else some attention other than themselves. Rebecca and I were just about to indulge in a little line, but I suppose you two don't need any artificial stimulants?'

'Not at all, Nialls. I'm quite prepared to relieve you of some of your over-priced goody bag. Chop 'em out. I don't know about Sophie, though.'

Sophie squeezed Malcolm's hand and gave him a kiss.

'Oh, for God's sake you two, it's pathetic. Someone should throw a bucket of water over you. Can't you behave normally for five minutes?'

'What's the matter, Nialls?' Rebecca said. 'Anybody would think you were jealous.'

Rebecca had poured herself a large glass of wine and was leaning against the mantle piece. She knew that Nialls probably fancied Sophie, and she was enjoying the moment.

'Isn't it that you'd rather be in someone else's shoes, and you're feeling a bit put out?'

Rebecca had hit the proverbial nail, although not completely in the right place, but Nialls was not going to go to the trouble of putting her straight. He knew why he was jealous, and it was not Malcolm's shoes he would rather be wearing. Not those dark-brown suede, Hush Puppy desert boots that matched Malcolm's jacket to perfection, as he stood there, majestically reflecting his newfound confidence.

'So, how's it working out Rebecca? Are you prepared for tomorrow?'

Sophie had joined her at the table, by the window.

'Just got to pack my bag and I'll be ready for anything.'

'No. I mean, are you all sorted. Have all the acts confirmed and everything? Who's actually playing, have you got anybody well-known?'

'Listen Darling. I'm not going to let the cat out of the bag. We don't want a stampede on our hands.'

'Would that be a stampede out the doors or in?'

'I'm not going to say anymore, except that the band playing tomorrow haven't gigged together since the Sixties, and they've never agreed until now, to a reunion. I tell you Henry Kissinger couldn't have done any better than me, to get these guys together again.'

'So, do you feel the whole event has captured spiritually what you intended, when you planned it?'

'I haven't heard many complaints.'

Nialls spluttered into his glass.

'Listen Nialls, most of the complaints I've heard about, have been to do with your behaviour.'

'Oh, Rebecca! You're so cruel!'

Nialls flipped through a pile of CDs and chose a compilation of Ibiza chill-out tunes. He was well on the way to wherever he intended to go to tonight.

Malcolm watched his friend pour himself a large glass of wine. Somehow he looked vulnerable. Nialls had developed a stoop, looked awkward, and was definitely avoiding him. Malcolm walked forward and led Nialls over to the fireplace, away from Rebecca and Sophie.

'Nialls. Are you alright?'

'Of course I am. Not that you'd be bothered.'

'That's nonsense Nialls, you know I am. I know that you can be a complete bastard most of the time, but it doesn't stop me caring about you. Look, why don't you knock this on the head and come out with us. You know it's going to get very messy if you stay here. Let's just go down the village, and have a few beers so that we can really enjoy tomorrow.'

'It's OK for you, Malcolm. You don't understand.'

'I know you should let your guard down for once, and realise that not everybody's out to get you. Just walk away. Come and spend some time with someone who genuinely cares about you, because this bloody madwoman certainly doesn't.

'God, Malcolm! If you only fucking knew.'

'Knew what. What are you trying to say?'

Nialls' mind was in turmoil. What should he do? He was at the crossroads, and this could be the most important decision he would ever have to make. He looked across at

Rebecca. She was staring at him, and he saw a coldness that made him shiver.

Malcolm turned to his friend once more.

'Just come Nialls. Just walk away.'

Gordonski filled his sack for the last time. As he dragged it across the garden, children could have mistaken him for a benevolent Santa Claus arriving late for Christmas, or even Guido Fawkes on an early reconnaissance mission. This would have pleased Gordonski, because he saw himself as a combination of both. Deliver the presents, then light the touch paper and stand clear. This, with a little Merlinesque magic, was his best metamorphosis yet. His face was black-ened with burnt cork, as he approached the clock tower from the cover of the Azalea bushes that edged the drive. The tower loomed out of the dark and he had spent the last few nights secretly altering the hands of the clock, which were now set at twelve. He hummed the theme from *The Guns of Navarone*, as a lone sentry marched along in front of him eating a vegi-burger. He made his way through the garden to the rear door of the tower, opened the door and climbed the stairs. The staircase finished on the second floor and in the corner was a ladder leading up to the small room, containing the mechanism. He pushed the trap-door open, and threw his sack up into the darkness. He had con-structed a camouflaged den in the corner, made up of pack-ing cases, and he used one of them to store his sack. He neatly unfolded his sleeping bag onto the floor and sat down. He was now ready. He reached inside his cloak, pulled out a piece of white cloth and tied it around his head. It had a red sun painted on it, and some black letters he had copied out of a book on Bonsai gardening.

By the early hours of the morning, Nialls and Rebecca were wasted, having drunk and snorted themselves to the brink.

Malcolm had tried to persuade his friend to go with them, but Nialls had become more aggressive and so, even-tually they left Nialls, to return to The Lamb. As they reached the front gates, they caught up with Simon, who was also heading for the pub.

'Hi Simon! Do you want a lift? Isn't Lynette with you?'

'I hope not. I've had about as much as I can take. I'm sleeping in the van again tonight.

'What do you mean?'

'I've got a job in the pub. Apparently these last few days have made Grumpy realise that as he can't really stand people, he'd be better off cooking in the kitchen. He likes doing food. It's worked well for him, and he's going to cook. So he needs a barman. I may as well give it a try. There's even a job for Tara if she wants it.'

———

Rebecca and Nialls were completely unaware of the time. Suddenly there was a knock on the door. It was Tara.

'Rebecca, Rebecca! Can you hear me? Can you let me in?'

'Who the fuck's that at this hour of the night? Fucking come in, whoever you are.'

Nialls was laying on the bed, waving a glass of wine about. There was a damp patch down the front of his trousers.

'I'm sorry Rebecca, but people are complaining about the noise.'

'Fucking–fuck–the–fucking–fuckers! Tell them to fuck off!'

Nialls raised himself up onto his elbow.

'Yeah, fucking cunts. They're all fucking cunts out there.'

'I'm just passing on the message, Rebecca, but you are making a lot of noise.'

'OK, OK! Alright, we'll keep it down! Now fuck off!'

Rebecca had a bottle of wine in each hand.

'They can all fuck off anyway because tomorrow, I'm leaving them to swim around in their own shit. Where do you fancy, Nialls? Anywhere you want? Let's go now.'

'Rebecca. I'll take you anywhere, anywhere in the world as long as you're paying. They're all losers anyway, searching for something that isn't there. They'd make more sense of their lives if they looked up my arse. I've got the stash, so let's go.'

Rebecca reached down on to the floor for her jacket, but Nialls grabbed it out of her hand before she could put it on.

'What are you doing Nialls? Let me have it. I'm cold.'

'You can't have this jacket. It's Malcolm's. He left it behind on purpose. He must have wanted me to have it.'

He fell back onto the bed, keeping a firm grip on the sleeve to prevent her from taking it.

'Don't be such an arse, Nialls. I'm really cold, and I need it more than you.'

She wrenched the jacket back from Niall's grasp, and they staggered down the stairs and into the car.

'Hang on, Nialls. We've got to make a detour. Take me to the clock-tower.'

Nialls started the car, screamed the engine up to thirty thousand revs, before putting it into third gear and stalling. They climbed out before realising they hadn't gone anywhere, and made for the gate that led into the garden.

'Where the fuck are you taking me, Rebecca? A day return to the vegetable patch? I was expecting something a bit more exotic.'

'Just got to get the holiday fund, and then we can be off. Follow me.'

She led him through the garden and up the stairs to the second floor, grabbing a torch that was wedged in between two ceiling joists.

'It's over here, my passport to the sun. Time to leave this one behind, as it's going out in the morning.'

She got on her knees and pulled up the floorboards, dragging out two bags.

'What the fuck's that, Rebecca? Let me have a look.'

It was full of bank notes.

'Nice one, Rebecca. Let's have another drink to celebrate.'

They took another swig on the Jack Daniels, before collapsing across the bags of money and there they remained, oblivious to the new day that was dawning outside.

—·—

Everybody had spent the morning so far relaxing in their tents, or sitting in their rooms. It had been a damp beginning to the day and a cloud of mist clung to the ground and mingled with the smoke of campfires. The breakfast van was doing a steady trade in bacon rolls, and The Tiny Tea Tent had run out of decaffeinated coffee. The whole atmosphere was subdued. Everybody knew they were waiting to witness a massive reminder of mans' vulnerability, and it was making them edgy with apprehension.

At about ten-thirty, Malcolm and Sophie drove up the driveway and in front of the house. They could see that a small crowd had begun to assemble on the lawn, but there was no sign of Nialls. They were just in time to see Phil and Phil disappearing towards the front gate on their bikes, loaded up with bags. They were both naked. They had decided to observe the eclipse from the hill that overlooked the village, and had packed up early. They did not intend to return for the music. They had not come for that. They pedalled through the village to the lane that led up past the school, and up to a small copse. This would be an excellent place to watch, and it would give them the inspiration to continue on their journey. They had planned a cycling tour covering the length of the country, to spread the word. They hoped to cover about fifty miles a day, and still retain the energy to conjure up a few dear departed souls before bedtime.

In an attempt to create the right ambience, Simon had built a pyramid out of scaffolding poles facing the stage, and covered it with black plastic bin-liners. Some of the gathered crowd were carrying cameras, in an attempt to capture the forthcoming blackness on film. They were discussing what would be a suitable aperture to photograph the complete obliteration of everything. The sun was practically rendered non-existent by cloud, but as the minutes ticked away, they settled themselves into preparing for the experience of a lifetime.

Malcolm and Sophie returned to Malcolm's room for the tape recorder, and to look for Nialls.

'I'll just knock on his door on the way out.'

Malcolm got no reply, so he tried the door. It was unlocked and he went in.

'Is he there?'

Sophie had followed him into the room.

'No, he's not. He's obviously not been here all night, but that doesn't surprise me. He's probably comatose in Rebecca's room.'

Malcolm picked up the damp towel on Nialls' bed and hung it over a chair. It smelt of Givenchy.

They walked down through the hallway. Tara was wiping down some tables.

'Tara, have you seen anything of Nialls this morning?'

'No, but we heard plenty of him last night. There was a hell of a row going on. They eventually shut up about four-thirty, and as far I can make out, they intended to drive off somewhere. They made an awful noise. Rebecca isn't in her room either, and Lynette found Nialls' car with the doors open, so God knows what's happened to them.'

———

Rebecca awoke with a sudden jolt and looked around the room. At first she could not remember where she was, but when she saw the tightly-rolled bank notes scattered all around her, she began to panic. She scrambled over Nialls and crawled to the window. The small amount of light shining into the room was beginning to dim. There was a table pushed up against the wall, and she climbed over it to peep around the corner of the sash. The crowd in the garden were staring up at the sky and covering their eyes with cardboard glasses. They were singing some strange aboriginal chant, accompanied by a group of men on the stage playing didgeridoos and shaking rainsticks.

'For fuck's sake, Nialls, get up! It's morning. We've got to go. Get the bags. The eclipse. It's starting, and everybody's in the garden.'

Nialls woke with an involuntary erection. It was either that or soil himself. He forced his eyes open and squinted at whoever it was wiping condensation from off the inside of the glass. His well-stoked brain, and the lack of light, convinced him he was looking at Malcolm, wearing his brown suede jacket. Nialls scrambled out of the sacks and lurched across the room, grabbing Malcolm by the shoulders and turning him round. But it wasn't Malcolm, but Rebecca, who focused her bloodshot eyes on his. But he did not want to see Rebecca and pushing her roughly aside, he pressed his face up against the glass. Nialls stared into the gloom as the last shafts of light began to disappear and as he watched, they glanced off the face of Malcolm who was standing in the garden gazing up at the sky, as his eyes reflected an iridescent glow towards the distant sun.

Nobody was really clear from where the first explosions started. They began with a general rumble behind the house, progressing to the perimeter of the garden and sending clouds of smoke into the air. A row of Poplars leapt eight feet into the sky, and an explosion at the rear of the stage knocked the entire aboriginal ensemble off their feet and into the Mosh Pit. After a brief recovery, they began shaking their rainsticks at the fading light, hoping to appease whatever Gods they had offended. A didgeridoo smashed into the pyramid, squashing the plastic panda mounted on the top. It had been placed there in an attempt to bring greater awareness to an endangered species.

Only Nialls and Rebecca heard the struggling mechanism of the long-ceased clock lumber into life. Horology had never been one of Gordonski's major interests, but the intricacies of the movement had captured his heart. He had lovingly restored it back to life, even if it was only going to be a short remission.

They heard it tick nine or ten times before it began to strike, but only the assembled crowd below would see that the hands were pointing to twelve. The sound of the bell striking its tune completed the surrealness, as all the heads turned to focus on the clock. Their glance was immediately diverted to a shape flying around the side of the tower. It was Gordonski, and the Angel of Death was amongst them. An avenging power come to claim its ransom, sitting on a toilet seat and suspended from a pulley. His cloak flapped behind him, and flames poured out from his pointed hat as he screamed a bloodcurdling cry, before disappearing behind the back of the old icehouse. Simultaneously, the icehouse left the ground and Gordonski's scream was lost as the explosion sent smashed masonry crashing into the trees behind.

Rebecca and Nialls watched him disappear into the darkness and then their eyes were diverted to something else appearing out of the gloom. It was a thin piece of glowing string, and it was getting closer.

As the fuse reached the semtex stashed above their heads, the force of the explosion sent the entire top-half of the clock tower crashing into the walled garden below. Rebecca would never feel again the penetrative sarcasm of Nialls' sting, and he would never again see that beautiful face, bathed in sunlight. They were simply blown into space and converted into matter in an instant.

———

'Maybe they did do a runner. It was certainly looking like they were going to. They're probably somewhere hot, having the time of their lives.'

The authorities had been left to sort out the chaos and the remains of Manderlay were being systematically sifted for clues. Malcolm had his hand resting on Sophie's knee, and he smiled as he thought of his friend drinking tequilla slammers on some tropical island.

'I'm sure you're right, but maybe his luck did eventually run out.'

It would be two days later before a man in a blue babygrow came across a partially charred thumb, with an immaculately manicured nail, amongst a pile of wreckage.

———

Malcolm and Sophie were driving along a dirt track on a Welsh mountainside.

'There it is. Over there, by the side of that hill.'

The Vision stood on its own, in the shade of a mountain, with the Welsh borders stretching out in front. A small plane was buzzing in the clouds overhead, and the gorse was beginning to turn.

—–—

The lorry pulled up on to the hard shoulder. Ahead lay the North, but to the East the cooling towers stood, a proud landmark reflecting the evening sun towards the city. The river flowed fast and strong here, skirting the industrial wasteland, past the Dale and towards the sea. A man climbed out of the cab and onto the grass verge.

'Thanks, Traat. Thanks for the lift, and have a good journey.'

'No problem, mate. Thanks for the story, very entertaining.'

The man had crossed the road before the driver noticed that he had left his bag behind. It was a Tesco bag and spilling out the top was some material. It was dark purple, covered in golden stars. The driver wound down his window and shouted to the man, who was already disappearing down an embankment.

'Hey Arnold! You've left your bag behind.'

But Arnold pretended not to hear him. He had already smelt the river and recent memories were deserting him, as the sound of the water rushing over the weir beckoned him on.

Forthcoming Spitfire Original

MEAL TICKET

David Charters

'*I'm afraid, Mr Nicholson, that you are going to have to learn the facts of life about divorce. Your children are still quite young.'*

She looked at her notes. 'Charles is ten and Sophie's eight. Charles is just about at the age when the courts will consider his preferences as to which parents he wants to live with. Sophie isn't. Unless you can prove definitively that your wife is an unsuitable mother, the presumption of the court will be that they should live with her. In legal terms, she will be named as the "parent with care".'

'Care?' Paul could not keep the bitterness from his voice. 'Does having an affair and breaking up the home qualify as "care"?'

Caroline Walters took a deep breath and continued. 'It's what used to be called custody – the modern term is residence...'

Suddenly, City banker Paul Nicolson's world collapses when Clara, his wife, falls in love with wayward artist, Nathan Black. Forced to make an agonizing choice between his children and his job, he ends up destined to lose both. But you can't keep a good man down! The unravelling of his elaborate plan for revenge and restitution becomes an epic journey through a world of high finance, the International Art Market, the tortuous legal wrangles of expensive divorce... even alternative theatre. All those who enjoyed David Charters' best-selling short story collections; *No Tears*; *I Love You, and Other Lies...* and his novella, *At Bonus Time No-one Can Hear You Scream*, will know his ability, with great pace and verve, to hold the readers' attention until the very last page.

October 2005   ISBN 1 904027 35 0   224pp   Paperback   £9.99

Spitfire

HAVE A NICE DAY

Barry Norman

What a place this was – a dream factory where everyone smiled incessantly because nobody dared look sad in a dream factory. But the trouble with a dream was that it only needed to take an unexpected little twist to become a nightmare . . .

William Pendleton, a television researcher, is sent to Hollywood to assist in the making of a programme about Willard Kaines, a rich and aged film star who is rumoured to be about to receive a special Oscar. However, things do not go according to plan. No one has a good word to say for Kaines and his second wife reveals an explosive secret about him which she has kept hidden for forty years. To add to William's problems, the presenter of the programme, Mark Payne, takes a violent dislike to him and threatens to ruin his career; his drunken producer is on the verge of collapse; a pimp of doubtful reliability moves into his hotel room and along with numerous unco-operative stars, he must also deal with Mark Payne's ever-demanding ego. As the tempo builds to reach the final, uproarious climax, William finally discovers what must be done . . . .

Barry Norman's name is synonymous with film. He hosted the BBC's flagship film programme for nearly twenty years until he announced his final departure from constantly sitting in darkened rooms. He has also written a number of best-selling books, including his autobiography. His novels, however, have been sadly neglected and this re-issue of one of his funniest is cause for celebration.

ISBN 1 904027 18 0 182 pp Paperback £9.99

Young Spitfire

BOWS AGAINST THE BARONS

Geoffrey Trease

He had killed one of the King's deer!
A cold sweat started out on his forehead, where his hand
had left a smear of blood. He stood as though petrified, won-
dering what to do.
Everything in the forest was sacred to the King. To fell a tree
was a crime, even to cut a branch. ...As for shooting one of the
deer! ...Only in the forest would he be safe. Sherwood was the
poor man's refuge. Folk said it was full of outlaws, old soldiers
who had no work, escaped serfs and men who had broken the
law – desperate men who would as soon slit his throat as take
him for their comrade.

First published in 1934, this rousing tale of medieval
England was Geoffrey Trease's first published work. Years
later, in 1966, he slightly revised the book and in his note to
that edition - reprinted six times – recalled its extraordinary
pull. 'Boys and girls wrote to me from all over the world.
Some could not because they did not know a word of
English - they were reading the story in their own languages
in Italy and Poland and Brazil. It was even turned into
Icelandic.' The tale of young Dickon, the clash between rich
and poor, and above all, the story of the great leader, Robin
Hood of Sherwood Forest presented as the author felt he
might have been, can now be re-discovered by a new generation of younger readers.

Geoffrey Trease's books were published in more than 20
countries and he was a past chairman of the Society of
Authors and a Fellow of the Royal Society of Literature.

ISBN 1 904027 26 1   160pp   Paperback   £6.99

Young Spitfire

JOHN DIAMOND

Leon Garfield

If ever I learned anything during that night, it was that if you should hear the noise of running feet, you should not be angry, but think that somebody down below might be gasping and groaning and struggling to save his life.

If you should see a boy raise his fists as if to bang on your door and then stumble away, it is not because he's a dirty little ruffian, but because he's just caught sight of somebody coming round a corner with a terrible hook.

'Really,' said Leon Garfield, 'what I try to write is that old-fashioned thing the family novel, accessible to the twelve-year-old and readable by his elders.' This classic tale of a boy who sets out to right the wrongs committed by his swindler father demonstrates how extraordinarily successful Leon Garfield was as a storyteller. First published in 1980, *John Diamond* won the Whitbread Award that year, as the best children's story book, and also the prestigious *Boston Globe-Horn Honor Book Award*. *The Horn Book* wrote:

Narrated with the verve and pace of a picaresque novel, [*John Diamond*] combines a cast of remarkable eccentrics with superb sensory descriptions . . . A series of heart-stopping pursuits through the twisting London streets, narrow escapes, encounters with the denizens of Whitefriars, Foxes Court, and Hanging Court Alley move the story at a precipitous rate toward a thoroughly satisfying and surprising resolution. Richly imagined and audacious in its balance of humour and suspense, the book is as absorbing as it is compelling.

ISBN 1 904027 32 6   208pp   Paperback   £7.99

Young Spitfire

THE VIPER OF MILAN

Marjorie Bowen

Perhaps it is only in childhood that books have any deep influence on our lives. ...When – perhaps I was fourteen by that time – I took Miss Marjorie Bowen's *The Viper of Milan* from the library shelf, the future for better or worse really struck. From that moment I began to write. ...I think it was Miss Bowen's apparent zest that made me want to write. One could not read her without believing that to write was to live and enjoy.
Graham Greene

Set in fourteenth-century Italy, the story is about the enmity between two princes, Visconti, the evil Duke of Milan and Mastino della Scala, the dispossessed Duke of Verona. The hatred of these two men is the absorbing basis of the plot, and the almost unbelievable cruelty and black-heartedness of the unscrupulous Visconti, help to make the impact of this story a really tremendous one.

ISBN 1 904027 24 5   384pp   Paperback   £9.99

THE WHITE CAMEL

Eden Phillpotts

With an Introduction by Joanne Harris

First published in 1936, this beautiful story of desert life by a master of English story-telling is written with a lyric intensity. The tale of Ali, the nomad boy and his white camel, will capitivate today's readers as it surely did nearly seventy years ago.

ISBN 1 904027 25 3   192pp   Paperback   £7.99

First published in Great Britain by

Elliott & Thompson Ltd
27 John Street
London WC1N 2BX

ISBN 1 904027 36 9

First edition

Book design by Brad Thompson
Printed and bound in Malta by Interprint